THE *Best*
{BRITISH}
Short Stories
2014

NICHOLAS ROYLE IS the author of more than 100 short stories, two novellas and seven novels, most recently *First Novel* (Vintage). His short story collection, *Mortality* (Serpent's Tail), was shortlisted for the inaugural Edge Hill Prize. He has edited sixteen anthologies of short stories, including *A Book of Two Halves* (Gollancz), *The Time Out Book of Paris Short Stories* (Penguin), *'68: New Stories by Children of the Revolution* (Salt) and *Murmurations: An Anthology of Uncanny Stories About Birds* (Two Ravens Press). A senior lecturer in creative writing at the Manchester Writing School at MMU and head judge of the Manchester Fiction Prize, he also runs Nightjar Press, publishing original short stories as signed, limited-edition chapbooks.

Also by Nicholas Royle:

NOVELS
Counterparts
Saxophone Dreams
The Matter of the Heart
The Director's Cut
Antwerp
Regicide
First Novel

NOVELLAS
The Appetite
The Enigma of Departure

SHORT STORIES
Mortality

ANTHOLOGIES (as editor)
Darklands
Darklands 2
A Book of Two Halves
The Tiger Garden: A Book of Writers' Dreams
The Time Out Book of New York Short Stories
The Ex Files: New Stories About Old Flames
The Agony & the Ecstasy: New Writing for the World Cup
Neonlit: Time Out Book of New Writing
The Time Out Book of Paris Short Stories
Neonlit: Time Out Book of New Writing Volume 2
The Time Out Book of London Short Stories Volume 2
Dreams Never End
'68: New Stories From Children of the Revolution
The Best British Short Stories 2011
Murmurations: An Anthology of Uncanny Stories About Birds
The Best British Short Stories 2012
The Best British Short Stories 2013

THE *Best*
{ BRITISH }
Short Stories
2014

SERIES EDITOR **NICHOLAS ROYLE**

SALT

CROMER

PUBLISHED BY SALT PUBLISHING
12 Norwich Road, Cromer, Norfolk NR27 0AX

First published by Salt Publishing, 2014

Printed in Great Britain by Clays Ltd, St Ives plc

Typeset in Paperback 9/12

ISBN 978 1 907773 67 9 paperback

1 3 5 7 9 8 6 4 2

In memory of Joel Lane (1963–2013)

CONTENTS

INTRODUCTION

THEY SAY THERE'S no accounting for taste and it plays a large part in the assembly of an anthology such as this. Zadie Smith's 'The Embassy of Cambodia', published last year as a handsome stand-alone volume by Hamish Hamilton, was beautifully written and you couldn't fault the author's grasp of the language, unless you objected to her use of 'presently' to mean 'now', but was it to your taste? (It did seem to be to many people's.) What was it anyway? A short story? A very short novella? About 8000 words in length and described by the publisher's blurb simply as a 'story', it came in 21 chapters tricked out with white space, generous leading and wide margins, to look more like a novella or even a short novel. It lifted the spirits to see a major imprint publishing an original short story on its own, even in its crafty little disguise; it would raise them even further to see the same thing happen with authors who don't enjoy the same level of media attention as Zadie Smith.

Smaller publishers, although they have less to spend, may also have less to lose. Daunt Books – better known, in the form of James Daunt, as a classy bookseller who came to the rescue of Waterstone's – has started putting out very smart-looking chapbooks containing individual short stories, among them Philip Langeskov's wonderfully tense 'Barcelona', reprinted herein. I hope readers will forgive my including a story first published in chapbook form by my own Nightjar Press – M John Harrison's 'Getting Out of There'.

Unthank Books, 3:AM Press, Oneworld Publications, Unlocking Press, The Fiction Desk, Tindal Street Fiction Group, TTA Press and Freight Books are all small publishers with the vision – and good taste – to take on authors and projects that would grace bigger imprints' lists if only the editors at those bigger imprints were not obliged to dance to the tune of sales and marketing. The above small publishers are all represented in the present volume. As are literary magazines *The Reader* and *Ambit*, as well as high-achieving online outlet *The View From Here*. Two stories were shortlisted in the Manchester Fiction Prize and the author of one of them, Adam Wilmington, walked off with ten grand as the winner. But the development of the year in short fiction – yes, more exciting, perversely perhaps, for this observer, than either Alice Munro winning the Nobel or Lydia Davis nabbing the Man Booker International – was the emergence of *Lighthouse*, a little magazine from Norwich publishing short stories, poems and essays of exceptional quality, including one (Anna Metcalfe's 'Number Three') that was later shortlisted in the Sunday Times EFG Short Story Award worth £30,000. *Lighthouse*, with its excellent editorial judgment and attractive modishly old-fashioned design, is a publication to cherish.

It's especially cheering that in the digital era, print publications, rather than merely clinging on, are flourishing, and there are more deserving stories being published than there is room for reprints in this book. I was much taken by two stories in the August 2013 issue of *Ellery Queen Mystery Magazine* – Jennifer Reeve's 'A Case of Mis-Identity' and Val McDermid's 'Ghost Writer' – as well as Jason Gould's 'All Items of Value Have Been Removed', in *Structo* 10, 'Two Parties' by Alan Beard, which appeared in *The Sea in Birmingham* (Tindal Street Fiction Group), and Krishan Coupland's 'Men of the Waste', shortlisted for the Bristol Short Story Prize and so included in the *Bristol Short Story Prize Anthology Volume Six* (Bristol Review of Books).

There wasn't a bad story in *The Longest Night* featuring five 'curious tales' by Alison Moore, Emma Jane Unsworth, Richard Hirst, Tom Fletcher and Jenn Ashworth; this handsome volume, illustrated by Beth Ward, was described as 'an entirely independent collaborative publication' with no named publisher or editor credited. Two regional anthologies provided a generous number of notably good short stories – *Root: New Stories From North East Writers* (Iron Press) edited by Kitty Fitzgerald, and *Connecting Nothing With Something: A Coastal Anthology* (Influx Press) edited by Gary Budden and Kit Caless, featuring new fiction, poetry and illustration inspired by the coastline of south-east England.

Some titles may reach small audiences, but they are labours of love and we are all richer for their existing. *Hoax* started up last year, a single A3 sheet folded to A5 and describing itself as 'a literary venture to present all forms of creative, text-based work as equal and to remove useless definitions of what creative work can be'. Further information at hoaxpublication. co.uk. Piece of Paper Press, run by author Tony White, is going strong after a number of years; last year saw it publish an original short story by Michael Moorcock, 'A Twist in the Lines'. *Interrobang*, possibly the world's first origami literary magazine, was created by York St John creative writing student Fionn Coughlan-Wills; like *Hoax*, this unfolds to a single piece of paper – glossy and printed in colour – but you try folding it back up again after a couple of drinks.

York St John is just one of the many universities around the country running lively and imaginative creative writing departments with excellent staff and talented students. Novelist, screenwriter and short story writer Hanif Kureishi made the news early this year with comments he was reported to have made at the Independent Bath Literature Festival.

Kureishi, who was made a professor at Kingston University in autumn 2013 and teaches creative writing there, was reported to have said, 'A lot of my students just can't tell a story.' He was reported to have gone on: 'A lot of them don't really understand. It's the story that really helps you. They worry about the writing and the prose and you think: "Fuck the prose, no one's going to read your book for the writing, all they want to do is find out what happens in the story next."'

This perhaps resonates with the experience of a friend of mine who applied for a job teaching creative writing at a university in the north of England. He confided that, when he went for an interview, there were four people in the room including the Head of English and himself, and three of them said they weren't that fussed about punctuation. The Head of English admitted to not knowing how to use a semi-colon. My friend was shocked and was quite relieved not to be offered the job and so have to decide whether to compromise his standards.

But the fact is there are some excellent writer-teachers on the staff at Kingston, as elsewhere, who must have been rather frustrated by Kureishi's comments. Why did he appear to bite the hand that feeds, adding, according to the *Independent*, 'The whole thing with courses is that there are too many teachers on them, and most are going to teach you stuff that is a waste of time for you'? Was he venting spleen, stating a sincerely held view, being mildly disingenuous or simply engaging in downright mischief? He did, after all, have a new book out, and newspapers never tire of the old debate: can you or can you not teach creative writing?

While the smart answer may be that you can teach it all you like, and the real question remains whether you can learn it, the fact is that my colleagues and I at the Manchester Writing School at MMU see remarkable results every year, and we're not alone in that. If you can write, the practice of workshopping and exposure to other elements of a creative writing MA will, in most cases, help you to write better.

This year's anthology is dedicated to the memory of Birmingham-based author Joel Lane, a much-loved writer of bleak and disturbing short stories – his preferred term was 'weird fiction' – as well as two outstanding novels and several volumes of poetry, who died unexpectedly on 25 November 2013 aged only 50.

NICHOLAS ROYLE
Manchester
April 2014

THE *Best*
{ BRITISH }
Short Stories
2014

THE FABER BOOK
OF ADULTERY

MARK FOLLOWED HER to the living room, drink in hand. The room was two rooms knocked together, running from white wooden slatted shutters at the front to a view of the lawn at the rear, scattered with toys. The long wall opposite was thick with shelves, the books backing onto the no doubt equally well-stocked shelves of the house next door. The terrace, in Mark's mind, extended away from them in both directions, like a paper chain of human figures joined at the hand and foot, a procession of paired mirror images. In all of them, people having dinner parties, couples flirting, children soundly sleeping.

Elizabeth had gone to the stereo, with her husband's iPhone, so he took himself in the other direction. He cruised the shelves, running his fingers over the spines, before allowing them to settle on one, as if at random. He levered it out, enjoying the feeling of resistance it gave as it slid against those packed tight on either side. When it came free, almost with a pop, the books alongside seemed to sigh into the space it left, their pages filling with air.

The book was Richard Ford's *Women with Men* – the handsome Harvill Panther edition. On the cover was a Doisneauesque couple kissing, or sort of kissing, on a railway platform. He flicked the book open with his thumb – the page edges smudged with age – to reveal a second photo, inside, of a barge on the Seine. Those low embankment walkways. That was where the true loucheness of Paris lay, he thought, in the flatness of its river water, so far from the sea – no overexcited tides, falling and rising, like the Thames.

Have you read this? he said. She was coming back over to him, her music selection drifting from the speakers.

Let me see, she said.

Yes. Look. And he showed him her initials, penned into the top corner of the first page. She thumbed on through it, giving a little grunt of recognition, or surprise.

Mark oriented himself against the mantel shelf, giving himself a clear view of the doorway into the hall, which turned and led down to the kitchen extension, where they had eaten: he and Laura and Elizabeth and Zac, and these two other women, Genevieve and Nicci, friends of Elizabeth's. The others were clearing the table and loading the dishwasher. Elizabeth, having cooked, was exempt, and Mark had said he would keep her entertained until they were done.

He took his first sip of the whisky Zac had poured him in the kitchen. The taste of it spread, making his mouth glow, as if he'd been given a very gentle anaesthetic, or stung by a swarm of infinitesimal and ultimately benign bees. Elizabeth's hair was the colour of whisky, but not whisky held up to the light: whisky seen looking down into the glass. He was quite drunk.

Why did nobody have drinks cabinets any more? He looked around the room. This was another difference between their generation and their parents'. Did this mean they were less adventurous in their drinking? Were their parents' hangovers worse, then? Grander, more splendid?

Elizabeth closed the book and handed it back. It's been a while since I read it, she said. And those American writers, sometimes it's difficult to hold onto a definite image of each individual story, you know.

All those endless adulteries, you mean.

I suppose so.

He could hear occasional yelps of laughter from the kitchen, short swells of conversation that gave birth to others: a healthy, stable wash of chit-chat.

I know what you mean, he said. Ford. Updike. Cheever. Yates.

Philip Roth.

Philip Roth. It's like they're incapable of writing a story that doesn't hinge, doesn't depend entirely for its moral resonance, on the traducement – is that the word? – of a marriage.

And you've never written a story about adultery?

No, but then I don't really do stories that much. And the novels are reasonably free of them, I think. But no. I'm yet to write my first adultery story.

She raised her eyebrows at him, and he considered the terrible, and terribly exact beauty of a woman's eyebrows, their pluckedness and trimmedness. Really, it made you wonder if binding their feet might not be such a bad idea either, after all.

Adultery and the short story, he said, in his seminar voice, and gave the whisky in his glass a swirl. Actually, I had this horrible realisation, in the class I've been teaching, that a good half of the stories I'd set them were about adultery. Carver, obviously. Not Updike – nobody teaches him any more, it seems – but Yates, Lorrie Moore, Anne Beattie. Yes, the women, too. What?

She was laughing, into her glass.

I was just thinking, how nice it is for the women that they get to have first names.

Ha.

No, I'm sorry. And what do they think of it, of their tutor foisting all this filth on them? Does it embarrass them?

God, no. If it was tutor-shagging-student stories, perhaps. But adultery, marriage, middle age, all that is so remote from their lives, it might as well be Chekhov.

She laughed again, the laugh turning into a sneeze. He removed a tissue from a box on the shelf beside them and offered it to her.

Thanks.

It's interesting, though, don't you think?

She finished blowing her nose. Interesting?

The short story, its use of adultery as the ethical question of the modern age. Not war, not death or grief – well, those too, but not, you know, bullfighting, or money, or violence. Do you think I'm obsessed?

I think that's a question you should ask your wife.

But before he could think of something to say to this, the others came through, Zac swinging the whisky bottle by its neck, then sort of half-throwing it up to catch it full in his hand.

Looks like you need some of this, he said.

Indeed I do. Thank you. Mark held out the glass for Zac to splash into, and smiled to the others. I was just banging on to Liz about adultery and the short story, he said. Actually, I've got this fantasy, this book I'm going to edit. The Faber Book of Adultery. The joke being, I suppose, that the subject is so all-pervasive as to make the selection entirely otiose. It could be pages taken at random from any book, published ever. They're all about adultery. A sweep of his arm, as if reading from a banner. The. Faber. Book. Of. Adultery. The Faber. Book of. Words.

They laughed, and he blushed, and warned himself to ease off on the adultery. Accordingly the conversation became general, and they grouped themselves and sat, in pairs and threes. Mark could feel the alcohol in his bloodstream, and the music thrumming along behind the conversation, as if to

4

underpin and corroborate it. Flirtation was a wonderful thing, he felt, and he was, he also felt, quite good at it. Flirtation was all about the navigation of invisible boundaries and contours, the skirting of a hill, the climbing of a stile. The only thing was that the line that stood between him and his friend's wife wasn't acting like a line. It was humming, glowing like a strip light, expanding and contracting, becoming more a zone than a line, something that could be stepped into without necessarily being crossed.

Even filching glances at Laura, he got no sense that he'd overstepped any mark. He sat there, sipping his drink and nodding along to whatever it was this Nicci was saying, but really he was listening to his body. His body was singing – or, not singing, but something like it, something like the harmonics you get from a piano. This heightened sense of – not desire, exactly, or desiredness, but something to do with desire.

You're flirting with yourself, he told himself, and smiled at the thought.

You're flirting with yourself, over her.

He watched Zac get up, laughing at something Laura had said, and go to the far end of the room. He leaned to tap at the screen of his iPhone, there in its dock, then scrolled with his finger. He tapped again, and the music changed: something harder, folky still, but with an electronic undercurrent that seemed to chivvy it along.

It was as Zac walked back over, affecting a cool/dumb clown-dance as he came, that Mark was struck by an appalling thought.

His wife, and his kids, treated his iPhone just the same as Elizabeth had treated Zac's: as common property. The kids even knew the pass code for it. They played games on it, when they were allowed, and Laura checked the weather and looked things up on the web if the laptop was off, or being used. And then there was that app they'd downloaded onto their phones that allowed each of them to see where the other's was, for if it got lost. How was anyone supposed to have an affair under such circumstances?

All those post-war Yank adulterers, with their elegant tail-finned cars, and their motels and pools, and their bright New England suburbs, they were all shagging away in what now seemed like a golden age. Nobody could have affairs any more, surely, any more than they could have drinks cabinets. He knew they did, in the abstract, but he certainly didn't know anyone who had. He couldn't see how anyone would even start to go about it.

It was a chastening thought, and his thank you kiss to Elizabeth, there in the hallway, was chaste, too, though he couldn't help but note the particular quality of the pressure with which she squeezed his arm, through the corduroy of his jacket, as they smudged cheeks, in a way that might have been code, or the code for a code. The still night air and back-of-the-head buzz of the booze and the warm clear rising thought of the impossibility of it all put a spring in his step as they walked home, and he clinched his wife's waist tight in to his, so she nearly tripped, and squeezed his bum in retaliation, and they laughed, and quickened their step again.

In the weeks that followed he thought about it more. He got out his Oxford Concise Dictionary, as was his habit at such times – when he felt an idea coming, beginning to take up residence in the part of him that wrote, that made him a writer – and looked up the etymology. It came from the Latin: Adulterare, to corrupt, as in to adulterate. Which was a nicely moral formulation: anything else added to a marriage being necessarily inferior, like cutting cocaine with baking powder, or worse. He'd assumed it shared a root with 'adult', but it didn't. That came from adolescere, to grow up. You had to be an adult to commit adultery, had been his thinking. After all, teenagers didn't do it, nor really did twenty-somethings. It was a grown-up activity, a mark of maturity.

He thought about how a story about adultery might work. If he was to have an affair, in this world of smartphones and itemised bills, and of couples who both held down jobs, and had kids, this world without motels and Cadillacs and back-yard pools, how would he go about it? If he was going to have an affair with Elizabeth, for instance, how would it happen? He thought of the readings and events he had coming up, and of other ones he could organise or invent, and he thought about how he would make contact with Elizabeth, safely and discreetly and deniably, or places they might bump into each other as if by chance.

Before any of these hypothetical situations could resolve themselves into anything like a plot, he found himself back at her house. It was a Friday evening, and he was babysitting Walter, their four-year-old, as the first leg of a trial babysitting swap. The plan had been that Laura would do it, but their own eldest, Morrie, was poorly, and Laura said she'd stay at home, and Mark should go.

Zac let him into the house, and told him to get himself a drink while they finished getting ready. It was the fortieth birthday of a friend from school, in a pub a taxi ride away. Elizabeth looked gorgeous in a wrap dress – he said as much after he'd kissed her hello – and she acknowledged the compliment by dipping her head to one side to fix her earring, a movement that dislodged a segment of hair that seemed to unfurl, in slow motion, down to her shoulder.

He stood on the front step to wave them off, feeling that strange feeling you get sending people out into the world from their own home, as if you'd become their doppelgänger, slipped yourself into the hierarchy. He watched till the taxi rounded the corner, then closed the door, gently, listening for the click of the latch. The house was his.

To begin with, he went to the kitchen and topped up his glass from the bottle Zac had pointed out to him. The place was messier than the night of the dinner party. There was a stack of children's paintings at the far end of the kitchen surface, stiff as poppadoms. More paper, with pencils and crayons, and left-over bits of the newspaper on the table. Two plates slotted slantwise in the sink, stuck with dried tubes of pasta and what looked like congealed custard. He opened a cupboard and looked inside, closed it, switched on the radio, then switched it off again.

He went into the sitting room, his sock feet making him feel even more like an intruder, and picked three recentish novels from the shelves, trying to guess which of them – Zac or Elizabeth – they belonged to. He took them to the sofa and flicked on the television. With half an eye on the telly he read their back covers, copyright pages, acknowledgements and openings, then put them down. He took his wine and went up the stairs. He stood for a moment outside Walter's door, listening for his breathing. He went inside and stood in the middle of the room. The boy was sprawled face down on his bed, in flannel pyjamas, with his duvet kicked down to the foot of the bed and his bum stuck in the air. Mark thought of his own children, of Morrie, and reminded himself to text home to check how he was. He pulled the duvet over Walter, who grunted and shifted in response.

One by one he pushed open the other doors off the landing: the bathroom, with its strange array of bottles and pots on the shelf and window sill; the spare room, clothes laid out on the bed in dry-cleaner bags; and then the master bedroom.

He stood looking at the bed, the two bedside tables, then he went to the cupboards and opened them. The doors on the right were Zac's, those on the left, hers.

He ran the back of a hand over the sleeves and sides of the garments gathered there, her clothes, then pushed his arm in, making a gap and widening it, to expose a delicate grey cardigan with mother of pearl buttons. His neck muscles were tight from the strain of listening for the sound of the front door. He slid his fingers inside the opening of the cardigan and ran them up and down against the weave of it. He had given himself the beginning of an erection. This is what he did, he thought, he vampirised other people's lives, sucking up incident and detail and squirrelling it away. He drew out his hand slowly, letting the fibres snag on his knuckles as they came, then brushed the clothes straight and went around the bed and sat down on it.

There, face down on the bedside table, was his own novel, his second and best one. He gave a laugh. This must be Elizabeth's side, mustn't it? He lifted a corner of the duvet and saw the beginnings of something liquid, a silk pyjama top. He switched on the bedside lamp and opened the book at the marked place. It was the scene in which the protagonist, Ricardo, was having his final confrontation with his father, accusing him of ruining his life by, well, by doing all manner of not particularly awful things, like being a bit strict, and making him play rugby, and sending him to a school he hated. He turned to the front.

'To Laura, always,' it said. The first was to Laura, the second to Laura, always. He'd set a precedent, and if he didn't keep dedicating his books to his wife, it would look odd. Why had he not simply dedicated it to his father, who was still alive when he wrote it, dead when it came out? His father, who had done so much to instil in him his love of books, and films, and so little to turn him into the kind of snivelling, self-pitying squib of character epitomised by Ricardo.

He flicked through the pages, to see if Elizabeth had left any mark of herself or her thoughts: an underlining, a folded corner. Nothing. People didn't have that kind of relationship with books, really, sad to say, not even him. Books, he felt, had usually stopped meaning very much to people by the time they were old enough to benefit from the wisdom they contained. People – grown-ups, adulterers – read books for the consolation they offered for the sad, true fact that they hadn't become the sort of the people they'd thought they would by reading the books they did when they were younger. He shook his head at himself. It was a stupid thought, the sort of thing he'd put in his book and his editor would insist he take out.

He put the book back on the table, stood and sighed, and looked around the room. The double-stacked pillows, the painting above the bed, the full-length mirror on its stand in the corner. There was something here, he thought. The marital bedroom.

He went down to the kitchen and found a couple of unscribbled-upon sheets of paper and a pen and went back upstairs. He sat on the bed and started writing.

The marital bedroom. Not so much a physical space as a mental one. A place where certain things happen. Some allowed, some proscribed.

Then:

He followed Frances into the living room. The curves of her backside. Crossed that out. The way the downward curve of her back changed direction, rotating through the three dimensions, to become the swelling pads of her derriere.

Just writing it brought back the sensation of arousal. The loosening at the insides of his legs, the hairs on his scrotum. He wrote there for ten minutes, sat bent over on the edge of the bed, then decided he had best go downstairs. He smoothed the duvet and double-checked the room before he went.

It was gone twelve when he heard the key in the lock. He was lying stretched out on the sofa, half-dozing, with a bad early Julian Barnes splayed open on his chest. He blinked awake and swung himself round and up. Felt for the wad of folded pages in his back jeans pocket.

It was Elizabeth. She stood in the doorway and smiled a little fuzzily at him.

Hi there.

Hi.

Everything okay?

He stretched. Yup. All fine. Not a peep. Good time?

She nodded, and shrugged off her coat.

I'll just pop upstairs and look in on him.

Sure. Mark followed her out into the hallway. Zac was nowhere in sight. He stood there, thinking, until she reappeared.

A load of them went on to a club, she said, as she came down, but I decided to call it a night. They're Zac's gang, really.

Right.

He'll regret it in the morning, of course.

Of course.

Now they were both stood in the hallway. He hadn't moved to get his things together, his jacket and phone. A moment arrived, and sort of hung between them. He waited it out, then said, with a carefully calibrated half-smile, So can I interest you in a nightcap?

A nightcap?

I quite fancy a drink, to be honest. He pulled a hangdog expression, watching her face, as if to show he was already resigned to her saying no.

Okay. What'll you have?

Well, I've had a couple of glasses of this very nice Sancerre, but I think I could push to a glass of that Talisker from the other night.

Talisker it is then.

He followed her into the kitchen, tracking the movement,

slightly weaving, of her hips and back – and, okay, her bottom – her furtive nips at her hair. This he wasn't good at. He could do dialogue, and drama, and introspection, but it was the transitional moments that got him stuck. Getting a character into the room. Getting them out of a car, in through the front door. It was laborious, self-conscious work. Nor could he assume that she would turn around and kiss him, just like that. If he wanted this to happen, he would have to make it happen – and that was the hardest thing. Now she had the bottle, and two glasses, and was pouring. When she turned, he would do it. But then if she went to the sink to get water? When she passed him the glass, then.

Water? Or do you prefer ice?

A drop of water. Lovely. Perfect.

There you go.

She held him out the glass and he took it and as he took it he pressed his fingers onto hers. And, at the same time, pushed his mouth down onto hers. That impossible, unthinkable action, like wilfully smashing your head against a wall, or the trunk of a tree. And, for a moment, she let herself be held there, be stopped, for a moment. Then she slowly pulled back, so very slowly he could feel the suck of the skin of their lips as they parted.

Well, then. What do you think you're doing?

I'm sorry. I just . . .

His mouth, he couldn't stop it, was hovering in the vicinity of a grin, as if waiting for permission to feel relief, or wicked embarrassment.

Ah, you just, she said. I see. Well, that's clear, then.

I just wanted to kiss you.

She lifted her arm to put her glass to her mouth, and his hand fell from it. She drank, swallowed, then tidied her lips with her tongue.

And what did you think would happen then?

12

Well, I suppose I thought that either you'd kiss me back, or you'd ask me to leave. Or, you know, slap my face . . .

She said nothing.

And, well, you've not done any of those things.

She slid the few inches along the kitchen counter until she was right next to him.

I'm not about to throw you out, am I?

Does that mean you are going to kiss me?

Ah, well.

They were standing so close now it was like being stuck in a crowded lift together. It would be impossible to even breathe without touching her. His erection was back, and he felt in it something like the power he felt when he was writing, and it was going well, the words revealing themselves one after the other on the screen, the text shifting up, line by line, to accommodate him.

It's not something I'm used to, kissing strange men in my kitchen. Or any men at all, really. Though I would like to kiss you.

And she did, curling her arm up to cradle the back of his head, and they brought their heads together in a whisky-tinted kiss that seemed to act, as he closed his eyes, like some kind of sacrament. He moved the hand that wasn't around his glass, on the kitchen counter, down to her waist. They were both making quiet noises of surprise and approval in their mouths, while their mouths, too, made noises, the incidental laps of tongues and lips.

He spoke, the words humming in the cavity of her mouth.

I wonder if you think we should go upstairs, he said.

She seemed to ponder this for a moment, then unkissed herself.

You want to go upstairs?

Mm.

Upstairs, as in to the bedroom? She distanced herself

further, a matter of inches, or centimetres, or less. Mark, I am not having sex with you upstairs, with my son asleep next door. She said this with a hoarse half-laugh that only served to mark the utter humourlessness of his proposition.

Well, obviously, he said. I didn't mean. I mean, we don't have to go upstairs.

Now they were talking over each other, she saying, What, so you want to have sex in the kitchen? while he was saying, I didn't mean that at all, and sort of paddling at the air between them, while she seemed to be trying to find a pose for her chin, her arms, her hips, that might best transmit whatever it was she might be thinking. She picked up her glass, empty, and drank from it. She poured more, in anger, then went out of the kitchen into the hallway.

Shit, look, he said, but he was talking to himself.

He followed her out.

So how was your evening, then? he said, hating himself as he spoke. I hate myself, he thought, and he shoved the pages of writing further down into his jeans pocket.

Oh, there was dancing, she said, and her anger seemed to have dissipated, or transferred itself somewhat. We danced.

She went into the sitting room and over to the stereo. She bent down – he watched the material of her dress shift to accommodate the flow of the anatomy beneath it – and brought out from a low cupboard a stack of CDs. Accommodate, he thought: horrific, unforgivable word. He was repeating himself.

She slid it . . . Christ, she *put* the fucking compact disc into the sodding machine and pressed play. Picked up her drink and came towards him.

So, Mark, Mark. Marky Mark. What's going on in that head of yours?

He smiled, as cover.

As cover, he smiled.

I've been thinking about you, he said.

Well, I've been thinking about you, too. I've been thinking about you especially hard in the last few minutes.

And before he could come back with some no doubt asinine reply to that they were kissing again. Thank God, he thought. Very gently, very deliberately, he lifted a hand and put it through her hair at the side of her hand. Her head. The side of her head. Ran his fingers through the strands, separating and defining them, as if to honour each one. She seemed to appreciate this, and began to push at him more with her mouth, implicating and exploring him, and making a use of her relative lack of height that he found just delicious. So much so that he gave, or let out, or emitted, a quiet grunt or groan. Or moan. Please more of a moan than a groan, he thought, reaching after the awful sound, to hear it again, fix it in his mind.

She was on tiptoe, one hand on his upper arm to steady herself. Her other hand on his waist. His shirt ridden up, she had her hand on his belt, the thumb inside the waistband, and she slid it around, as if unthinkingly, towards his back pocket. He shifted his stance, to stop her getting even slightly near the pages of his story – not a story, not yet; just notes, really – and this brought the front of his jeans into contact with the front of her, the what, the declivity of her? She gave a sort of moany groan – she was doing it now, too, whatever it was – and it carried within it, the sound, particles of what sounded like laughter. She slid her hand back around and pressed it against him, flat on the raw denim.

Oh god, she said, talking now to his shirt. What are we going to do with you?

Eyes closed, he found a way to press himself harder against her hand, and she pressed back, actually holding him, as best she could, through his jeans, showing through the action of her palm her intimate understanding of the matter. He pushed even harder, hating himself, but wanting above all to find some way of expressing himself, his intentions, his delicate reservations, past history, world view, thoughts on the nature of signification, the problem of endings, Wittgenstein, Kelly Brook, the de Stijl movement, the novels of Michel Houelle-becq and Chris Cleave, any or all of this.

He shifted himself and tried to reciprocate, moving his hand to the front of her dress, but she outflanked him, still kissing, shaking her head in the kiss – Uh-uh, she said, or otherwise intoned – twisting her hips to deflect or dissuade him. He turned his head to the side, and felt his body be jerked forward two, three times as she tugged his belt out from its buckle. He thought of dressing and undressing his children, the thousands of instances of it, their patience and passivity in the face of it, the way they held out their legs, or raised their arms. She opened his fly, pop-pop-pop went the buttons, and he said, well, something. Who knows what he said. To her or himself. Something about a text not sent. An exclamation, exhortation, appeal to the deity.

Is this what you want? she said, and he bit his lip, unwilling to trust himself to words. She had his what, his cock? his dick? his fucking prick free of his underwear now and was working, quite unconscionably, away, with a solicitude that seemed to go quite beyond intimacy, that was almost incestuous. His hand was on the mantel shelf. The other on her shoulder, bracing himself.

Please, he said.

What?

Please.

Shh, she said, and he heard, too, the quiet susurration of a tissue being drawn from its box. He opened his eyes in fright and saw books, hundreds of them, up, down, left and right. None of them his, but each one of them chock full of adultery, even the ones entirely free of it. His gaze skittered desperately across their spines, pressed hard as a cliff face, nowhere

safe, nowhere to hold onto, to come to rest. This can't be it, he
thought, as his fingers gripped tight on her shoulder and she
leaned into him, thinking no doubt of the carpet, closing the
gap between them, and as he felt her forehead buck gently
against his shoulder he thought: not this. This can't be what
it's like.

JAY GRIFFITHS

THE SPIRAL STAIRWELL

A TRUE STORY

IT HAPPENED IN Bristol, during the Blitz. Every night, Len drove an ambulance to collect the dead and the injured. He would be given a slip of paper with a typed address, a message sending him across the city to houses bombed with explosives or incendiary devices. His job was to find whatever remained.

One night, having done several journeys through the siren-scarred night, he returned to base and went to the control room. The controller was a slow, careful woman. He held out his hand impatiently for the next message-slip with the next address on it. The address he was given was his own.

The sky is falling, the sky is falling, the sky is falling. He had often read this story to his daughter at bedtime. He couldn't get the line out of his head now.

'Does the sky ever fall in real life?' she had asked.

'Never, my little princess, never.'

He had stroked her silky hand. She put all her small fist in his and her trust made him a lion, as he carried her up the cast-iron spiral stairwell to her bedroom, with a window to the stars.

Now he holds the message-slip in his hand. Motionless, he

stares at the controller. She doesn't know that where a stranger's address should be, he sees his own. He is seized by an agony of heroism which turns his mouth to metal in a moment. He says nothing but takes the paper and walks to the ambulance. His knees don't shake but they don't bend either.

Anti-aircraft lights are scoring his deep, dark veins and all his lovely inner night is torn open.

All sounds recede. The fall of information on deafened ears. The typed letters indent the paper like the beloved marks of baby teeth on the books in his study.

Then panic. The siren, screaming itself white in the black night, is screaming inside his silence.

Dry-mouthed, he wants to take the message back to the controller, and tell her she's an idiot, that she made a stupid mistake. Then he wants to rip up the message, tear it to shreds, burn it and stamp on the ashes. But even if he does, the message won't go away. *The writing is on the wall. A written warning. It is written, it is written, it is written.*

Suddenly, the paper seems alive to him and he clutches at it, fearing to drop it. He twists the paper between two fingers as he pushes his round glasses up over his nose and grasps the wheel. *Why am I holding onto it? Am I likely to forget, for God's sake* – and his mind swings with his hands on the wheel turning the corner as fast as he can – *am I likely to forget what it says? It is my most precious memento. All I will have left of my world is the little scrap of paper which describes it.*

He grips it for dear life. The message is now an icon, the print of an address burnt onto his mind like the print of a dress which will be burnt on to the body of a small girl in Hiroshima. The future is in the present. East is West and the girl is his own daughter. Lateral explosions. Collateral damage. East of the sun and West of the moon, he hums, madly. 'Love . . . makes one little roome an everywhere,' and his whole world is in that address.

I am the only one who knows what this message means. And what it means is that I am alone in a world deworlded. He can read the message forwards and backwards, from the present into the future and from the future into the past. This is the message of infinite destruction and he will carry the message wherever he must.

Driving across Bristol, he is driving from the world of the living to the world of the dead. Tension fuses his hands onto the steering wheel as the skies, prised apart from the heavens, crash to earth.

The sky is falling now. On all my world.

Of all the houses in all of Bristol, you had to drop bombs on mine. That house was my whole world, you bastards. You bastards, you bombed my whole, entire world.

His round-toed shoes gunned the accelerator, when suddenly a tabby cat ran into the low headlights and he slammed on the brakes. *Damn it to hell, must this war take everything? Even a little pussy cat?*

He is there. He is there. He is there.

Part of the roof is on fire.

The house is still standing.

Hope corkscrews through him, hurting him.

He pulls open the door and then he sees.

His whole world is trembling in the balance.

All the glad world held to ransom in that moment.

Hanging by a thread.

For an incendiary bomb has fallen on the house but – *by all the angels who ever loved me* – he gasps, the bomb has fallen in the dead-centre of the cast-iron spiral stairwell.

There it burns. Caught, burning its fury, exquisitely, caught in the nick of time, in the nick of place. Tucked in the spiral banisters, the bomb rocks and fizzes.

Underneath it, deep in the cellar, dark and implicit as a womb, his wife and children are tucked together: his world and worlds to come. The children are whimpering: he sees his daughter first, her eyes full of fear and fireworks, transfixed by the bomb. It is seared onto her retina and I know that for the rest of her life she will never understand how people can actually *like* fireworks.

'Dad is here, Dad is here, Dad is here,' her brother shouts out, breaking the spell, and she sees him as never before. Hero. Mountain. Tree. Lion. Dad.

His wife is calculating if it is safe to edge out of the cellar now. The children don't think: they run to their father, he lifts them to kiss them, but they are not kissable children now, they are small, frightened animals, and they burrow into his body, tucking themselves into the deep dark of his overcoat.
'You'll be right as ninepence, my darlings, right as a trivet, right as rain, right as . . .' and his voice was too choked to go on.

'The sky *did* fall, Dad. Might it ever fall again?'
'Never, my little princess, never.'
It was months later. He was taking his little daughter up the stairwell to her bedroom with a window to the stars. Memory turns in spirals, like a stairwell, like the double helix of DNA, like whorls of galaxies. As he carried her, he remembered not only her near-death but also her conception.

His wife was looking sternly at him, telling him he was a bit tipsy. So he tickled her. And tickled her again till she giggled. I imagine them giggling when a little spurt of starlight shot out of him, giggling seeds which laughed their way into her earth-night and one shooting star, with perfect aim, found its way right into the centre of her whorls and inner spiral stairwells, exploding on the scene, a tiny bomb of life: sherbet, yeast, champagne, fireworks, starworks. *Ping!* My mother.

RICHARD KNIGHT

THE INCALCULABLE WEIGHT OF WATER

HE HAULS HIS aching body forward to the dam wall, up the grassy bank in the warmed silence of a July afternoon. He's too old for climbing hills. Ann has been pushing this idea for years. She's waiting for him now, in the café next to the car park, and he knows that by the time he makes it back down there he will certainly have taken too long. She'll get up and sigh and tell him, tell him that he's too old, as though that somehow explains everything.

Ann has asked him several times over the years why he likes to climb up high. Once, years ago, she came with him out of interest, in the time when they first tussled with each other's strangeness and were happy in that struggle. It was before they'd even thought of marrying, years before Oliver was born. They'd eaten a sandwich, he remembers now, in the lee of this same dark wall, the mist swirling around their young, loose-limbed bodies. She'd mocked him gently about the view he'd promised and he knew by the end of that day that she would never come with him again, preferring the company of the radio, her books or her friends. But he still remembers that image, still sees it now tilting back like a framed photograph; Ann at its centre shivering with the thick-cut sandwich pinched between forefinger and thumb, not liking his walk but loving him still. That trip was conceived from the possibilities of love.

Perhaps she's right, he thinks, looking up and feeling the beginnings of a slight mountain breeze that cools his sweating face. The sky is a densely packed blue, almost solid and unmarked over the blackened grit-stone wall. He senses the incalculable weight of water that squats behind that wall, unseen, menacing. He's been here before in winter wind and heard it lapping, lashing the stone and agitating for release. But today, a fine day like this, he imagines it will be lifeless, a darker likeness of the unblemished sky.

He should recognise the birdsong by now. Are they curlews? He can't remember if it's the right season, but he doesn't wonder about it for long. He's walked up here many times, but not really for the bird life. He squints under the sun, mapping the route in his head along the ridge to the west of the reservoir and back down to the car park. Flying ants swarm there in late summer but he hopes it's still too early for them.

It's so quiet up here he imagines he could whisper her name – her straightforward name, no need for a gratuitous 'e' – and that it would slice through the stillness and she'd somehow hear it down there. He thinks it, he even parts his mouth slightly, but doesn't push the necessary air out. In the right pocket of his walking trousers he grasps the phone that Ann makes him carry and switches it on. It's mid-afternoon and now it feels as though the heat is humming as he waits for a sequence of glaring screens to load.

It had been Ann's idea to come out today. There was no use just sitting around waiting, she'd said. They had her mobile number, the one she used all the time now. These days he was more often than not bemused as he watched the world alter, swinging away in a direction he couldn't quite understand, but Ann had always just accepted how things moved. As Oliver said, usually after they'd both failed to hear his call ringing on the kitchen handset, there's little point having a home telephone these days. Oliver often sent Ann text messages, which were sometimes relayed across the patterned wool carpet that separated their chairs. Early that afternoon she'd made the suggestion – which was more of a decision really – and put his boots in the car and driven them to the visitor centre. The boots had been the sign. He knew then she wanted to be away from him.

He cups his hand around the old Nokia and turns his back on the sun. As ever, there's no signal. The small icon of an antenna in the top left corner of his screen droops like a plant wilting in the heat. She'll work it out, he thinks. She won't be worried; she knows how it is. God, she's enough to worry about herself. He puts the phone back in his pocket. High above his head an aeroplane trails an erect stream through the blue and he wonders which resort it's heading for. For a second or two he closes his eyes against the glare of a summer idyll, the awful images of everyday happiness.

His heart thuds and he suddenly feels light-headed. He reaches the wall, holds out a hand to its rough contours. The breath of the breeze cools his brow and he steadies himself there, peering out across a vast sheen of thick, peaty water. This strip of the world, this strange flat landscape, is as empty as ever.

This is what he comes for.

The stillness consumes him for a moment and he lets it, lets it sink in until it rings through his skull.

Ann thought they'd have rung in the morning.

'You'd think they would,' she'd wondered aloud at lunchtime through the tinny babble of the kitchen radio, as he cut woody cores from slices of tomato. 'Why keep people hanging on? It isn't fair. Thoughtless, really.'

He didn't think she needed to hear a reason and muttered his agreement. She was talking to make noise, to fill spaces. Now he feels the sweat between his eyebrows and his eyelids, takes off his glasses and wipes it away with the back of his wrist. He hadn't realised it was quite so hot when he set out an hour ago. He hasn't brought water with him. Another hour and he'll be back in the café with a cool drink, but he's dreading it already. He fears the evenness with which Ann will accept the news, whatever that is, and turn her mind to the future; to plans, ideas, images that he can't even bear to picture. Up here the world is unmoved, unmoving. Up here his mind is at rest briefly, out of range, lacking a signal. He blinks and puts his glasses back on.

At first he sees it as a small island. It's summer after all, a rare fine one, and the water level in the reservoir is already quite low. Over by the west shore there's a slim, black mound, maybe twenty yards out in the water. Curious, he walks further along the embankment. He has to go in that direction anyway, to get to the path that runs along the ridge. At the end of the wall he stops and shields his eyes from the glare of the sun.

The black coat is filled with air. Who would throw their coat into the reservoir, he wonders? Nearer though, dropping onto the small rocky beach, he recognises an arm, a white hand. He stumbles on a stone, his arm shooting out instinctively as he rebalances and stands, struck suddenly immobile by the lifelessness of the corpse. His heart pounds, as a kind of reassurance, a chaotic celebration of his own life. He hesitates at the edge of the gently lapping water.

Before he knows what he's doing, he's ankle-deep in the reservoir. The black water ripples into wide chevrons in front of his shins. Each short stride takes him inevitably towards the startling prospect of a dead body. He stops for a moment and looks back, as though there might be clues suspended in the humid air; about when this happened, how it happened, why it happened. But there's nothing. He turns back to the corpse.

The white hand he'd thought was floating is in fact resting on a black bin bag. The body could have been here a long time, he suddenly realises. The moment of death might have passed months ago, when a coat would still have been needed. Would he worry about keeping warm in a winter coat just before his own planned death? He stays there, the water below his knees, the question stilling him for a second. He feels a compulsion begin to rise, an urge to wade just a little further and tug at the coat, at the hood that hides the face. But he's fearful of the nothingness, the dreadful emptiness he might see there.

There's no rush up here. There's no life to save. The phone in his trouser pocket buzzes urgently and he almost falls, his boots slipping a little on the unseen bed of the reservoir. The noise is disproportionate, comical even, on a hot and windless hilltop and him up to his knees in water as sludgy and black as leftover coffee. He takes the phone from his pocket again, his eyes still fixed on the corpse ten yards away. He begins to make out the arch of the buttocks beneath the coat where the legs begin to slump under the surface of the water. It's definitely a man. He's convinced of that fact, for no clear reason.

With two careful prods of his thumbs, he unlocks the screen of the phone and despite the sun's glare he can just see there's a new message. He opens it.

From: Ann
just rang its ok hurry up want to go morisons

Instantly he senses fizzing molecules of air above the reservoir being sucked over the near horizon of the black wall. He gasps and stumbles on the uneven bed of the reservoir. Staring once more at the corpse, he is momentarily excited by something; his own jagged, unbalanced, uncalibrated heartbeat, perhaps.

There's little he can do here now. His impulse to reach out and touch the dead man is fading. He no longer has a desire to witness the hidden legs, the other arm, the true shape of a barren body, the gruesome and bloated white face that he pictures with a gaping mouth, a mouth that once spoke and relentlessly breathed air. He's no longer curious about the contents of the bin bag.

He grins at Ann's dreaded practicality, the unstudied normality of her text, the careless spelling, the missing punctuation. No x. Only two short words reserved for such significant news. He replaces the phone in his pocket. As they rotate in the water he watches his legs and sees the peat-saturated water swirl gently around his shins. Back on the rocky beach, he turns and looks again. It's still there, that small, black island. It's not a mirage, despite the shimmering air of summer. It's as real as the phone in his pocket, as the acrid water now slopping in his boots, as the car that will soon carry them – him and Ann – to Morrisons.

Descending the stony ridge path to the car park, he thinks about the dead man in the water. He knows he should call the police. He should tell Ann, too, which would deflect the conversation they ought to have. It would delay her shopping trip, that was for certain. He isn't clear how, but he knows that if he makes the call now, if he tells his wife, it might take them away from each other. As he nears the car park, he still hasn't decided what to do.

In the café, Ann's there, nursing a cup of tea with one hand and texting with the other. She stands up quickly as soon as she sees him enter. Her eyes glisten as she takes in his boots, moments before she smells the peaty water.

There's the sigh.

'Isn't it about time you packed it in, all this climbing up away from the world?' she snaps, even though it had been her idea in the first place.

She steps forward, not meeting his eye yet, and just for a moment he sees her doubtful eye cast over him, the young man he once was at the edge of his world. But he doesn't understand what happens next. She splutters, drops her shoulder like she's been shot, and he reaches out and catches her, holds her still. She sobs, only for a second or two, brief instants of the afternoon. He says nothing now. The café is empty, just the two of them left in there. He holds her for some time, listening to the clatter of dishes coming from somewhere beyond a door at the back of the room, trying to feel the heartbeat of his wife. She breaks away finally and sniffs. She laughs at herself, a short cough of a laugh behind a folded tissue, before she dares to catch his eye.

'What did you see up there?' she asks, beginning to move past him towards the door.

Someone will call the police soon. It might be him, but if he does call it won't be today. They'll go to Morrisons instead. Perhaps tomorrow he might tell Ann what he saw up there, if she cares to ask again.

'Nothing much,' he whispers, watching her back as she strides away through the door into the blinding light of the afternoon.

VICKI JARRETT

LADIES' DAY

A WET, GUSTY wind barges across the race track and slaps the crowd for being daft enough to have pictured this day as sunny.

The women, the *ladies*, are woefully exposed to the elements in thin dresses that flick and snap around goose-bumped fake tan, not a coat to be seen, clinging on to head gear, reinserting clips and pins, trying to hold it all together against the odds.

Three of us from the baby group – me, Kaz and Ashley – shelter behind a bookies' booth.

'Remind me again why we're here,' says Ashley, leaning on my shoulder for balance as she picks a wad of muddy grass from the heel of her stiletto.

Kaz glares at her. 'We're here to have a day off. Away from the kids, the husbands, the housework and everything. We're going to have fun, right?' She scowls at the two of us until we nod agreement. 'Anyway, the tickets cost a bomb so at least pretend like you are.'

Ashley examines the muddy streaks on her fingers. 'I need a drink,' she says.

I give her a baby-wipe from the packet in my bag.

I should've stayed at home, phoned Kaz and said I'd got a cold, or Sean's shifts had been changed at the last minute. Something. Anything.

Sean had come up behind me as I fiddled with my hair in the hall mirror. 'Mmhmm. Looking good,' he said, wrapped his arms round my waist and pressed in against my back. His hands travelled upwards as he nuzzled into my neck.

I steadied myself against the wall. I'm not used to heels so my balance wasn't great to start with. I peeled his fingers off and wriggled out of his grip.

'Thanks, that really helps.' I tried a laugh to soften the sarcasm in my voice but it came out bent. I don't know what's wrong with me. I'm angry all the time these days and it's not his fault. My reflection frowned at us both from the mirror. It's not anyone's fault.

'What?' The mirror-Sean raised his open palms behind me. 'Well, you look sexy,' he pretend-huffed, stepping back.

'No I don't. I look like someone's mum.'

The dress was bought for a wedding last year and was supposed to be *floaty* to blur the edges of my post-baby figure but it just hung on me like a worn-out flowery dishcloth.

Sean smiled. 'You *are* someone's mum, pet.'

'I know that.' There was that irritability again, showing through like a spot under too much concealer. 'I meant someone older. Someone . . . else.'

A moment of silence opened up and out of it poured this sadness, like the sky had just emptied straight down on me. The anger washed away but I was drenched, the stupid dress drooping and dripping. I jerked in a breath and blinked a couple of times. Sean squeezed my shoulder and for a second I thought maybe he understood but I didn't have time to find out because there was a cry from upstairs. We both froze and tilted our heads to listen. A couple more whimpers and then silence. We looked at each other and nodded.

I went back to jabbing at my hair clips. I had no idea if I'd done them right. We were all supposed to have hats for today and I did try but hats make me look fake. I even tried a few of those feathery things Kaz showed me. 'It's a *fascinator*,' she said, 'like I'm not fascinating enough already,' and laughed that loud laugh she's got, daring anyone to contradict her. All the time, this phrase, *morbid fascination*, kept pushing into my head and the fascinators, the *morbid* fascinators, started to look like exactly what they were: bits of dead bird. So, I compromised with these tiny enamel flowers, three of them in different purples. Hopefully they're enough to show I made the effort.

We make our way to the line of bars and food stalls strung out behind the betting ring, backing on to the red-brick pavilion. Two plastic cups of fizzy wine pretending to be champagne and a double vodka later, the weather isn't so bad.

'Another?' I wave my empty cup at the others. I'd be feeling quite relaxed if it wasn't for these heels.

'Nah. Those prices are ridiculous,' says Kaz. 'Ashley, phone your Barry and get him to pass something over the fence for us.'

When the rumour had first gone round about security guards at the gates searching handbags and confiscating any alcohol, the options were discussed at our Tuesday afternoon baby group.

'You know if you open up boxes of wine, they have plastic bags inside?' Kaz had said. 'I could get a couple of them, strap one to each leg, up high so they couldn't be seen. They're not going to actually frisk me, are they?'

The other mums looked sceptical but cracked up laughing when Kaz stood up and waded around the hall like a fat gunslinger.

Liz, an old hand on baby number three, came up with another scheme. 'Those blue bricks you freeze for coolbags?

Empty them out, fill them with whatever and stick them in with the picnic. You'd get a fair bit in that way.'

In the end, we didn't put any of the plans into action. We did get our bags searched though, which was just rude.

The Barry plan is a good one. If we keep buying drinks in here, I'll run out of cash before I manage to place a bet. I wouldn't bother, but it's not, strictly speaking, my own money.

Sean lifted his jacket off the banister and pulled his wallet from the inside pocket. 'You got enough?'

'I took some out of my account,' I muttered, looking at my shoes.

He knew as well as I did there's nothing left in there. I've not worked since Tom. That was the deal and it isn't like what I do at home, looking after Tom, cleaning, cooking, all that, isn't work. We both agreed. It's fine. It's only times like this, not that they happen often, when there's something just for me and it takes money. I can't ask. Cannot force the words out my mouth. I'd rather go without than have to ask. It's humiliating. I know it shouldn't be, and Sean does nothing to make it that way. But it still is.

'Take it,' he said. 'Put a few bets on for me.' He was trying to make it okay by turning it into something I could do for him, like a favour, or a job. He understood that much. 'I'll expect a share of your winnings when you get back.'

He pressed the money into my hand and I took it, said thanks and shoved it into my handbag. There was an awkward silence and I turned towards the stairs. 'I'll just—'

'You'd best not,' Sean said. 'Don't want to wake him.'

'I'll be careful,' I whispered, already half-way up.

Tom lay on his back, arms thrown up above his head, as if the afternoon nap had taken him by surprise. His sleep breath snuffled in and out in a steady rhythm. I leant over the cot and felt that familiar desperate lurch in my stomach. Despite the satisfaction of seeing him grow, I can't help wishing he'd never change, that I could protect him from time and everything it'll bring, even though I know it's impossible and I've already failed. I reached a hand out to brush his curls but stopped short. Leaving would be much harder if he woke.

I stepped slowly backwards towards the door, in the pattern dictated by which floorboards creak and which don't. Almost there, my heel came down on the soft toy from hell. It started up, high-pitched and insistent:

It's a small world after all

Christ, bloody thing. I hear that tune in my sleep.

It's a small world after all

It's become the soundtrack to my life. I snatched it up,

It's a small world after all

and fumbled with the off switch.

It's a small, small—

Finally!

Tom turned his head and raised one arm, like he was waving, but his eyes were still closed and he puffed out a sigh and settled back to sleep.

Me and Kaz stand near the paddock, waiting for Ashley to get back, watching the horses being led in circles, snorting and stamping, manes knotted in bumpy braids, tails wound up tight. Women drift in and out of the betting booths and bars, carrying drinks and fluttering betting slips. The rain has gone off and a weak sun is making the grass sparkle. The scene looks almost like it was supposed to.

'That one!' Kaz shouts. 'We should bet on that one.' She's pointing to a brown mare skipping nervously around the paddock. The horse's skin looks tight and thin, every sinew and vein visible, eyes rolling, nostrils flared. As she goes past I catch a sharp whiff of sweat and earth and hot grassy breath. She's making a horrendous sound, chewing at the metal bar between her teeth. Flecks of white froth collect at the soft corners of her mouth.

'Why that one?' I ask.

'It just had a shit. I heard they go faster if they have a shit first.' Kaz folds her arms and looks knowledgeable.

'Well, less weight, I suppose.' She might have a point.

'Perhaps we should try to scare another one,' she says.

'What for?' I ask, looking at the other horses, bristling with trapped energy. 'Why would you want to do that?'

'So they, y'know, *go . . .?*'

Sometimes it's hard to tell when Kaz is joking. But for once we don't have to stop and explain, or apologise. We're both crying with laughter, holding onto each other's arms, when Ashley arrives carrying a rolled-up cardigan.

'Guess what Barry says to me?' she demands, but doesn't stop for an answer.

Me and Kaz straighten our faces.

'He says *Talk about special treatment. You get to have your own day. Blokes don't get anything like that. We don't get Gentlemen's Day.* Can you believe that? Poor you, I says, all you get is every other day.'

'What did you get then?' Kaz interrupts, plucking at the edge of the cardigan to reveal the red top of a vodka bottle.

Ashley steps away, pulling the wool back over the bottle and giving it a pat, cradling it like a baby.

An hour later, Ashley sits cross-legged on the tartan rug, one strap hanging off her shoulder, talking about her Barry and how he's great with the twins but the house will be a bombsite when she gets back because he can't multi-task. When she starts talking in circles, Kaz takes over about her dad's cancer and how her brother's no help at all since their mum's gone and she has to drag the kids backwards and forwards to the hospital. She talks fast, eyes wide, lips wet with vodka and Coke. I think she'd like to stop talking because now she's rounded the last turn and we can all see what's waiting on the finish line. She stops abruptly and stares off across the track then knocks back the rest of her drink before clambering to her feet and swaying off to find the Ladies'. I start talking about Sean and Tom and how I'm thinking of going back to work, which surprises me. I hadn't realised I was seriously considering it. None of us are used to talking without constant interruption from children. Combined with the drink, it's like running too fast downhill.

The horses thunder past, throwing up crescent-shaped clods of turf high into the air, the jockeys hunched on their backs in bright colours like parasitic beetles. The ground shakes, like drums from underground working their way up.

Kaz arrives back waving a race programme. 'Right! We need to pick which horse to bet on. I think we should go for Liberty Trail, but I like the sound of Blue Tomato too.'

I pour more drinks and Ashley blows her nose.

'So, twenty quid each way?' Kaz pauses but gets no answer. 'I've no idea what that means either so don't look at me like that.'

I watch the horses as they loop back round for another circuit. I think I can see that mare from the paddock. She's out in front and my heart starts beating faster as I watch her straining ahead, a hurtling mass of muscle and sweat. She's tearing through the air, ripping it apart. It's like she's trying to tear a hole in front of her and escape through it, to some other place where something else, something more is waiting, a place where maybe she can stop running. It's always that bit further ahead. The promise of that.

M JOHN HARRISON

GETTING OUT OF THERE

Hampson came back after some years, to the seaside in the rain, to this town built around a small estuary where a river broke through the chalk downs. Everything – everything people knew about, anyway – came in through that gap, by road or rail; and that's the way Hampson came too, down from London, midweek, in a rental van, unsure of what he would find for himself after so long. He had options, but since he wasn't sure about them either, he rented a single room on one of the quiet wide roads that run down from the old town.

The day he moved in, he realised that not all the things he had brought back with him – bits of furniture, endless half-filled cardboard boxes sealed with gaffa tape – would fit in there, so he drove the van to a self-storage under some railway arches where the London Road left the centre of town. It was a bit back from the seafront, the usual kind of place, not very modern, with untreated breeze-block cubicles of different sizes, behind doors that were little more than plywood. He spent a morning carrying things around in there, then looked into the office on his way out. Behind the desk he found a woman he recognised.

'My god,' she said.

At the same time Hampson said: 'I knew you when we were kids!'

'You wouldn't leave me alone,' she said.

'I was quite stricken.'

'I know you were,' the woman said.

Hampson paid the bill. 'I was seven years old,' he said, 'and you were, what? Thirteen?'

She laughed. 'I bet you can't remember my name either.'

Hampson had a couple of tries but she was right. As he was leaving, she called after him, 'It's Beatrice.' And then: 'Are you going to be stricken again?'

Hampson said he didn't know how to answer that one.

'You haven't changed,' she said, as if he'd already done something which demonstrated it.

The house – it was called 'Pendene', everything had to be called 'dene' round there – was large, square, detached, surrounded on three sides with empty parking space and, at the back, a long, overgrown garden. It wasn't much. Hampson's room wasn't much either. It lay at the end of a long, badly lit second-floor landing, which still smelt of food cooked there in the 1960s: a section of a room – perhaps twelve feet by ten, painted white, accessed from a fire-door with the remains of broken bolts laced down the inside – so literalistically partitioned out of the original Victorian space that the light filtered in from about two-thirds of a bay window. The day he moved in, before he went down to the storage with his things and met Beatrice again, he had looked out of the window and watched a woman, thirtyish, long hair and nice legs in skinny jeans, walking diagonally across the road towards him from a house twenty yards down.

The garden wall, so overgrown with ivy it was bowing into the street, cut off his view of her. Shortly afterwards she was followed by a man in a pale blue shirt, who vanished in the same way. The next time Hampson looked up she was walking towards him again. The wall obscured her. The man followed about a minute later, and the wall obscured him. This happened three times, in bright sunshine. Hampson never saw either of them walk back towards their house. They didn't speak to one another. Up the street – towards the square where the buildings began to look a little less bleak, more as if they housed families of human beings – the gardens were full of camelias and early-flowering clematis.

For the first three or four days he didn't do much. He had a job to go to, pushing software in a local design firm, but it wouldn't start for a week. He pottered around, refamiliarising himself, feeling his way across the joins between the old town – with its herringbone brick and lapboard architecture, its carefully cultivated links to notable soldiers and writers of the Edwardian afternoon, and its quiet graveyard backwatered behind yews – and the new, which wasn't much more than a housing estate, some car parks, and a loop or two of bleak, dusty pubs and charity shops tucked between the chalk cliffs and brutalist sea defences known for lost geographical reasons as Shining Dene. There wasn't a lot to it, but Hampson already knew that. The promenade. The beach with its reclaimed Victorian railway track. A couple of Regency crescents on a hill which attracted a dry cold wind.

If you were bored – and Hampson soon was – you could go up on to West Hill and stare out towards France. One lunchtime he went into the English Channel, a pub about a hundred yards back from the clifftop, and Beatrice was sitting there at the back. He bought a drink and went over. He asked if she minded him joining her, she asked him why she should mind. Unable to disentangle anything from that, he said:

'This is a weird place.'

'It's a town of the dead,' she said.

'I meant the pub,' Hampson said.

At the back it was hollow with plastic beams and tobacco-stained artex; a whitish sea-light crept in among the tables nearest the window, overexposing the floorboards, the sleeping dogs, the customers' feet. Every support pillar was papered with posters – 'Club Chat Noir', 'Maximum Rock & Roll' – and a sign behind the bar advised, 'No bloody swearing'. For a moment Hampson and Beatrice stared companionably around, then she said:

'So. London.'

'London,' he agreed.

'I'd kill to be in London,' she said. 'Why'd you leave?'

He couldn't answer that. He hadn't answered it for himself. 'I suppose you get sick of it,' he said. 'You get sick of pretending it's not crap.' But it had been less about London and more about not fitting into your own life, not being described by the place you live in. Not being seen into life, by others or yourself. He had been lonely there even though he knew people: but Hampson told her a different story. 'Vomit's the London keynote,' he said. 'If you like to stand in a puddle of someone else's in a tube train on a Friday night, London's the place to be.'

'But why come here ?' she said. 'Nothing happens here.'

'Nothing happens there, either.'

She laughed at that. 'Except the vomit,' she said.

'The vomit's world class. Good solid stuff. We can be proud of that.'

She made a face.

'I don't think I'll have another drink.'

'Of course you will,' Hampson said.

After that, he often popped into the storage at lunchtime. He took a couple of things out then put them back the next day. She teased him about it.

Hampson was a small man, perhaps five foot six. He couldn't see anything wrong with that. In her high-heeled shoes Beatrice sometimes had an inch or two on him. He was excited by her and didn't see why he shouldn't show it. They chatted.

They shared this funny small-town teenage history. It was all very pleasant and explicable but it wasn't going any further. Then, after a fortnight or so, Hampson was dawdling through the centre of town on his way to the cinema to see a film called *Shame*. It was a warm evening, just after dark, with a light rain and static patches of mist out to sea. As Hampson crossed one of the High Street junctions, Beatrice walked straight out of a house about a hundred yards in front of him. In the moment the door slammed, she was just a figure to him, in a pencil skirt and some sort of jacket with a pinched-in waist; then he recognised her from her walk, short tapping steps echoing back to him. He followed her without a thought. They were soon out of the centre, heading along the Bourne past the Ship Museum into the old town, where she knocked on a door; waited for a moment or two; called, 'Emily? Can I leave them with you tomorrow? Emily?' and receiving no answer went up a steep, narrow little passage and out into one of the Regency enclaves that faced the sea. It wasn't an area Hampson remembered. She was too far ahead to call her name; anyway, shyness kept him from calling out to anyone in public. He thought he would make himself known when he caught up with her, but he never did. Instead he hung back, listening to the sound of her heels on the pavement. He never saw where she went. The cloud broke: moonlight gave the deserted streets a flattened perspective, as if the two of them were in a picture: suddenly Hampson became anxious and turned off.

Next day he went to the storage at lunchtime and asked her out.

'You took your time,' she said. 'What about Sunday afternoon?'

They rode the West Hill funicular railway to the park at the top of the cliffs. She stretched her arms. 'It's great,' she said, 'that you can get so high above it all.' A moment later she was gone. Hampson stood where he was, waiting for her to come back. There was a strong smell of cut grass, then fried food from the cafe at the top of the funicular. If he looked off to his left he could see her sitting on a bench about a hundred yards away. Behind her the town fell away towards the sea. Was she looking back towards him? He couldn't be sure. Suddenly a flock of gulls poured down the Bourne and circled over the shops and houses, screaming and calling; then spread out along the esplanade and diffused like fog.

'I just went off for a bit of a wander,' she said when she came back.

'No problem,' Hampson said.

'It's a bit neat, this park. Don't you think?'

'I quite like it.'

'I was just sitting on a bench down the path,' she said.

Two or three boys kicked a ball about on the grass behind them, and in front the sea was dissolving into the sky behind the tall black net shops and the art gallery. 'That yellow lichen on the roofs down there,' Hampson said, 'I wonder what it is?'

She laughed.

'I thought you were a local,' she said.

From there they went up on to the golf course, where groups of children hunted around all weekend for lost golf balls, paying particular attention to the base of the old black smock mill. There was a constant wind which seemed, Beatrice said, to come all the way from France. 'Look!' she said. From up there you could see clearly how the houses flowed between the downs, filling up the valley with humanity or something like it. Hawthorn and sloe grew on the edge, low, lichenous, wind-sculpted, dense. Lower down a fox sat calmly in a small sloping field between woods and allotments, watching some people tend horses. There were little valleys, warm, still and full of life, a few hundred yards from the sea. 'Anything can happen here,' she said, 'safe and out of the wind.' They ended up at the Open Art cafe, which offered an all-day breakfast sandwich, fragile-looking wildflowers in old glass bottles and the Sunday afternoon gathering of the Philosophical Society.

'What's the topic for this afternoon?' someone asked Hampson, as if he and Beatrice were members too. For him, Hampson said, to some laughter, it would have to be the existential quality of the art on the walls: several versions, in different sizes, of a sunbather sitting naked on the shingle, seen from behind, hugging her knees, framed in such a way as to render the whole experience anxious and claustrophobic – the sunshine, the beach, the wideness of the air, all denied. They were all called 'Woman From the Sea', with a hashmark and a number.

'Well I enjoyed that,' Beatrice said when they were back in town.

'Come out one evening,' Hampson suggested.

'I can't,' she said. She stood awkwardly on the pavement outside a pub called the Plough, waiting for him to kiss her cheek; then laughed and walked off up the hill. 'But we could do this again,' she called back. Then she stopped and turned round and added: 'I've got kiddies. Two.'

He couldn't imagine that. He sat in his room later that night, watching the TV with the sound turned down, and tried to remember what she had looked like when they were younger. He couldn't remember much of anything. A smile, a pleated uniform skirt. Wet light shining off the seafront benches, streets steepening away north and east into middle-class cul-de-sacs. A gang of Year Ten girls laughing about something they had seen, or perhaps done, in the Shining Dene public toilets where moths with fawn pillowy heads and eyes like cheap red jewels lay stunned and immobile on the windowsills of the lavatory stalls. If he tried, he could remember how he felt – it was a small boy's crush – and someone giving him a sweet; but he was afraid that if he tried too hard he would begin inventing things, so he put it out of his mind and went to bed. A couple of evenings later he waited beneath the old railway arches until he saw her come out of the storage place, then allowed her forty yards' start and followed her home. There was a qualitative difference between this time and the last: he understood what he was doing. Also what he was feeling. Curiosity. Excitement. On top of that, a kind of peculiar self-satisfaction, as if following her made him superior.

It was cold and lively up there. The shabby white stucco façades, the columned doorways peeling and cracked in daylight, had under the moon a pure, abstract look. By day you could tell from their mismatched curtains and rows of doorbells that they had been divided as thoughtlessly into flats as 'Pendene'; at night they curved away like fresh illustrations of themselves in watercolour and architectural ink. Beatrice approached a house. He watched her put key to lock, listened for her footfall in the hall, waited until a ground-floor window lit up; then turned up his coat collar and went back down into the town.

After that he followed her most evenings. Sometimes he was tempted to make his way straight to the house and wait for her to arrive; but another feeling kept him honest: he wanted the sound of her heels, the lucky emptiness of the streets, the sense of the two of them being figures caught moving on an almost abstract ground. Her life seemed simple. Hampson couldn't see much of it. The children ran about playing some game upstairs. They had a television up there. Beatrice called out to them from the bathroom or the kitchen. They seemed happy. Later, she might sit for an hour on her own in the yellow-lit front room, staring ahead of herself. Crouched painfully in a soft patch of the bit of garden at the back of the house, he found himself shaking with attention. His hearing sharpened until he thought he could hear her breathe. When she leaned forward to pick up a magazine he could feel his heartbeat rocking his upper body. Walking home afterwards, he felt dizzy – as if he had been released from some vast effort – and at the same time quite unreal. It would have been easy to believe that, at night, the town had no existence except as a picture – or not one but several of them, stacked planes, layered and imbricated in the rising salt air and faint sound of waves, implying three dimensions yet completely two-dimensional.

One evening as he hid in the garden, he realised someone else was in the room with her. She was listening to someone he couldn't see; someone, perhaps, who had been there all along; a male voice, first questioning then reassuring. From then on, Hampson wondered if he too had company. Though he never saw anyone, might other men be crouched in the garden near him at night, their attention as excited and obsessive as his own?

All the time he was following her at night, they had an easy familiarity by day. They sat in the English Channel at lunch-time, eating a pint of prawns each. When she could organise childcare they visited the art cinema and had arguments about Michael Haneke. It was a normal relationship, although Hampson often felt she was trying to tell him something without actually saying it. She took him to a famous house a few miles inland. This confection of butter-and-honey stone, built by an Edwardian author to enclose the memory of his dead son, had first passed into the hands of the Bloomsbury group – who, in their anxiety to control the cultural conversation and contribute to English post- Impressionism, had painted watery greyish designs on the wallpaper and doors – and now belonged to the Nation. Standing in extensive gardens, behind warm brick walls and tall yew hedges, it boasted an oast house, a box maze and a fully operational watermill from which visitors were encouraged to buy flour.

Beatrice and Hampson took the Saturday tour, after which she led him through a little wooden gate into one of the more intimate gardens, which featured a rectangular pool and some statuary among exuberant cottage garden plantings. There, she sat him down on a bench.

'Look!' she said. 'I love this!'

Hampson wasn't so impressed. The rim of the pool had been tiled by amateurs – an effect less of Tuscany than of the mouldy bathroom in a Spanish holiday villa – and all you could make out in the clouded water was a kind of feathery weed moving to and fro. It might have been growing on something, Hampson thought, some shape he couldn't quite bring to mind. Overseeing the pool from a short plinth of home-made concrete was a ten-inch figure without head or legs but with detailed, slightly disproportionate male genitals. There were similarly broken or partial bodies all over the garden – both sexes reduced to loins and buttocks half hidden by foliage.

'Isn't it calm?' she said.

'Very calm,' Hampson agreed. But he hated the place and couldn't wait to get away: within a week he was having a dream in which it seemed less like a garden than the site of a crime. Limbs had been torn off for reasons unfathomable; the aesthetic of careful disarrangement – of humorous disarray – tried but failed to dissimulate the rage that lay behind it all. Hampson knew he wasn't looking at a celebration of Mediterranean influences and classical forms, or even the operations of a disturbed mind. One night he woke up understanding the difference between the garden and his dream of it: in the dream all those dismembered trunks and torsos were real. The knowledge exhausted him. He groaned and turned over. He fell asleep again. He had begun the night throwing body parts into the pool: he spent the rest of it trying to force an object the colour of a plastic lobster into an open pipe.

When he woke again it was six the next morning and the

sun was out. He walked down the hill to Shining Dene, where he found two old women already swimming from the shingle. They ran laughing into the sea, carrying between them a child's bright blue-and-yellow plastic inflatable upon which were printed the words HIGH VELOCITY SPORT, which they lost for a moment in the surf; then, still laughing, ran out again. They shouted and waved to someone on the cliff above, stumbled about in the shallows chasing one another. Hampson, puzzled by their energy, sat under the sea-defences, pulling up clumps of chamomile and yellow horned poppy. Down among the roots he found beads of a material resembling cloudy plastic, washed in by the tide. It was difficult to tell what they had been; on the shingle, the difference between organic and inorganic was constantly eroded by water, weather, sun. This idea made him think about the object in his dream. It had looked crustacean but felt fleshy and limp. It had been about the size of a seven-year-old boy. The old women finished swimming, dried themselves and tugged on their vast shorts. Soon after that, he began avoiding Beatrice during the day and stopped following her at night.

He couldn't have said why. He was angry. He hadn't liked the pool, he blamed her for the dream; he was angry that he had to follow her.

He didn't phone and he didn't answer when she phoned. He took the train up to London once or twice a week. It was the same as ever: he would spend the evening in Soho getting pissed, wind up outside the Bar Italia with all the other digital creatives, clutching a beaker of hot chocolate too glutinous to drink. He would grin vaguely into the warm drizzle and wonder what to do next. He missed her. He missed their walks together. In a week or two, he felt, he would be all right again: meanwhile this was the best his personality would let him do. Eventually she came to find him.

Thursday, after midnight. The corridors and studios of 'Pendene' exuded a false warmth; the smell of old cooking oil hung in the corners. The residents were locked down in silence for the night, while, outside, strong winds came blustering down the Channel from the Hook of Holland. Hampson sat in his room playing Death Camp 3 for the X-Box through an old Sony TV set, out of which issued faint hissing noises he couldn't fix. When Beatrice knocked on his door he opened it but sat down again immediately. She was wearing black jeggings and a short white lozenge-quilted parka with fake fur round the hood. The cold came in with her. 'I don't know how you got in,' was all Hampson could think of to say. He kept his eyes on the screen, after a minute adding: 'They're supposed to keep the outside door locked at night.'

'You're going too far with this,' Beatrice said, looking around as if the room were part of it.

'How far is that?' Hampson said.

'Don't be puerile.'

She lifted the lids of the as-yet-unpacked boxes of books, poked the bin bags into which Hampson had compacted his clothes when he left London. 'It's like the back room of a charity shop in here,' she concluded. 'You should be ashamed of yourself.' She switched the electric kettle on and the TV off, then knelt down in front of him so that he had to look at her. Her hands were cold. He wondered briefly if she had come to have sex with him. Instead she smiled with a kind of painful intensity and urged him: 'Listen to me.'

'How are the kiddies?' Hampson said.

'Listen,' she said, 'no one can show you anything if you won't involve yourself.'

'I don't know what you mean by that.'

She shrugged and let go of him.

'Come and find me when you do,' she said.

A few nights later he turned on the TV and a woman was

striding around in a derelict house shouting, 'We could put a pa sha in here! Plenty of space for a pa sha!' For a moment Hampson had absolutely no idea what she could be talking about. Then he saw that it was the bathroom she was in.

He turned the TV off again and went out to look for Beatrice, and soon he was following her once more, every night, up the quiet steep streets on the landward side of the town, or along the deserted sweep of the seafront. They were a hundred, two hundred yards apart, the two of them, in the night wind and strange light. Everything was very silent. There never seemed to be an ordinary passer-by. Hampson felt rapturous, even though, after a while, he saw that after all they weren't alone. Other men were following her too, a dozen at a time; some women, too. Though Hampson saw them, they didn't seem to see him. They had the look of the figures in Stanley Spencer's 'Beatitudes of Love' paintings, shabby, collapsed and watery, rather grotesque. He wondered if he looked like that to other people.

To a degree, he felt relieved by this turn of events. He felt as if some weight had been lifted; a weight and perhaps a barrier. But his dreams didn't improve. He dreamed of Beatrice's children, who he'd never seen: they were a boy and a girl, toddlers in matching woollen coats, their little gloves dangling on elastic from the ends of their sleeves. He dreamed of the beach at Shining Dene. He dreamed of a hollow below the Downs, where the sun fell through dense, wind-sculpted hawthorn on to ashes, on to candle grease dripped over the stones of a temporary hearth. An event enacted itself in front of him, some episode which transfigured everything, in which a madwoman strode across the golf course to the smock mill, carrying her coat across her arms like a child. Soon there were lots of women, all carrying their coats that way, like sleepy children across their arms; but now they were throwing them off a pier into the sea. Lines of people followed one other person down to the sea, where they first sang an old Morrissey number, 'Every Day is Like Sunday', and then something, coat or child, was let fall into the water. All this dream-content seemed so distant! At first it was musing, lyrical but simple and matter-of-fact. It seemed strange but kind: the arms of the coats fluttered and gestured as they fell: they were like the expressive arms of performers in a charming traditional drama. But then someone was being killed and dismembered at a distance, in a rusty enamel bath or perhaps an empty brick sump. Hampson was helping with it. Great chunks of translucent, whitish flesh were falling heavily apart along clean cutlines. They were weighty and substantial, but there was no blood. It was more like fat. On waking he thought, I can't do this any more. He didn't really know what that meant: it was just the kind of thing you thought. But he knew he had to get things out into the open.

'You know full well what's going on,' he said, when they were alone in the storage place next day. 'You always knew.'

She smiled. She looked at him sidelong.

'I don't get it,' Hampson said.

'Why should you?' she said. 'Why should you get it, after all?'

'You've made me into a voyeur,' Hampson said. 'That's not what I am.'

'I know. You're a man escaping the London vomit. Ask yourself if that's all you are.' She came out from behind the counter and offered him her hand. When he took it, she led him through the office and into the storage itself. Rows of shoddy cubicles stretched away in all directions, their plyboard doors fastened with little cheap padlocks. 'People leave stuff here for a decade or more,' she said. 'When they come for it again, their lives have changed. They might as well be going through someone else's things. A lot of it they don't even recognise. They don't know why they didn't just throw it all away and save themselves the trouble.'

'Other people are following you too,' Hampson said.

That made her compress her lips and turn away abruptly. 'I don't want to know,' she said. 'I don't want to know what you see.'

'What have you got that they want?'

No answer.

That night he followed her down towards the sea. She knew he was there, and he knew she knew: there was a satisfaction to that. He knew she was smiling, though she never looked back. He was one among many, but Hampson didn't mind: he had seen them all before, trailing after her up and down the windy streets; they were easily recognisable. He could also identify other groups of followers, following other individuals. Some were women, some were men; some were members of the Philosophical Society. It resembled a midnight paseo, in which everyone in the town went down on to the vast, brutalist sweep of the sea-defences and filed along them in the transparent, motionless dark. After crossing Marine Drive to the seaward stub of the High Street, they all paused for a moment on the apron between the car park and the Brazilian JuJitsu Academy, halted, apparently, by the smell of the salt. For a moment they had an air of being discarded, agitated by a breeze too faint to feel in their world. And the thoughts you had when you watched them were the same, like the continual blowing or silting-down of the chalk detritus from the cliffs. Groynes of piled rock, with acres of flint shingle strung between them so that from above they looked like webbed fingers, reached out from the land; the sea, though calm as a pool, gave the impression of hidden disorder. Beatrice walked down between her followers to where the shingle steepened. Everyone was smiling. They were all watching her. They all shared the secret now, even Hampson. He watched Beatrice walk slowly into the water until it closed over her head. Her hair was left floating for a fraction of a second, then it vanished too. But he knew not to follow her, or call out to anyone, or otherwise raise the alarm. When he turned away at last, he was alone on the sea-defences and it was morning. The blunt chalk headlands, already busy with commuter traffic, stretched away east, decreasing mistily into the distances of Peacehaven and Hastings. He looked at his watch. Beatrice was waiting for him in the shadow of the sea wall. She had the two kids with her, peaky-looking little things about two years apart, one girl, one boy, who stared up at him as if they were thinking something that couldn't be put into speech.

She said, 'I thought I might find you here.'

'Are you following me?' Hampson said.

Beatrice laughed. The kids laughed. Hampson tousled their heads. They went all four of them and got some breakfast. He had never thought life was infinite. He had always understood that focus was the key, although he was prepared to admit he had often focussed on the wrong things. Earlier in life he had felt too much anxiety over that. From now on he wouldn't feel enough, even though he knew his focus was slipping off the right things. Like everyone else he would begin to look forward to the evening, two or three glasses of wine. He would eat too much.

SIÂN MELANGELL DAFYDD

HOSPITAL FIELD

OWNING SOMETHING ANCIENT adds weight to life. Your tree: nut-skinned, sturdy, harmony in a pot, which has grown up to be tiny, perfectly asymmetrical and squat, with teardrop, razor-edged leaves, which has grown up beautiful, is finally being delivered home. You stuff all your other belongings into a rucksack: underwear, toothbrush, books, and you negotiate customs, ticket turnstiles and packaged sandwiches while your two hands are firmly wrapped around its roots in a blue glazed terracotta pot. You think it looks like it ought to have been a teapot, not a plant pot; blue as sea in summer, shining about its soil. Your fingers sweat all the way home but you hold it and hold it, adjusting your fingers when their bones ache.

Your girlfriend asks you how old it is.

'It's very old,' she says, 'it must be.' You tell her you have no idea and probably won't, unless it dies and you get to cut its trunk to count the tiny age circles, 'but really, really, do you think I'm ever going to get to do that?' you ask her. You both agree on 'old'.

On the mantelpiece it goes, then, next to a painting by a school-friend artist and a black and white photo of your grandmother looking young on a boat. Against a white wall, you are pleased with its shape and how the light from the window throws its shadow diagonally and larger than life. The tip of its right out-reaching branch throws the longest shadow, hitting the rim of a photograph by a semi-famous Cambodian. The chair you sit on to play your guitar lives in the right place so that when you look up again from folk songs and breathe deep, there it is, perfectly crooked and alive in your home.

Your bonsai dies or it seems to be dying: you're not sure which. It takes seven days to get to such a state. On the morning of the eighth, the little feet of its blue pot are covered in leaves, and the palms of the leaves are closed. On the ninth morning, even more. You break your waking ritual. Instead of going first thing to loo-kettle-radio-shower, you pop your head into the living room to check the damage. You've learned to expect disappointment before your eyes are fully open. On the floor, leaves crunch like grains of rice into your parquet gaps.

Your girlfriend says you should be talking to your tree, and laughs.

'Which language?' you ask. She suggests English is a poor second to Japanese but you could give it a go since singing hasn't charmed it into feeling at home.

You tell it about your day, about the man across the way on the seventh floor who had a heart attack and had to be taken out of his flat in a crane through the window, his chest naked to the freezing air and pumped by a machine. You even ask it if it's listening and then prod the soil which is just as it should be, according to the instructions.

Day fourteen and leaf three shrivels and drops in front of your very eyes. It scrunches to powder between your thumb and forefinger and flakes back to where it fell in the first place. You leave the dust there.

Something must be done. You journey to the other side of the city after work, to a place you hardly ever go – journey to the very end, just because you're after a specialist and that's where he's to be had. It's where the canals merge, large maples and damp benches, and street sweepers hosing the roads down between passengers and cyclists. The shop is the size of a locksmith's, has mini grass-plants you don't recognise hanging from upside-down pots on a washing line. A miracle man works here, clearly.

'I have come to ask about my bonsai,' you tell him.

He asks if you bought it here.

'No.'

'Did you bring it with you?'

'No.'

'Where is it?'

'At home, losing its leaves.'

'That'll be the problem: your home,' he says. 'Take it outside and it might survive. At the very least don't keep it cooped up,' this man said, pressing his black fingernails into his palms, 'not for more than, say, seven days on the trot.'

You repeat 'cooped up' in exactly his tone: high-pitch disgust. You wonder whether he imagines you in an apartment with trees in chains, just like the silver birches in the Biblio-thèque François Mitterrand.

'I need to lock up,' the man says, as if he's seen into your soul and seen padlocks, and you watch his hands as he fiddles with the keys. You trust those hands.

You report back over dinner.

'It *is* hot here,' your girlfriend says, '*very* hot.'

'You've never said that before,' you tell her.

'But it *is* though,' she says and blows out with puffed cheeks.

'*This* isn't hot,' you say. You point at the thermometer which shows something between seventeen and eighteen degrees and you knew it would. 'My dad has it fixed on twenty three.'

'We're not talking about your comfort, or your dad's.'

'Is it too hot, then?' you ask her.

She tells you that in your place she would have worn a jumper instead of cranking up the heat. That, for sure, this shows that you're more urban than she is. But, no it's not *too* hot, no. You're not sure if she's lying and start watching her differently. She sleeps untidily at night: kicks down the duvet. You pull it back up. Another clue is that she gasps in her sleep. How could she, you tell yourself, how could she?

In the morning she makes coffee while you crouch in front of the bonsai.

'It's not personal,' she says. 'It's science.'

'You mean nature,' you suggest.

'Same thing,' she says. 'It's just the way things are.'

You tell her elms die outside. There's a foreign disease out there that gets them.

'But not the miniature elms maybe,' she says, 'they're made of stronger stuff.'

You don't give in; you consider the balcony but you don't do it. It's a decorative plant, so what's the point of it if it can't be seen? So, contained in this beautiful, perfect flat, with artwork by foreign photographers of children with stories in their eyes and no shoes, your bonsai loses its last-but-one leaf.

You bend low and analyse the tiny point of contact between leaf and bark; try to find what is it that gives up right there. You fail, but find yourself staring until your lower back aches. You're tempted to pluck out the remaining leaf, to get the whole thing over and done with. But this posture isn't natural for you, and actually really hurts, so you stand up straight, resist the urge to touch the tree, and grab your coat to head to work. On the bus, you tell yourself that you really are killing it and should have stuck it on the balcony.

The last leaf is on the mantelpiece on your return. The tree is gone, the marble polished where the pot stood. It's been manhandled again, this time carried by sweaty hands to share a garden with grasses, with bruised heads of great burnets, liquorice milk-vetch covered in sun-spots, devil's-bit, blood-veined eyebright, clots of comfrey and meadowsweet frothing above it all. It's abandoned there until it feels better. Once in a while, she brings it in; places it in the middle of the kitchen table and tucks into a plate of poached egg on toast, dandelion and sorrel salad, picks at her nails and the muddy feet of the bonsai pot; drinks tea. She grows nut-skinned; sometimes wonders – did you ever know that you were the one who changed everything – and takes another sip of tea. Sometime around the bonsai's hundred-and-fiftieth year, you die, mid-crane-lift outside your apartment window.

ROOF SPACE

I AM UP here in the roof space. I am Michael.

I am waiting for my father to come up into this space above where we live. To join me with the tracks and trains, the arrivals and departures, the timetabled lives, these journeys.

My father has often come up here into the roof space and we have constructed this world of coming and going, this necessity. These platforms and disciplines, these engines and carriages and flags, these entrances and exits, these sidings and announcements, these inventions.

I am up here in the roof space and when my father arrives there will be announcements and whistles and precision and everything will work and for hours at a time we will be in command.

Not like downstairs. Not like the house beneath. Not like the rooms and the demands and the crying. Not like the father then.

I am up here in the space above all that. I am waiting for my father to command and the way the trains obey and the way that the station clock is a sort of god and we all know where we are. But even now I do not tell my father about the passengers.

He does not see them. He would never understand.

He understood clocks. He understood watches. They are like

small gods making sense of our days. He understood table manners and declensions and the meanings of bird migrations.

He does not have time for fictions and jokes and tricks and with the exception of the trains in the roof space there is very little he shares with me.

In the roof space there is glow and shine and so much to keep an eye on and so many things that might go wrong. Beneath the roof space lights and timetable and things to maintain and check on, each evening and at weekends, my father so happy, more than content, sometimes humming, always in control, always ahead of things. He seemed to trust me.

The trains went to Trusby and Hillier, Ollerby and Chribton, Sawmills and Hallways, Gap Hill and Pebble Cove, Lower Beedington and Broiler Hill, Upper Sidcomb and Lower Hawton.

There was a summer and a winter timetable but the places remained the same.

Sometimes our station was snowed in or there were floods down the track. Once the station was decorated for the coronation. There might be delays also, caused by a driver being ill or a dead pig on the line or a fallen tree but these were rare events. The station was operational every day except for Christmas Day and January 1st and the day mother ran away.

Sometimes I was involved in the ordering of more track or extending the platforms and there were additional notices required informing passengers about waiting rooms and toilets and a few notice boards about local events; a visiting circus, the local football and cricket clubs, bus timetables and the local taxi service. Sometimes the white line at the edge of the platforms needed repainting. The station clock kept perfect time, of course.

Downstairs was half light and doubt and where was mother? And bad meals and silences and bed-wetting and where was mother? And sometimes father got into bed with me. I kept thinking of the trains, the timetables and the way that the passengers got off and on the trains.

Downstairs was no visitors and eating the same food and the garden slipping into wilderness and the only place to get to was the roof space and the noise of it and the hurry hurry of it and my father talking nonsense more and more and the way sometimes rain got in and always the gleam of the track, its glory, its determination.

He does not see the passengers. He does not hear the small children. He does not get up into the roof space as much as he used to.

One day I noticed one of the women passengers. She looked so much like, like mother. And the man she was with I think was Malcolm Roberts who used to give out the hymn books in chapel. There was a small boy with them.

I've been doing a lot more things recently. New track, changed timetables, more trains, a small booth providing drinks and snacks and now a major new timetable system so we all know what is happening.

There have been a few strikes. Sometimes the passengers miss their trains or the platforms have been changed and I can see the passengers getting all confused and have to tell them what's what.

Last month, I think it was, there was a passenger who had fallen onto the track. Platform six. Train for Bidford, Castlemere, Coddlington, Upper Holt, Bramington and Studley. Beautiful early-evening rural run. Usually packed full. Hits the man full on. Terrible for the driver, of course.

Kept the passengers calm. Said it was an incident. Before the police arrived. Before the body was carried away.

I am up here in the roof space. I am Michael. I told him not to get into my bed. I told him to stop it. I warned him lots. And when I closed the trapdoor and wouldn't let him up here he screamed like a brat. Filthy language.

Then when I had almost forgotten he existed he somehow got up into the roof space and went off down Platform Six. He was walking very fast.

I should have given him more time or stopped the train departing on time. I should have sent one of the four porters running after him. I should have closed down the entire system until he came back.

But all the passengers had got on board and the train went off and it was time to announce new arrivals.

I should have contacted the signal box.

I should have stood up in the roof space and screamed I FORGIVE YOU.

But I did nothing.

I sat there all night and then very early in the morning I saw them carrying something into the station.

All twisted and split.

I keep it in a small box, over there, with all the other broken things.

ANNA METCALFE

NUMBER THREE

MISS CORAL GETS up from her desk on a cool October afternoon. She walks over to the kettle and drains steaming liquid
into a clear plastic flask, the tea leaves swirling within. Moon
is crouched in the corner of the office, a small book of poems
on her knees. *Dead Water* by Wen Yiduo. She learns the lines,
breathing out the words.

'Time to go,' says Miss Coral. 'The Director can't catch
you here again.' Her tiny frame and button-bright face
do not convey the threat she intends. Moon looks up. Her
eyes, a little too far apart and as flat and smooth as her
forehead, sit open and blank. She gets to her feet. She
can't have grown an inch since she got here, Miss Coral
thinks.

Moon is a scholarship student, transferred from rural
Wanzhou. To the Director's surprise, she arrived in Chongqing by train, unaccompanied. She was standing on the platform, carrying her belongings in a bamboo basket strapped to
her back with coloured rope. When the Director asked Moon
why her parents did not bring her, she replied indirectly.
They allowed her to take the train instead of the bus, she said,
cutting through the mountains to cross the Golden River in
four hours instead of six.

Though Moon has been at Number Three Middle School

for two years, she remains the new girl. When she arrived, her grades in Chinese and mathematics were already exceptional, but she had no knowledge of English. Miss Coral was engaged to help her improve until she reached the requisite level for her age. It was felt that once her skill set was complete she would fit in. She never did. One or two of the other students like to mock her country accent; the rest remain aloof. Moon doesn't seem to mind. She neither seeks friendship nor refuses it and wanders the extensive grounds of the school wearing a look of mild surprise, as though perpetually reliving her first day.

Their evening English lessons became the first of Miss Coral's extracurricular duties. They met every day at six o'clock in the break between afternoon and evening classes. They waited for one another by the entrance to the school library. They chose always to sit at a table towards the back of the lower ground floor, far away from the computers and the teen fiction shelves and where few other students gathered. They leant over a new copy of *English Now!* and Miss Coral made frequent corrections to the textbook's spelling and grammar with corrector fluid and a ballpoint pen. To make time for Moon, Miss Coral had to hand over one of her English Literature groups.

A month after their lessons began, rumours started to circulate that the rival school across town had employed what they called a Real English Teacher. Letters from parents of students at Number Three Middle School arrived, threatening the withdrawal of their children. Number Three was supposed to be the best, they said. Why didn't they have such a teacher on their staff? A meeting between the governors and the school's patrons took place and a partnership began with Teach China. Anglophone language teachers would come and go in six-month-long rotations. Miss Coral was charged with the running of the programme. These foreign teachers must receive a good impression of Chinese hospitality, the Director said.

Within a few months of Moon's arrival, Miss Coral had been removed from the classroom completely. She acquired an office at the end of the Director's corridor from which to conduct her duties as International Hostess. The Director was keen that she should not take the redistribution of her skills as a sign of promotion, so he liked to hint among her colleagues that she had been withdrawn from teaching on grounds of incompetence. It was to be understood that, if it wasn't for his greatness of heart and generosity of spirit, she might not have a job at all.

Miss Coral and Moon moved their evening English lessons from the back of the library to the office. Miss Coral would leave the door open, to save Moon the shame of standing in the corridor like the students awaiting detention. When Miss Coral entered the room she would find Moon hunched over her homework, sitting squat in the corner with her papers placed neatly in front of her on the floor. At the beginning of each lesson, Miss Coral had to invite Moon to sit down with her at the desk. Moon worked hard, improved quickly, and soon there was no more need for lessons. Yet, Miss Coral kept up the habit of leaving her office door open in the evenings and often she would come back from afternoon meetings with the Director to find Moon in the corner.

'Time to go,' Miss Coral says again. 'I have to be at the airport in an hour.' Moon watches as Miss Coral sips a mouthful of tea and twists the metal cap back onto the flask. She hooks the flask's wire handle over her wrist like an expensive handbag. From the desk, she gathers a small purse, a plastic folder full of papers and a laminated sheet of A4. She slots them into a canvas satchel. Moon makes a small bow towards her, a shimmer of a smile on her lips, then leaves. Less communicative than ever, Miss Coral thinks.

Miss Coral takes a taxi across town. The city is different again. Another skyscraper, another bridge underway; new routes to serve new destinations. The shanty town shacks of Tianfu, half flattened, are making way for settlement housing. Though she has been here five years, there are moments when life in the city comes as a shock. In her home town, a few hundred miles into the country, her father is a hospital porter, her mother a department store janitor. She goes to see them twice a year and sends money when she can. Soon, a main road will be built connecting the town to the city and perhaps then things will be different.

The driver winds in and out of the traffic with the front window down and bursts of cool air flow over her shoulder as they cross the Jialing. A late afternoon sun casts a haze over the urban sprawl. Smog and fresh dust linger, hovering over warehouses, slums and disused factories as they leave the inner city and approach the airport.

Miss Coral arrives with twenty minutes to spare. She finds a good spot at the edge of the ribbon that marks the arrivals gate, takes small sips from her tea, and waits. When the announcement comes for the London flight she delves into her satchel and produces the laminated sheet of A4:

WELCOME TO CHINA
MR JAMES

Amid crowds of Chinese businessmen, a young white man emerges from the sliding glass doors. He is tall. His light brown hair is roughed in greasy tufts and bruise-purple smudges darken the corners of his eyes. For a moment, he appears lost, then he picks out Miss Coral's sign from the lineup of hotel taxis and family reunion balloons. He smiles. Coming together on the Chongqing side of the airport ribbon, Miss Coral extends her hand towards him as he, simultaneously, drops into a bow. 'Welcome to Chongqing,' she says, tapping him stiffly on the arm as he rights himself.

In the taxi on the way back to school, he sleeps. She watches him, wasting her welcome speech on the driver. *It is an honour to welcome you to China, Mr James. Number Three Middle School is delighted to have a foreign teacher on the staff and, though I know you are yet to begin your teaching career, we are sure that your presence will inspire and encourage the students to improve their language skills and broaden their cultural perspectives.* She stops short of the section where she had intended to explain her role as International Hostess and allows herself, instead, to note the stubble on his neck and chin, the tear in the left knee of his jeans.

When they arrive, she takes Mr James straight to his apartment on the eleventh floor of the residential building. Only the most senior teachers get their own apartments, the rest bed down six to a room. When she opens the door to his large, unshared space, she expects him to be pleased. He takes a quick look around, runs a palm over the arm of a beige, faux-leather sofa and asks when the flat will be cleaned. She pretends not to have heard this and instead hands over his timetable and a list of codes to the electric school gates. After midnight, she warns, he'll have to call the doorman to let him in. Mr James raises an eyebrow but says nothing. They both sit down. Miss Coral places the six-month contract on the glass-topped coffee table in front of them. It must be signed by tomorrow in order to get the visa ready, she says. With a shrug and a yawn he turns to the back page and crams a string of Latin letters into a space made for three Chinese characters.

A week later, sitting in her office with Moon in the corner, Miss Coral receives a phone call. It is Mr James.

'Hello, Mr James,' she says.

'I need to talk to you,' he begins. 'It's about the money.'

At the mention of money she gets to her feet. Moon looks up from her place.

'So, I've been chatting with my friends,' Mr James continues. 'They're all English teachers. In private foreign-language facilities, mostly. You know, Wall Street English and such. The point is that it seems they're all getting a couple of thousand more than me a month.'

Miss Coral recoils. His words strike her as rude. She states firmly that she would prefer to discuss this in person and asks him to designate a convenient time.

On the way to his flat, she wonders whether or not to tell him that he's already being paid more than almost all of the other teachers at the school. She considers trying to explain that this is not a private language facility, attended only by the rich children of the city's elite. That Number Three Middle School has little enough money going to students like Moon. Too patronising, she decides.

When he opens the door, Miss Coral finds the displeasure in his face more violent than she had expected. It seems out of proportion. If she were to ask the Director for a pay rise on his behalf she would be sacked for her audacity on the spot. 'Mr James, I don't have long,' she says. 'Seeing as you already signed the contract I'm afraid there's nothing I can do.'

Mr James opens his mouth to speak but presses his lips together when he sees that she is not finished. She sits down. He joins her.

'Given that this is an ordinary Chinese middle school, and not a supplementary private language facility, there are some perks you may not already be aware of,' she says.

He opens his eyes a little wider, releases some of the tension from his jaw.

'We have a full month off for Chinese New Year in January,' she says. 'And when the students come back they have two weeks of exams, during which you are not expected to teach.'

'And will I get paid in that time?' says Mr James.

'Yes,' Miss Coral replies. Mr James appears placated and starts musing over the details of a six-week-long trip across South East Asia. Miss Coral, pleasantly surprised by the ease of this negotiation, gets up to leave.

'Look,' he says. She stops and turns her face to his. 'I just can't help but feel it was dishonest, you know, you not telling me I'm getting below average wage.'

'It was written in the contract,' she replies, her eyes smarting at the accusation. His phone, sitting on the coffee table, bleeps loudly. 'And it is not below average,' she says. Mr James taps at the keys of his phone before placing it back on the table. He returns his attention to the room. There is a silence.

'Look,' Mr James says again, studying her face with intent. Miss Coral notices that his eyes rest a moment on her lips. 'I don't want to fall out in my first week.'

When she gets back to her office, Miss Coral finds that Moon is still there, squatting, birdlike, in the corner. The small of her back is flat against the wall, heels off the floor, weight on the balls of her feet. As usual, she has a book perched on her knees. As Miss Coral arranges herself at the desk, Moon gets up, scattering loose tea into the flask. A rush of hissing water hits the bottom of the plastic cup and Miss Coral watches as it fills.

At the beginning of November, Mr James calls Miss Coral to ask if she would like to go to dinner with his friends. Show us your favourite haunt, he suggests. She meets them by the school gates. Mr James is there with two blonde girls – Sybil, who is French, and Carey, an American – and three unshaven young men who introduce themselves as Johnny, Kit and Max, leaving their nationalities undisclosed. Miss Coral takes them to the best Fire Pot restaurant in Shapingba. The menu comes on a clipboard: it is a check list of items grouped into vegetables, meat and side dishes. They all turn to face Miss Coral.

'How spicy do you like it?' she says, placing ticks and numbers beside a dozen or more items on the menu.

A cauldron of red broth arrives: a ferocious-looking concoction of sesame oil, fresh chillies and Sichuan peppercorns. It is held between two waiters while the centre circle of the table is removed and a gas canister placed beneath. The gunmetal cauldron fills the hole in the middle of the table and the flame from the gas brings bubbles, thick and slow, to the surface of the soup. Skewered ingredients appear on platters. Cloud ear mushrooms, winter melon, lotus root and pak choi. Miss Coral shows them how long to cook each one, plunging her chopsticks into the soup and deftly removing chilli-soaked hunks of blood-red pumpkin and yam.

Empty bottles of beer gather beneath the table. *Pi jiu* seems to be the only Chinese word they know and they order in bulk, counting in English, making hashed attempts at the Mandarin. She tries to teach them Chinese fingerspelling for numbers, mapping the shapes of the characters with her hands.

For most of the evening, Miss Coral says little and busies herself sharing out food from the pot. She listens as they compare culture shock crises – *Why is everyone always shouting? – Someone touched my hair on the bus – I'd give anything for a cheese and pickle sandwich – Make mine a PB and J.* Miss Coral is surprised to find how much she enjoys hearing the critique. No one asks those kinds of questions in Chinese. The French girl, Sybil, is sitting on her right. As another round of beer is ordered, Sybil leans towards Miss Coral. She speaks softly. 'Do you like living in China?' she says.

'I've never lived anywhere else,' says Miss Coral.

'Don't you want to travel?'

Miss Coral says she has no plans to do so. Before Miss Coral can elaborate, the French girl asks her what she does in her spare time.

'I like translating things,' Miss Coral says, after a pause. 'And perhaps that's as good as travelling. Perhaps it's better. No jet lag,' she says. As she speaks she addresses the simmering broth. An old university professor still sends her bits of translation work, she says, but she can't tell the Director, or anyone at Number Three Middle School. On a whim, last year, she applied to do a Masters in Translation in Beijing. She got accepted, but she can't take up her place. Miss Coral laughs at herself. She has a good job, she says, thinking of the teaching she once loved. When she looks up at Sybil, Miss Coral sees that she is no longer listening, is paying more attention to balancing domed mouthfuls of rice on her chopsticks.

The end of the evening comes. Miss Coral and Mr James share a taxi back to the school. The night guards open the gate and Miss Coral gives them a tip. They walk up the wide avenue towards the residential building. They ride the lift together. When it stops at his floor, Mr James says goodnight, stopping the doors with his foot. He leans over and kisses Miss Coral on the cheek. She smells the beer on his breath.

'Fuck,' he says, 'I forgot you don't kiss in China.' He walks into the dimly lit hallway, laughing to himself.

Miss Coral takes the lift up to the twelfth floor. She tries not to wake her roommates as she slips into bed, fully dressed, listening to the sound of the other teachers breathing in their sleep.

December proves troublesome. One afternoon Mr James comes to her office. A student is causing him concern and he has come to ask that something be done; he thinks perhaps the boy has Down's Syndrome. Miss Coral does not recognise the phrase and asks Mr James to write it down. After he has gone, she looks the words up, and is confused by myriad translations in Chinese. She arranges to observe the class in question the next day, during their History lesson. She takes care to pick a slot in the timetable when she knows that Mr James will be busy teaching other classes somewhere at the other end of the school.

Miss Coral immediately picks out the student concerned. He is a large boy, unusually tall, sitting at the back of the room. He swings on his chair, writes nothing down, is ignored by his classmates and History teacher alike. When a stream of incomprehensible noises escape his lips, the History teacher turns and gives a sharp reprimand in Mandarin, silencing the boy. Mr James, of course, can only discipline in English, and perhaps this is the problem.

Miss Coral speaks to the Director, who presents a simple solution. The boy can be removed from Mr James' lesson as soon as he causes trouble. The Director gives Miss Coral a key to a cupboard in an adjacent corridor where the boy can sit until English is over. It would be prudent to lock him in, the Director says.

When Mr James is next scheduled to take the class, Miss Coral waits for him to arrive outside their classroom. In her careful English, she explains the lesson she observed and the Director's advice and hands over the key. Mr James stares at her. Miss Coral is aware of the muscles in his mouth tightening. He looks towards the classroom door then brings his eyes back to meet hers: 'I'd rather he screamed for an hour than lock him up in a cupboard. That's fucking disgusting,' he says. Mr James enters the classroom, slams the door behind him.

It is not until she is back in her office that Miss Coral allows herself to cry. When Moon opens the door, she lingers a moment on the threshold. She takes up her usual position in the corner and keeps her head down as Miss Coral pats dry her cheeks and smoothes the front of her shirt. When Miss Coral has straightened herself, Moon still does not look up. She has her head dipped over her book, tracing the lines with her finger and making occasional notes in the margins. For the first time, Miss Coral is aware of the calming presence Moon exerts on the room. Miss Coral gets up and leaves. When she returns, she is holding a small wooden stool and a cushion.

'Stand up, Moon,' she says and Moon obeys. She places the stool and cushion in the corner and Moon smiles in a way that Miss Coral has not seen before. It feels as though the sun has moved a little closer to their window.

Towards the middle of the month, Mr James demands a Christmas holiday. The Director allows him the 25th and 26th. He pushes for the 24th. Miss Coral, receiving his urgent text messages and voicemails, is too afraid to ask for more. When she plucks up the courage to approach the Director again, it takes less than a second for him to refuse her. When Mr James phones in sick on December 24th, instead of docking his pay cheque the Director docks hers. Everyone will know, she thinks. That night, Miss Coral makes sure she is in bed, feigning sleep, long before her roommates arrive.

In January, Mr James leaves for Vietnam – 'a six-week romp down the East Coast, Halong Bay, Nha Trang and Ho Chi Fucking Minh', as he puts it to her in an email. Miss Coral returns to her hometown for Chinese New Year. By the time she leaves, the school is almost empty. She has been working hard on her latest translations, making the most of the office. Moon, too, has stayed behind, helping where she can, making creative suggestions. They share a taxi to the train station before embarking on long cross-country journeys in opposite directions.

Two weeks later, when Miss Coral comes back to school, she finds a postcard from Mr James on her desk. Halong Bay. He gives her the date of his return. He will miss the start of term, he says, *because the flights are too expensive*. She breaks the news to the Director by email. He informs Miss Coral that she will have to cover the classes and that Mr James' wages will be docked by a quarter. Nervously, Miss Coral paraphrases the Director's response into an email for Mr James, to which she receives no reply. When she next hears from him, he is already back in China, and has other things on his mind.

In his absence, his apartment had become home to a swarm of flying ants. He arrived to find the floor carpeted with insect corpses and the air about him thick with the survivors. *What,* his email said, *is the school going to do about this?*

On the third day of term, Miss Coral is already exhausted. What does he want her to do? Go over there and sweep up the insects herself? She writes back, conveying her sympathies but making it clear that the maintenance of his apartment does not come under her job description. She recommends that he buy insect spray and offers to hire a cleaner on his behalf, though he would have to pay. Beyond that, she is powerless. Miss Coral clicks 'Send' and finds that her head is filled with images of ants raining from ceiling to floor. They are flooding the room like the sand of an egg timer.

When Mr James' contract comes to an end on March 31st, Miss Coral throws him a farewell party. She flits between classrooms, brandishing a basketball shirt bearing the school logo on which students paint parting wishes and well-worn quotations in permanent fabric marker. Everybody writes something. Across the left shoulder blade, Moon writes a line from Confucius, with a translation in brackets: 'Wheresoever you go, go with all your heart.'

In a large classroom on the second floor, they convene. Some groups of girls have prepared traditional Chinese songs to sing. Others come laden with white cardboard boxes containing sticky piles of egg custard pastries and sanguine jujube dates. Black and white sachets of White Rabbit Candy garnish the tables and bottles of sweet jasmine tea line the window sills. Mr James appears genuinely moved. Miss Coral hands him a card she made herself, done in traditional Chinese calligraphy. Inside the card, her message conveys her thanks, on behalf of Number Three Middle School, for his freeness of

ANNA METCALFE – *Number Three*

spirit and passion for equality. *It is of utmost importance,* she writes, *for Chinese students to speak good English, so that they may have more colourful opportunities in their futures.*

When he gets back to England, Mr James sends her an email returning her thanks. She opens it from the office computer. He will never forget such a pretty little face, he says, and Miss Coral puts her hands to her cheeks to mask the flush she feels rising as she reads.

In early April, Miss Coral is called to the Director's office. A letter has come from Teach China, from their Chinese delegate in Chongqing. He hands it across to Miss Coral and demands that she read it aloud.

> To the Director of Number Three Middle School,
>
> Following a letter of complaint, demanding considerable compensation, we must express to you the concerns of our client. Mr James reported to us that he was dissatisfied with his rate of pay. Further more, he was somewhat disappointed by the arrangements for the Christmas holidays. (Christmas, we would like to remind you, is one of the most important events in the Western calendar.) The accommodation provided was less than satisfactory, a statement for which he provided photographic evidence. In dealing with these matters, Mr James claimed that he felt underrepresented at the school, being unable, himself, to communicate with the authorities in Mandarin.

'That will do,' says the Director.

Miss Coral feels something like a stone lodge in her throat. She prays she won't be asked any questions. Her mouth is too dry, her throat too small for speech.

'I'm sure you know what this means,' the Director goes on.

'You will be paid for the rest of the month, but we ask that you leave today.'

It takes less than thirty minutes for Miss Coral to pack her belongings into a large canvas rucksack. She peels the sheets from the bed and folds them neatly into a pile. She lingers for as long as she can in the office, re-organising paperwork and deleting old emails. When the door clicks open, she flinches, but when she looks up there is no one standing in the doorway.

She pulls a piece of paper from the notebook in her handbag and tries to think of what she might say to Moon. But even if she could find the words, she decides, where would she put the note? And how could she possibly know that Moon would be the one to find it? She folds up the paper and slots it back into the notebook.

When the office is clean and bare, Miss Coral opens the window to refresh the air. She places the clear plastic flask and an unopened packet of tea leaves beneath Moon's stool in the corner. As she leaves she lets the office door swing wide.

In the taxi across town, through the smog and the half-hearted spring rain, stopped in traffic on a bridge crossing the Jialing river, and gazing over at the far-side embankment, Miss Coral has time to note that the Tianfu slums have now been flattened completely.

DAVID CONSTANTINE

ASHTON AND ELAINE

1

ASHTON – NOT his real name, but even supposing he ever
had a real name, nobody in this story knew it – Ashton was
found behind Barmy Mick's stall late afternoon on a Saturday
in the week before Christmas, as the market closed. Mick's
son Kevin, a boy of eleven, found him. He went to fetch some
sheets, boxes and sacking, to begin packing up, and when he
lifted the tarpaulin, under which they were kept dry, there lay
Ashton, shivering. Kevin covered him up again and went to
tell Mick. Dad, he said, there's a coloured lad under the tarpaulin. Mick took a tilley lamp from a hook over the stall, and
with it, drawing off the covering, illuminated Ashton, who lay
on his back with his eyes wide open. Fetch your mam, said
Mick. She was soon there. All three then, father, mother, child,
stood looking down at Ashton in the light of the lamp. Day was
ending in a drizzle. The lamp had a haze, a tremulous mist, of
light around it.

Ashton wore a stained thin jersey, stained thin trousers
that were too short for him, unfastened boots that were far
too big. No socks, his bare ankles looked raw. He shivered, and
stared upwards. The mother, Alice, bowed over him. What you
doing there, love? she asked. Ashton, who was perhaps Kevin's

age, said nothing. Mick handed the tilley to Alice and knelt down. What's your name, son? he asked. Again Ashton said nothing; and it was not possible to tell, from his expression, whether he understood the question or not. He seemed to be clenching himself tight, as though trying not to shiver, and his face perhaps showed only that: the effort, and the failure. Mick stood up. I'd best go and fetch somebody, he said. Alice handed the lamp to Kevin, kneeled, drew one of the packing cloths over Ashton, up to his chin, and laid her hand on his forehead. Ashton closed his eyes, perhaps – who knows? – to safeguard a kindness behind his lids. But he could not stop shaking and his face, which, eyes shut, looked more exposed than ever, still manifested the struggle.

Mick came back with a policeman. Alice stood up. Kevin shone the light over Ashton. The policeman squatted down, removing his helmet and cradling it between his big hands in his lap. Ashton opened his eyes. Can you talk to us, sonny? the policeman asked. Can you tell us how you got here? The rain came on heavier. Ashton said nothing, only stared, and shook, the thin cover showed it, crumpling and twitching. Better get him moved, said the policeman, rising, putting on his helmet, turning aside, speaking into his walkie-talkie. Alice knelt again, rested her hand on Ashton's forehead. He closed his eyes.

The ambulance, first the siren then, in silence, the twirling blue light, drew attention to the scene behind Barmy Mick's stall. A score of people assembled, keeping their distance, in a half circle, all gazing, none speaking, two or three held lamps, in which the rain shone. The ambulance men, in their uniforms, were as imposing as the policeman. One knelt, Alice moved aside, he drew off the cover, and in a murmur asked questions, which got no answer, meanwhile feeling over the child's limbs and, very delicately, under his spine where it rested on the sacking. The other removed his loose boots – so bruised the feet – and with great care the two together slid him over on to the stretcher laid by. Then they lifted him and walked the ten paces to the ambulance's wide-open doors, Kevin following with the boots. The doors were closed. Slowly, quietly, the ambulance felt its way out of the market. At a distance the siren began to howl. Everyone dispersed. The last shoppers went home, the stallholders resumed their packing up.

2

The consultant on duty at the Infirmary that afternoon was Dr Fairfield, a paediatrician, a local man who, on the way to begin his shift, had called at the maternity hospital to see his daughter who had just given birth to her first child. The sister in charge undressed Ashton, still speechless, staring and shaking, and stood back, watching Dr Fairfield's face. Many times she had watched him assessing the state and the immediate needs of a child; and on the way home and sometimes in the night when she thought of her work, she saw the child in question, or perhaps a whole series of them, all hurt, all harmed, all distinct in *how* they suffered, but as the register of that, almost as the accumulating sum of it, she saw Dr Fairfield's face when he first kneeled to be at the same height as a child standing before him or looked down closely from above at a boy or a girl laid on a clean sheet on a trolley. And now, watching him as he contemplated Ashton, the sister saw something like puzzlement, like wonder, in his eyes. Many years in the job, he looked, to her, in the case of Ashton, to be being pushed to the edge of his knowledge and comprehension, to a sort of frontier, beyond which lay only a wasteland devoid of any human sense. Unspeakable, he muttered. The boy stared up at him and shook as though under the skin he was packed with raddling ice. And still his face looked tormented

77

by the effort not to shake, as though if he shook it would be the worse for him, but to halt the shaking was beyond his strength. Among the marks on his body those on his wrists and ankles, of shackling, were perhaps, being intelligible, the easiest for the eyes and the mind to bear.

A trainee nurse came to the door. The sister kept her away and brought her message to Fairfield that the police were in reception. Tell them I'll come down when I can, he said. But it won't be soon. They'll want the clothes and the boots, I suppose. And could you ask her to find Dr Adegbie. Ask Dr Adegbie will she come up, please. Then he turned back to Ashton, spoke softly to him, rested a hand on his shoulder and began to study what had been done to him and what a doctor might be able to do to mend it.

3

Back then disappearing was a lot easier than it is now. You walked down a street, took a bus, sat among travellers at a railway station, unfilmed. Of course, children who were reported missing would be looked for by the police and some-times also by the general public in organized search parties; but the unreported missing, why should anyone look for them? And a child who, as in Ashton's case, arrived from nowhere, speechless, unless he was on a list with a photograph or a description or sketch of what he might look like – and Ashton, the police ascertained, was not on any such list – how should a place of origin be found to return him to? The two scant bits of clothing and the cruel boots said nothing. The police labelled them and put them in a cupboard in a plastic bag. And at the Infirmary Ashton was given, first, pyjamas and later, when he could walk, clothes that fitted him comfortably so that in his outward appearance he did not look odd among the other children on the ward. He walked well enough, in a hunched and hesitant fashion, but he did not speak, though the doctors found his speech organs to be healthy. He had, moreover, keen hearing and very sharp eyes. But he would not speak. He watched. 'Watchful' was the word that came to mind whenever a doctor or a nurse remembered Ashton in the Infirmary. He was easily frightened, he had resources of terror in him that on unforeseeable occasions suddenly might be broached; but his usual state was watchful, his eyes looking out in a restless wariness.

4

The peat and gritstone country even today, crossed busily by trunk roads, motorways and flightpaths, surveyed unceasingly by satellites, if you once raise your eyes to it from the west side or the east, it will lie in your dreams and in the imagination high and level ever after, as a foreign zone, as a different dimension of the life of the earth. The cities for more than two centuries with blackening labour pushed up into it, climbing its streams, and the ruins are up there still. In the cities the moors feel very close. In the age of the smogs you might not often have noticed them, but the smogs are a thing of the past and from railway platforms now or from high office windows, look out east or west, you are bound to notice that the moors are there. You are very close to a zone and a form of life in the world which under the human traffic and the human litter goes down and down many thousands of feet, unimaginably dark, unimaginably old, and with not the least memory or presentiment of love or pity.

In 1850 a mill owner by the name of Ferris did the usual thing and built himself a mansion outside town high above the dirt and the noise by a stream that had not been spoiled and with the open moor accessible from his garden through a small back gate. The house, which to please his wife Mr Ferris christened Astolat, was of the local stone whose appearance for a while was light and sparkling. But the smoke Mr Ferris had hoped to escape came up there on the wind, some days the very air had a bitter taste, and Astolat blackened in the look it gave to the world. Between the wars, when the mill was done for and the family went bankrupt, the Local Authority acquired it cheap, changed its name to Hollinside, and used it first as a convalescent home for men whose lungs had been ruined in the mines and the mills, and then, after the Clean Air Act, as a children's home. Quite soon the rhododendron leaves no longer dripped soot whenever it rained, the women no longer wiped the lines before they hung the washing out to dry, and the children, taken for hikes across the moor, no longer blackened their hands when they scrambled on the crags. The stone of the house stayed black, but upstairs and downstairs the many rooms let in the light through generous windows, the tiles and cladding of the conical towers reflected every weather, all indoors was brightly decorated, and the spacious sloping and terraced gardens received the southern and the western sun. The brook, steep-sided, was fenced in safely for its passage through the grounds; but the tones of voice of it, soft or ferocious as the weather dictated, lingered in the dreaming memory of the children long after they had grown up and gone elsewhere.

When Ashton came to Hollinside in the latter part of January 1963 the stream was utterly hushed in ice under feet of snow. That winter had begun in earnest on Christmas Eve, deep snow, a hardened ungiving earth, week after week, the birds dying in thousands. Hollinside, warm and cheerful indoors, stood in a scoop of frozen stillness, from where, tracking the stream, very soon you might have climbed on to England's backbone, three hundred miles of it, the long uplands, snow on snow on snow, under bright cold sunlight, bright chilling starlight, and the visitations of blizzards out of blackening skies on a wind that cut to the marrow of every living thing. Ashton, never speaking, looked enchanted by the snow. Warm and safe, the bustle and chatter of the room behind him, he was seen standing at the window, viewing a silence that perhaps, after its fashion, seemed to him kindred to his own. The wariness went out of his eyes when he contemplated the snow. He watched the frozen powder of it falling in sunny showers from the trees when the birds, small handfuls of imperilled warmth, swooped on the crumbs thrown out for them on the cleared flagstones.

Fuel and food, the doctor, the nurse, the workmen, the visiting teachers, came up to Hollinside after the snowploughs out of town. And twice a week, Mrs Edith Patterson was brought down early from Lee Farm on the moor, by her husband, Fred, in his truck, to help with the meals. She met Ashton on a Friday – he had been at Hollinside three days by then – and on the way home that evening she spoke about him in tones which caused Fred, driving very cautiously through the banks – almost a tunnel – of snow, to glance at her often. There was an excitement in her voice, and she seemed, as she talked, to be trying to understand why meeting Ashton was so important. He doesn't speak, she said. And it's not that he can't, it's that he won't. And when Fred asked how he made himself understood, she had to think about it. I don't rightly know, she answered. I don't recall that he smiled or nodded or shook his head. But he takes everything in. His teachers are sure he's learning. When he's upset, he starts shaking. But when he feels all right, he looks at you like you were a blessing on him.

Night cannot fully descend over fields of snow. It seems to hover, quivering, lit from below. The farm lights showed. The dwelling made a brave appearance, its barns and byres and useful sheds clustering round. Elaine stood watching at the big kitchen window, her gran, Edith's mother, holding her shoulders and also, above her, looking out. As the truck drew

in and halted on the crunching snow, Elaine waved her right
hand.

5

After the blizzard of 24 January the roads were impassable.
Edith could not get to Hollinside, nor Elaine to school. The
stillness around Hollinside deepened. Ashton stood at the
window looking out. How immensely blurred all the out-
lines were! The ground fell away in soft undulations over ter-
racing and steps. Mrs Owen, the Matron of the home, came
and stood by him. He looked up at her. She saw that he was
tranquil. She smiled at him, he looked away again at the vast
soft forms of snow. Seeing him there, two or three other children came to the window, so that Ashton stood at the centre
of a small group. And nobody spoke. Tranquilly the children
and the Matron regarded the stillness which overnight, by a
silent fury, had been enlarged and intensified. Thinking about
Ashton later, when he and the snow had gone, the Matron felt
a sort of gratitude, she felt gladdened and encouraged by him,
because she was certain that in him then, in the hush after the
snowstorm looking out, some hope had started in the life that
he kept hidden.

Four days after the blizzard, Ashton's teacher, Miss McCrae,
rode in shotgun, as it were, on the first snowplough to get
through to Hollinside. She noticed a change in him – nothing
very concrete or easily describable, more like a shift of light
over a surface of ice, snow or water. He did not speak; but
a keener alertness and a more trusting openness had come
into his face; and his movements, of his hands especially, were
quicker and more expressive. She told him about her adventurous journey up to Hollinside, and seeing him so attentive,
she chose her words very precisely. Soon after midday she was
to ride down again, the snowplough in the meantime having

pushed on to some of the outlying farms, Lee Farm among them, clearing a way. Leaving, Miss McCrae did as she had often done before. She took a sheet of white paper and wrote in a clear hand: Goodbye, Ashton. I will see you again the day after tomorrow. Two things happened. First he nodded and smiled. And on that unprecedented sign Miss McCrae would have ridden down between the ten-foot walls of snow on a high of happiness. But more happened. Ashton did more. He took the pen out of her hand and below her message, quickly and neatly, he wrote: Goodbye, Miss. I will see you on Friday. Then he gave her back the pen, bowed his head, clasped his thin shoulders and shook as though all the cold of the moors had suddenly entered him.

The big yellow snowplough came lurching up the drive. The children crowded to the windows to watch Miss McCrae climb in and be carried off. Passing through the hall, she told the Matron what had happened. He can write, she said. And very fluently. It was his secret. And now he is terrified because he has given himself away. The Matron hurried to the schoolroom. Ashton was not there. Arlene, who hadn't wanted to see the snowplough, it frightened her, said that he had run off and Miss Roberts had gone after him. He was upset, Arlene said. He was making a funny noise. The Matron found him in his bed, Miss Roberts standing over him. He had drawn the blanket up over his face, gripping it very tightly. Nothing could be seen of him except his black knuckles. But the blanket itself, tugged and convulsing, gave the two women some idea of the thing possessing him.

Edith came in next morning, having missed her usual day because of the snow. They told her about Ashton's sudden writing and what it had done to him. Though he sat at the breakfast table with the other children, Edith saw that he had withdrawn into himself. He would not let anyone see into his eyes. Of course, he was by no means the only child ill at ease. Across from him sat Albert, continually making faces, but as though for himself, as though in some private place he were trying them out, all he could muster, until he might hit on one that would have the power to placate the world. And three places along from Ashton there was Barbara, who never stopped muttering, never stopped cocking her blonde head this way and that, listening, as it seemed, to arguments about herself, harsh judgements and harsher, and her in the middle, listening, defenceless. But all that day Edith watched Ashton. And when Fred came to fetch her and with infinite care very slowly drove home through ravines of snow, she said she had been thinking about it again, she felt so much better lately, and would he come in and see Mrs Owen with her tomorrow, and talk about Ashton.

Next morning early, Edith in her canteen apron and Fred in the dark suit he wore for all solemn occasions, talked to Mrs Owen about Ashton. It would be company for Elaine, Edith said; and remembered she had said this last time when they went through the whole procedure, all the forms, and pulled out when a boy might have come to them, her nerve failing. I'm better now, she said. And added, into the pause in which Mrs Owen considered them, Aren't I, Fred? Fred nodded, took her hand, and nodded again. When he's better, said Mrs Owen to Edith and Fred, why don't you take him up to the farm for a day? See how he likes it, see how you all get on.

They left it at that. But when Fred came back again in his work clothes to fetch Edith at 5, Ashton was standing in the big bay window, looking out. Their eyes met. Fred nodded, smiled, and raised his left hand in a greeting like that of an Indian chief who comes in peace. I'll swear he nearly smiled, he said to Edith, driving home.

6

Towards the end of February then, the freeze still looking set
to last for ever, early on a Saturday Fred and Edith fetched
Ashton out to Lee Farm, for a visit. Edith sat in the back with
him and about half way home, as he stared in his silence into
the climbing and winding narrows of packed snow, she told
him in a few words, to prepare him, about Elaine. He faced
her at once, very close, so that she felt abashed and almost
fearful that by her tone of voice and her words, only a few quiet
sentences, a child could be so instantly and wholly rapt into
such attention. It was as though he could see her daughter in
her eyes. She patted his arm, and pointed through the window
at a sudden gap and a perspective over a vast tilt of snow on
which showed traces of drystone walls and, far off, there stood
a house, the limitless bare blue sky curving over it and behind
it. That's where Elaine's dad was born, she said. He only moved
to Lee Farm when he married me.

Elaine was watching for them at the window, with her gran.
She waved in great excitement as the truck halted. Getting out,
Ashton was hidden from her, and he kept between Edith and
Fred coming into the house. Edith felt the silence deepening in
him. She ushered him ahead into the big warm stone-flagged
kitchen. And then it was as though the adults vanished, that
is how they remembered it later, they stood back and aside
and were not there, only the children were, Elaine in her best
dress, a soft dark blue, short-sleeved, her left arm ending at
the elbow in a bulbous flipper, her face, under black abundant
curls, of startling beauty, hesitant, fearful what this newcomer
would make of her, this stranger, the black boy from nowhere
who would not speak – he stared, he widened his eyes looking
into hers, for a long while, so it seemed, but not that he was
considering her, weighing a verdict, rather that she was flooding into him, through his eyes, into his silence, and when, as

it seemed, the look of her had filled him, then, very foreignly, as though this were the custom in a faraway long-lost other country, he closed his hands, crossed his arms against his breast, and bowed his face out of her sight.

You've been baking, Mother, said Fred. Edith undid Ashton's duffel-coat and hung it up. Elaine snatched hold of his left hand in her right. Come and see, she said. I know you don't talk, but Mam says I talk enough for two so we'll be all right. Come and look. And she dragged him out of the room.

7

A few days later, sitting in the schoolroom at a desk with Miss McCrae, Ashton reached across her for a sheet of paper and a pen, and wrote: Elaine showed me through the window where she went sledging. Then her dad said he would come out with us if we liked. So the three of us went out. I wore my new wellingtons in the snow. Elaine's gran made a cake. Elaine's mam said I could come again if I liked. Elaine's dad said would I help him with the sheep? They are having a bad time in the snow. Here we feed the birds. – He wrote quickly and neatly but with a pause between each sentence during which, deep in his throat, he made a sound which at first was like the low insistent working of a small engine, and then more like a purring, a humming. The letters he made were not at all pinched, flattened or cramped. They were rounded, well-shaped, and making a word he joined them fluently. When I watched them forming, Miss McCrae said to the Matron afterwards, it felt like watching him breathing. His letters are airy. Anxious that, as on the first occasion, Ashton might fall into a horror at what (and now so much more) he had disclosed, Miss McCrae hid her feelings under a brisk teacherly manner. Good, she said. Ashton, that is very good. And now I'll tell you what we'll do. She fetched a light blue folder from the cupboard

86

and on it, in black capitals, she wrote: ASHTON'S WRITING. So all your work goes in here. He looked at her. His lips were pressed tight shut; but, beginning to be able to read his eyes, she believed she saw triumph in them, a fierce and precarious triumph. She held open the folder, he laid that first sheet in it. I will see you again on Tuesday, she said. Perhaps you will have more to write about by then.

Driving back into town for her next pupil, Miss McCrae recited the sounds that Ashton had made. Pace, pitch, rhythm and tone were all variable, which made for a great expressiveness. She improvised on a few of the possibilities. It pleased her best to begin quite high, in anxiety, move lower into exertion and concentration, settling then into contentment, a purring contentment, the lips tight shut, the tongue quite still, the humming and purring of contentment, in her throat.

8

Miss McCrae could not reach Hollinside on the following Tuesday and nor, the next Saturday, could Ashton be fetched for his weekly visit to Lee Farm. Quite suddenly, in the first days of March, the thaw came and the sound of it, almost at once, was the roaring of flood. Under its carapace of ice and its muffling of snow the stream through Hollinside enlarged its bulk and soon became visible through fissures and abrupt collapses as a dark thing mottled grey and white, battering every impediment loose, ferrying all away, breaker and bearer in one, deeper, faster, more destructive and cluttered by the minute. From above, behind glass, adults and children, equally spellbound, watched.

The moor let go its dead. The trees that, tough as they were, could not withstand three months of ice, they died inside, they stood only as skeletons, gone in the roots, not holding, and the ice that had killed them, becoming water, broke them effortlessly and as mere flotsam, draggled with other life, delivered them downstream. Beasts came too, the bloated ewes, and the small stiff lambs evicted out of the womb into the snow, with bloody sockets, eyeless, they came down swirling any way round and any way up, and a long-legged colt, or somebody's dog or cat, and once, swelling monstrously, a cow, hastily the moor got rid of them. Half a shed came down, a ladder, fencing, a chicken coop, any one of which might clog a bridge so that things nobody wished to see lodged there publicly for days. The lanes themselves, as their packed snow dissolved, became fast tributaries into the bigger rivers, the Irwell, the Tame, the Etherow, the Goyt, that now, afforced, finally could heave their effluent and torpid sludge thirty, forty miles into the sea.

Ashton watched. Among others or alone if he was let, he stood at Hollinside's big windows, watching. And at nights, closing his eyes, still seeing what he had seen, he listened to its roaring, for nearly a week the melt roared near below him, by his side, with sudden particular cracks and poundings, a clatter at times, a grating and once a sustained long undulating shriek. When he slept it was the motor of his dreams, he surfaced out of sleep and still it roared, he sank again, dumbly comprehending it.

Then the fury was done with. The stream through Hollinside became its former self, a modest thing with a low and amiable voice, and over it, that first early morning of quietness, louder than it, the birdsong started up that had been held back for weeks, the first singing of birds after a winter that had killed their kind in thousands, they sang and sang on the threshold of spring in the echoing pearl-grey, silver-grey, rosy grey light. The stream made a pretty tinkling, running quickly and almost out of sight between its accustomed banks, and over it, early morning, early evening, the surviving birds made a triumphant din of song. Along the slope, under the big windows, ran tidemarks of the stream's few days and nights of violent aggrandizement, lines of leavings, some of them hideous, some ugly bits of junk, torn remnants of birds, little sodden cadavers, which the caretaker and his two sons cleared away in sacks into a skip so that the children shouldn't see them. But Ashton, the watcher, had.

9

Towards the end of April Ashton moved to Lee Farm. He had a room of his own next to Elaine's at the front of the house looking out miles over the moorland and down towards the valley and the vast conurbation. The room was light and neat and would have been their second child's, had he lived. Ashton still went down to Hollinside for lessons with Miss McCrae on the days when Edith helped with the meals. But he slept all his nights at Lee Farm. On three further days Miss McCrae or another teacher came to him there. That was where he lived.

After tea, Ashton and Elaine shut up the chickens for the night, and brought in the eggs. He helped Fred usher the cattle in through the muddy yard for the evening milking. He learned quickly, they were soon used to him, he flitted among them, watchful, settling them. Then he stood to one side, the cows snuffled and clattered, the machine hummed, Ashton attended. He takes it all in, Fred told Edith. I never saw a lad look like that. You'd think I'd let him into wonderland. And on Saturdays, warmly kitted out, he rode on the tractor with Fred into the top fields, to see to the sheep. Fred halted, Ashton jumped down and tugged a bale of fodder off the lifted pallet behind, leaving it where it fell. The sheep came running, they raised a great noise. Ashton climbed up again, to the next drop. When all that was done, Fred left the tractor and he and Ashton went together over a stile out of the green fields into the open moor. On the north slopes the snow still lay, very bright in the sun against the drab grass and heather. The wind felt chillier in the open. They found three dead lambs and left them lying. All their wool and flesh, the small body of them, would be gone soon. They'd be clean bones, disconnected, scattered. Fred strode off, Ashton keeping up the best he could, and halted, looking down into a snow-filled hollow. The snow had shrunk since his last visit, but still nothing showed that was any concern of his. Across the snow, from perches on the gritstone, two carrion crows regarded him and the boy. They're the ones, said Fred.

Elaine asked her mother, How old *is* Ashton? Nobody rightly knows, was her answer. About your age, I'd say. – So he could be going to school like me? – Could be, said her mother, could be. Elaine did her homework at the big kitchen table while her gran and Edith got on with things. Ashton sat opposite her, drawing or writing. At first his humming and purring were a wonder to her. She didn't know what to think of it, so she had nothing to say about it either, only stared at him. But soon she got used to it, bowed her head over her work and sometimes, very quietly to herself, made a humming of her own.

Ashton drew a drystone wall with a hogg-hole through it, in great detail, all the clever fitting of the stones, and behind the wall rose the moor, and on the skyline, larger than life, sat two crows. And in his airy flowing script, with long pauses between each sentence, he wrote: Elaine's dad doesn't move his arms when he walks. He keeps them still by his sides. He stoops a bit. He goes up the hill at a steady pace. I have to run to keep up with him. He says when he was my age he was always out on the moors. He knew every rock and every stream. He says when it's a bit warmer he'll take me up there with Elaine. Then he'll teach me all the names.

Elaine looked at Ashton's writing upside down. It's better than mine, Ashton, she said. Whenever he saw Miss McCrae she opened the skyblue folder and he put his new work into it.

Once Elaine's homework was to learn a poem by heart. It's quite a sad poem, she said. But Mrs Entwhistle says it has compassion. Elaine read two lines silently, then looked away from the book and said them aloud. Ashton watched and listened. You could test me, she said, if – Unbidden, he came and sat next to her, on her left side, so close their bare arms touched. With the index finger of her right hand she pointed along the lines of verse. Their heads inclined together over the words. Then, unbidden, he covered the poem with his left hand. She looked up and in a poetry voice said:

When I sailed out of Baltimore,
　With twice a thousand head of sheep,
They would not eat, they would not drink,
　But bleated o'er the deep.

Into the pens we crawled each day,
　To sort the living from the dead;
And when we reached the Mersey's mouth,
　Had lost five hundred head.

Yet every day and night one sheep,
　That had no fear of men or sea,
Stuck through the bars its pleading face,
　And it was stroked by me.

Ashton shook his head, disclosed the text, she studied it, he covered it, she tried again. In that way she got the poem by heart and recited it to the company over tea. Ashton helped me, she said.

After that, some evenings when she had done her homework, she fetched one of her old reading books, sat Ashton by her on her left side, and pointing along the lines read aloud to him in a clear and schoolmistressy voice. Well? she said.

He nodded solemnly. It's hard to tell with Ashton, she said to her mother. He's a quick learner, her mother answered. But perhaps he knows it already, said Elaine. Best assume he doesn't, said her mother. Besides, it won't hurt to learn it again.

Elaine's class were given a project: Memories. They had to ask one or two grown-ups, the older the better, to remember things, happy or sad, childhood, going to school, getting a job, getting married, good times and bad, and you had to write them out in your English book, perhaps with photographs; or better still, if you could, make a recording of the person remembering aloud. Fred bought Elaine a small tape-recorder and said she should ask her gran to talk about growing up in the city when Queen Victoria was the Queen.

Elaine practised on her mother, to get used to pressing the right buttons and saying, Recording now! This was at the kitchen table. Ashton watched and listened. Where did you and Dad meet? she asked, in a professional sort of voice. At the British Railways Club in Gorton, Edith answered. At a dance. Then there was a silence. Ashton and Elaine looked at Edith. Go on, Mam, said Elaine. You have to say more than that. You have to talk. He came down off the moor, said Edith, looking for a wife. And he found me. Was it love at first sight? Elaine asked. Edith leaned over and pressed Stop. Mam, you're blushing, said Elaine. Go and ask your gran things, said Edith. She's a better talker than me.

A couple of evenings later Elaine called Ashton into her room. She was sitting on the bed. Listen, she said. She pressed Play. Her gran's voice started, the accent very pronounced, it was her somehow brought closer, the tone of her, almost too clearly her, and only her. She was saying, Your mam had no father growing up. She was only eighteen months when he was killed. She only knew him in photographs and what I told her about him which wasn't much. My father looked after her quite a bit. He'd come to our house for tea every Friday. Gramp, she called him. He always went through the market on his way and she'd be waiting for him on her scooter at the bus stop. He bought her oranges. They were in a brown paper bag in a shopping bag and she hung them on the handlebars of her scooter. Then she went on ahead of him. She come in round the side, shouting, Mam, he's here! Mam, he bought me some oranges! Elaine pressed Stop. She looked up at Ashton. His eyes were very wide, his lips were pressed tight shut.

10

Every year on the Sunday nearest to 12 July, weather permitting, the family went for a picnic on the moor, for Fred's birthday. That year the sky was a cloudless blue. Fred, as always, invited Edith's mother. You coming, Mother? he said. Fine day, you'll enjoy it. And she always said, It's your day, Fred. You three go. I'll stay home, thank you very much. But she baked a cake which they took with them as part of the picnic. So the day had its ritual. But that year there was Ashton. You four go, she said.

They parked in the usual place just past the Boggart Stones, mid-morning, hardly any traffic, no one else on the moor. First things first, said Fred. And he took out the spade and the sack. Back then nobody thought you shouldn't help yourself to a bit of peat if you wanted to, for the garden, for potting. Still Fred didn't like to be seen doing it, which made Edith laugh. He strode off up into the moor, into a black rift he thought of as his own, where the peat was thick and firm and where from the road he was invisible. Edith stood by the truck getting everything ready. Sunhats, she said. One each, snow white. Elaine grabbed Ashton's left hand and hauled him away, past Fred, digging, his sack already beginning to be bodied into shape by the rich black after-life of plants, the layered seasons, the

93

compacted goodness. The children ran off. You know where we'll be, he shouted. He watched them climbing away, his surviving child and the foundling, dwindling away and above him over the rough terrain. He saw, and then faintly heard, a lark rising over them. He wished they would turn and wave, but they were intent on the climb, so small already and diminishing further, the girl a dot of skyblue, the boy a dot of red. Once he saw her stumble. Ashton was on her left side then. Fred saw her reach for him – she must have seized the sleeve of his shirt with her flipper fingers, steadied herself – and they went on, until, in the hillside, a soft ravine of peat took them out of sight. He knew the ground, every character and variation of it, as well as he did every syllable of every word of the language of his daughter's body, the growth of that vocabulary year upon year as she shaped herself to live with, and become ever more dextrous, agile and expressive despite, the born deformity. But not till they reappeared, scampering higher, did he resume his digging.

On the rocky knoll the children turned and waved down to the truck, Fred heaving in his sack of peat and the spade, Edith standing by with the hamper till he should be ready to help her with it up to the picnic place. She waved and Fred did, and the children, on cloudless blue, waved back again, semaphore of love across the sunny slope, its textures of black and brown and many greens, its vigorous yearly renewal through the blonde dead grass, the bracken unfurling, the scent-dizzy bees in the heather, the black groughs, gold gorse, soft white cotton grass and, from where the children stood, the untold acres of ripening bilberries. Looking west from up there you can see the trig point on Broadstone Hill, turn south over the reservoirs to Featherbed Moss, east gives you Wessenden and the grains and the brooks that flow into it: so you might triangulate the Pattison family's happiness that sunny day. And north, over Broadhead, Rocher and Black, over Butterly,

Warcock and Pule, by moss and hill, on and on, to the north you might open it more and more and for ever.

That night Elaine was woken by Ashton crying out. It was sounds, not words, but sounds such as she had never heard from him before, terrifying, utterly confusing her, so that for a while – too long – she did not know where she was or even who she was that she should be hearing cries of that kind. She jumped out of bed, ran from her room and was hurrying to fetch her mother – but saw that his door was open and, in the light from the landing, that he was sitting up and covering his face with his hands. Seeing that, to be an immediate help, she went in. Ashton, she said, it's all right. There's nothing the matter. You're all right. She stood by him, leaned over, he uncovered his face and she saw the depths of terror that had been in hiding behind his hands. You're all right, she said again. I'll fetch Mam and Dad. But he closed his two hands on her hand that barely emerged from the left sleeve of her nightdress, enfolded the bulb and the slewed fingers in his warm grasp, shook his head, again and again shook his head, shook through and through, she sat by him on the bed and could feel him shaking as though all the cold of all the long winters of earth had taken possession of him. He would not let her go to bring help from a grown-up person. She sat with him, old as him, till his shaking lessened, his eyes in hers, her eyes in his, he watched himself better out of hers, she saw it happening, his terror being evicted. Sat, watched, till he was quiet and he let go her hand. Then abruptly he lay down, closed his eyes, slept.

Next morning he gave her a sheet of paper on which in his airy and flowing script he had written: It was only a bad dream. Even when you are happy you can have bad dreams. Please don't tell your mam and dad. Elaine read it, nodded. OK, she said. Then she added, Ashton, why won't you talk? It'd be more fun if you talked.

11

Six weeks later Edith was ironing in the kitchen. She had her back to Ashton. He sat at the big table, drawing. In summer Edith liked to iron by the window, for the light. And she was watching for Fred coming home with her mother and Elaine. Silence, but for Ashton's humming and purring as he worked; and that was an accustomed sound, like the crackle, sighing, sudden collapses of the fire in winter, or the chickens scratting around in the yard, accustomed, one ingredient, only occasionally singled out for particular thanks, in her own reassurance. Then suddenly, from behind her: Mam? She stiffened at the shock of it, but held steady, looking out through the window at a row of geraniums in pots along the south-facing shed. She *would not* look round. Well? she said, taking another of Ashton's shirts from the basket and laying it out on the board. Mam, he said again, in an accent as though he were flesh of her flesh, Mam, our Elaine says if I start talking I could go to proper school and you and Dad would let me go in on the bus with her. – Elaine doesn't know everything, Edith answered, over her shoulder, ironing his shirt. It's not up to us to say if you'll go to proper school or not. – But if I start talking? – Well it certainly won't happen without you start talking. So the sooner you start the better, in my opinion. She reached for the next thing, a pair of his shorts. Our Elaine says you and Dad'll take us bilberrying this Sunday, he said. Very likely we will, she answered. – I can read, you know. All the books Elaine gave me, I can read, he said. I should hope you can, said Edith.

The truck pulled into the drive. They're back, Edith said. Only now did she turn to him. She saw how he questioned her face. Don't shut up now, love, she said. Not now you've made a start. Then your dad and I will ask about school.

12

On Saturday 23 November Edith took her mother to the market
I called Ashton after, where he was found. Many Friday evenings Edith's grandfather, coming round for tea, had brought
her oranges from there; and many Saturdays, as a child and
until her marriage, she had gone there with her mother. It was
the best market on that side of town, worth the trip. So two
or three times a year, for a treat, mother and daughter drove
down from the moor.

Barmy Mick – the third (at least) of that name – was the star
of Ashton Market. His wife backed him up with teas on the row
behind, and his son – a Kevin, a Jack, a Keith, a boy of eleven or
twelve as he always seemed to be – helped out at the front until
he grew sick of it, till he really did think his dad was barmy,
till it embarrassed him scurrying among the women with their
purchases; and then he vanished and was replaced by another
son who looked much like him. Going back two or three times
a year to Barmy Mick's, however old you got, you might well
feel some good things last for ever and will never change.

Mick's customers were all women. He faced them over his
trestle tables, over mounds of ladies-wear, in the sun when
there was any sun, under the awning and lit by tilley lamps
in the seasons of rain and cold. In frocks or macs, in hats that
might be as fancy as Easter bonnets or nothing but thin plastic
bags, they stood there wanting him to make them laugh.

Edith and her mother stood on the fringes, but were soon
enfolded into the midst as other women came and went.
Barmy by name, he was shouting, barmy by nature, and as my
missus tells me twenty times a week, You get much barmier,
they'll take you away. So buy 'em while you can, ladies, not
three, not five, not ten, it's fifteen pairs I'm offering and the
socks to match, any colour you like so long as it's red, black,
yellow, purple, puce, lime-green or orange, and all fluorescent,

and I'm not asking ten quid, I'm not asking five, God help me, mother, I'm not even asking two pound ten, call the yellow van now, I'm asking one pound seventeen and six, for the fifteen pairs and the socks to go with 'em, match 'em how you like or go for the contrast, each foot different, suit yourself, give the old bugger a treat, it's Saturday night. That lady over there, son, that lady who looks like Audrey Hepburn, fifteen is it, madam, and the socks just as they come? And Alma Cogan, just behind you, thirty, did you say? Take that lady thirty, Kevin, and here's the socks, it's Saturday night, give the old bugger a heart attack and off you go out and find yourself something younger.

Audrey Hepburn was standing near Edith. She had a friend with her, more a Diana Dors. It's his last chance, she was saying. If this doesn't perk him up I'm off with the butcher. Kevin pushed forward with her purchase in a paper bag. One pound seventeen and six, missus, he said. – You're sure they're all in there, sonny Jim? – Kevin shrugged. Count 'em if you want, he said. Audrey Hepburn did, holding them up. Kevin waited patiently. Puce goes nicely with black, he observed. Edith was watching him. That must be the lad who found our Ashton, she said. Her mother nodded. Very like, she said. Kevin moved on to the blackly bouffant Alma Cogan, and already Mick was calling him back. Leave them ladies alone, he shouted. Thirty pairs over here, another fifteen over here, Brigitte Bardots, both of 'em.

Edith drew her mother away, out of the crowd. It was starting to drizzle. You wanted some of your ointment, Mother, she said. And I thought I'd get some chrysanths. And then we'll have a cup of tea. But she halted on the outskirts, watching the boy dash in and out of the pack of raucous women, his father's patter accompanying and directing him. He ran to and fro, quick as a ferret, bringing the purchases, taking the money, giving change out of a soft wallet on his hip, a nifty boy, shrewd and grinning, self-possessed too, with a sort of reserve in himself, as though he were thinking this won't last for ever, one day I'll be off. Still Edith hesitated. Should I not tell him who we are? she asked. Tell him our Ashton is doing well and say thank you for finding him? And Mick, and his wife who does the teas, should we not go and say thank you for looking after him and fetching the policeman and the ambulance so that he got seen to quickly and came to us? Edith's mother shook her head. Best not, I'd say, she said. The less we go back there, the better, in my opinion. Have a cup of tea, if you like, then you'll have seen all three of them, where it started. But don't go introducing yourself. That would be my advice. The less talk about our Ashton, the better.

Raining again, ladies, Mick was saying, and twenty-six shopping days to Christmas. Kit yourselves out now for the festive season. Fifteen pairs for one pound seventeen and six and the socks to match. Look very nice indeed under the mistletoe in a paper hat. Mick's your man for the Christmas spirit. All good stuff, all hand-made, all guaranteed to give lasting satisfaction. One pound seventeen and six! As my better half never tires of saying, They lock 'em up when they get like you, our Mick. Nowhere cheaper in the whole North West, except maybe Liverpool, and what woman in her right mind goes traipsing off to Liverpool?

Kevin dashed again through the crowd of women, towards Edith and her mother on the fringes. Edith looked hard, to remember him, she took in his intentness, his sharp canny eyes, the quickness and confidence of all his movements. When he was close, he caught her looking at him. She smiled at him, Thank you, Kevin, she said under her breath. And with her mother she turned and left the market.

LOUISE PALFREYMAN

THE JEWEL OF
THE ORIENT

IT WAS RAINING, a fine drizzle that could only be picked
out against the sullen glow of the streetlamps, their pumpkin
brightness glaring into the dark. Beneath the lights, reflec-
tions of orange diffused across wet concrete. It glistened with
moisture that pooled in little eddies, black rivulets trickling
towards the drains. I was sitting at the desk in my bedroom,
looking out from the first-floor flat of a terrace in the Pen-
nines. It was positioned in a narrow side street which rose
from the main road leading down to the centre of the village.
On my first visit I had pictured mill workers wearily trudging
home to pots of steaming broth and pale mucky faces at the
table. Taken with this image, I told the letting agent I intended
to move in the following month. But now I was here, there
was something claustrophobic about being crammed in on
top of each other, rising up the hill in a stack of stone and
slate.

A skinny white cat darted across the street, ears flat against
the shower that was fast becoming a downpour. I watched it
climb the steps to the front door of the house opposite, and
it mewed to be let in, its call a strange harsh sound. Within
seconds the door opened a fraction, and a long, slender arm

extended downwards in welcome. The cat shot past, and the door closed.

I had seen her around the past few days. Moving tends to mean you spend a lot of time out on the street . . . to and fro, to and fro. She'd nodded at me one morning as I was tackling my book collection. No words were exchanged, and I could see from her frame that she wouldn't be much use to me anyway. So I nodded back and carried on with my labours, trying to look manly as I lifted a box and carried it inside, imagining my shoulders to be broader than they actually were.

The following day we met, by chance, in the local shop, a faded general store with a freezer full of ready meals, a poor selection of wine, and postcards at the till.

'You've just moved in, haven't you?' she said.

Ten out of ten for observation, I thought.

'Yes,' I said. 'Is there a pet shop around here?'

'Oh! What have you got? A cat? I've got a cat. He's called Freud.'

'Ah, a cat with depth,' I said, starting to flirt though in truth I thought it a ridiculous name. She laughed.

'Yes, he's quite something . . . So? What is it? A cat or a dog?'

'Fish, actually. Siamese fighting fish.'

'Oh, ok . . .' She seemed intrigued. It was a great chat-up line, with the right girl. 'I haven't seen you move a tank in.'

'No, the tank went in before I did and the water has been settling. The fish are gradually going in, from smaller containers. They fight, you see, especially when they're stressed. You can't keep males together, so mine are all female.'

I was very worried about my fish. It had taken years to build the current community. I worried about water temperature, fin rot and aggression. In nineteenth-century Malaysia people bet their homes on the outcome of sparring matches that could go on for hours. The King of Siam was a great collector and sanctioned the fights as something of a national sport. I kept all this to myself.

'No males . . . interesting,' she said. 'Your very own underwater harem. Well I don't think they do fish food in here and the nearest pet shop is about fifteen miles away . . . Maybe they'll eat each other, if they get hungry. Anyway, see you around.' She paid for her milk and left. I found her a bit strange, but that didn't stop me wanting to fuck her.

She lived at No.9 and as the rain intensified I looked at the ferns in her front garden. They were clumped along the steps to the front door, and had taken on a prehistoric sheen in the streetlight. I rolled a pencil up and down an A4 pad of paper. I was trying to write. It wasn't happening, and I wondered why I had positioned my desk by the window. A movement in the bedroom opposite mine caught my eye. I remembered why. She came to the window and closed the curtains. She must have seen me but she didn't give any indication that she had. I felt inches from her. The curtains were ivory and almost completely transparent. I didn't know why she bothered. She stretched and yawned, then lay on the bed on her stomach, her bare feet playing with each other as she leafed through a magazine. Her hair fell over her shoulders, meaning I couldn't see her cleavage like I had done the night before, when her hair had been tied back.

She read for a while and then slipped the magazine to the floor and rolled over onto her back, rubbing her neck which must have stiffened with the awkward posture. I imagined my hands on her skin. I rearranged my legs beneath the desk. She was wearing a vest top and no bra beneath it. Her hand traced over her stomach as she lay, staring at the ceiling. What was she thinking about? After a while she sat up and, with her back to me, slid the top over her head, revealing the long, elegant sweep of her spine. Her hair tumbled out of the vest and cascaded down her back, feathery like the fronds of freshwater plants. *Heteranthera zosterifolia*. Star grass.

'Turn round . . . turn round,' I thought, unable to look away, unable to move. She stayed cross-legged on the bed with her back to me, dressed in only a low-slung pair of faded joggers. She was the kind of woman who looked extremely sexy in beaten-up leisurewear.

'Infinitely fuckable,' I thought, my palm moving along the ridge in my jeans, my fingers hovering at the zip.

She turned round after a few moments and sat facing me. My hand fell still. Between her breasts was a rude and clamorous scar. It ran in a straight line from her sternum to below her navel. I felt insulted by its presence, outraged that it should have marred such perfection. Its red, welt-like prominence was clear enough to make out behind the thin veil of the curtains, which also failed to shield her eyes. She was staring across at me, watching for my reaction. I stayed at my desk, and stared back at her. My hand, concealed from her view, was still at the top of my flies. She brought her hand to between her breasts and rested her fingers at the top of her scar.

I felt uneasy, but I was transfixed. I ran my fingers down the length of my zip. She ran her fingers down the length of her scar. I traced a finger back up my zip. She traced a finger back up from her navel to between her breasts. My fingers tweaked the zip fastening. She pinched the top of her scar. I started to undo my zip. She started unzipping her skin. My hand stopped, hers continued. As she moved her fingers down the red trail on her abdomen, light spilled out until, on reaching the end of the scar it was as if a door had been opened, just slightly, leaking light from within. As her scar opened wider it became a shaft that bisected her bedroom window and shot out into the darkness of the street, catching the raindrops in its path.

Freud jumped on the windowsill. He sauntered through

the beam, tail aloft, and sat at the other side, facing it. He stared intently into the swirl of light. Freud's owner stared at me. I stared back at her, then at what was coming from her abdomen. Brightly coloured fish started to appear in the light, swimming in air as the rain fell, the frill of their fins fanning out in an invisible current. Freud raised his paw and batted them this way and that. They moved as one, flashing their iridescence in the steady stream, shining blue and green, orange and red. *B. splendens*. The Jewel of the Orient. Siamese fighting fish . . . my Siamese fighting fish. I looked over at the tank in my bedroom. It was empty and the light was out. When I looked back across the street, Freud had gone and the room was in darkness. His owner was nowhere to be seen. I looked down at the tarmac of the pavement in front of her house. The only light now came from the streetlamp, and I could just make out flickers of movement in the eddies and rivulets as my beautiful jewels rolled and gasped in the gutter.

WHAT'S GOING ON OUTSIDE?

KAREL SAT AT the card table peeling his third orange. His hands were large and powerful, his fingers nimble and dextrous. By the time he'd finished, the flesh of the orange was clean, pithless and perfectly round. For a short time he admired his handiwork, then split the orange into segments. He ate them with a speed that suggested he feared one might be stolen. When done, he sucked the juice from the fingers of his left hand and with his right removed another orange from the plastic sack at his feet.

'For the love of God, Karel,' Eugene said. 'How many oranges can one man eat?'

Karel looked up from his fourth orange, his nail already under the peel. The older man – canted, pocked face, grey eyed – was stretched out on the right-hand bed, a newspaper just below his eyes.

'Would you like one?' Karel said. 'I have plenty.'

'Speak Russian, Karel!' Eugene said. 'It's almost midnight. It's much too late in the day for English.'

'Would you like one?' Karel said in Russian. 'I have plenty.'

'You know I can't abide oranges,' Eugene said. 'You know

I can't even stand the way you peel your oranges. So just be quiet, okay? Be quiet and eat your fucking oranges.'

The answer was nine: one man – or at least the one who was Karel – could eat nine oranges in one sitting. The last two are not pleasant: too sweet by that point, too sticky on the fingers, no matter how many times you wash them. And their room was the furthest away from both bathroom and kitchen. Those last two oranges are something like an ordeal; but Karel always likes to push things. That's what his father used to say. What Eugene says, too.

'Does it not give you a stomach ache?' Eugene asked, setting aside his newspaper and tapping a cigarette against the wall.

'They're on special offer downstairs,' he said. 'A whole bag for a pound. And they're good oranges, too. Try a piece.'

Karel held out a segment of orange, Eugene pointed to his lit cigarette.

'They're good for you,' Karel said. 'Vitamins and things. You should eat fruit. It's good for you.'

'Nothing is good for you,' Eugene said. 'Everything's going to kill you one day. Don't you read the papers? Don't you watch TV?'

'No one's died from eating oranges.'

'Perhaps no one's eaten as many as you have. Maybe you'll be the first man to die of oranges. The first man to eat his body weight in oranges and then drop dead.'

Karel laughed and his shoulders went down and up like he was working the jackhammer. He stopped and went back to his orange.

'Your father would never have eaten fruit the way you do.'

Karel looked up from peeling. He smiled.

'He'd have eaten the peel as well,' he said.

'Don't you be disrespectful,' Eugene said.

He shook his head and picked up his newspaper. Karel watched him move from the bed to the window. It was a

broken sash, three floors up. They had the best room because
Eugene had been there longest and got to choose his room-
mate and where he slept. When he'd first arrived, he'd shared
a bedroom with five other men, sleeping in shifts, the smells
and noises like something from a farmyard. Now there was a
wardrobe and a dresser, a card table and just two single beds,
a window out of which to look. Eugene opened the sash and
hung out, smoking his cigarette. He could smell the exhaust
fumes from buses, sweet pastry being baked. Most of all he
could smell Karel's oranges.

'What's going on outside?' Karel asked.

Their room was above a greengrocer with a view down onto
the main road. The shops were Turkish, Kurdish, Greek; open
all hours. There was always something to see, either down at
street level or in the flats and bedsits opposite their window. In
the smaller window at one o'clock to them, a man was jigging
a small child up and down. He wasn't wearing anything on
his top half and was animatedly, though to Eugene mutely,
singing as he bounced the child around.

'There are a few lights on. The man with the baby's there.'

'The wife?'

'No. No ladies tonight.'

'There never are any ladies, are there?'

'No. They're all such *teases*, aren't they?' Eugene said.

Karel sat at the card table peeling his fifth orange. His hands
were large and powerful, his fingers nimble and dextrous.
By the time he'd finished, the flesh of the orange was clean,
pithless and perfectly round. For a short time he admired his
handiwork, then split the orange into segments. He ate them
distractedly. When done, he sucked the juice from the fingers
of his left hand and with his right removed another orange
from the plastic sack at his feet.

'I'm not sure I can take another night of this,' Eugene said.

'You say that every night,' Karel said. 'Every night the same.'

'Is it any wonder?' And talk Russian, you sound like a dope in English.'

Eugene tapped a cigarette against the wall as Karel chewed on the first segment of his sixth orange. Karel said nothing. He said nothing again. And for the third time.

'So out with it,' Eugene said. 'You look like a fish. A big stupid fish.'

'There is nothing to say,' Karel said. 'Nothing important at least.'

Karel started on the seventh orange. The peel did not come away in a perfect roll. The peel looked ragged, like a label picked from a beer bottle.

'How long have we lived together? How long have we known each other? You are my son. My blood is not your blood, but you are my son, as close as is possible. Like Joseph to Jesus. I know, Karel. I know that something is on your mind. Your father looked the same way when things were on his mind.'

Karel put down the half-peeled orange and stood. Triangular torso and bullet-headed, smooth pink skin. The woman he did odd jobs for called him The Tank. She liked to watch his forearms as he moved gravel from one part of the garden to another, drinking tea with her friends as he worked. She was a good woman. She reminded Karel of his mother.

'It's nothing, Gen. Nothing really.'

'Say nothing then. Say nothing for the rest of the night. Let's sit ourselves in silence! You can look like a dopey fish all evening.'

There was half of the orange left. It sat on the plate by its ragged skin. He looked up at Eugene and then back down at the orange. Were he to say something the conversation would last the night. The thought tired him enough to leave the last of the orange.

Eugene opened the sash and hung out, smoking his cigarette. There were two men arguing outside the greengrocers. One was carrying a large leather bible. A bus rattled past, a van with a defective exhaust.

'What's going on outside?' Karel asked.

'Two men are arguing,' Eugene said. 'I don't know the language, but it's an argument.'

'Anything else?'

'There are a few lights on. The man with the baby's there. His wife too. They're all singing. She has a top on, but he doesn't.'

'How do they look?' Karel said.

'They look tired,' he said.

Karel sat at the card table peeling his tenth orange. His hands were large and powerful, his fingers nimble and dextrous despite their stickiness. By the time he'd finished, the flesh of the orange was almost pithless. He split the orange into segments and ate them with a speed that suggested he feared one might be stolen. When done, he sucked the juice from the fingers of his left hand and with his right removed another orange from the plastic sack at his feet.

'And you're just going to sit there, are you?' Eugene said. 'Eating your oranges? Eating one after another?'

The tenth one tasted of nothing; the eleventh one the same. Karel was not even bothered by the stickiness of his fingers. There had been twenty oranges in the plastic sack and he felt he could eat them all.

'What's wrong with eating oranges?' Karel said.

'It's the way you eat them,' Eugene said. 'Your father would be ashamed at the way you eat them, the way you peel them, with your long nail.'

'Nina likes the way I eat oranges,' Karel said. 'She says it's like art.' He picked up the perfect coil of peel to show Eugene.

'Does she know how many you can eat though? Does she

have any idea of the smell? And speak Russian for the grace of God!'

'She's normal. She likes the smell of oranges,' Karel said in Russian.

'She says that now, but believe me she'll soon—'

'Can you just be quiet and let me eat my oranges?' Karel said and looked the other way. Half of the orange remained. He could not even think about eating it. It would dry up there, pucker in the summer evening's breeze.

Eugene tapped a cigarette against the wall, went to the window and opened the sash.

'Are you seeing her tonight?'

'We're meeting at ten.'

'You're going out that late at night? You need to be up in the morning. We have a job.'

'I'll be awake.'

'No good will come of this. Let me tell you that.'

Eugene lit his cigarette and looked out of the window, down onto the street. All the men and women, all the boys and girls. He wondered what Karel's mother would make of it all. What a woman, what Nastia, would make of this house of men. The smells and manners, the grubby nests of sheets. Nastia who called, whose face appeared at the computer screen when he was out. Eugene was always out when Nastia and Karel talked. He did not want to see her, hear her. The way she spoke, the way the words sounded from her mouth. Not like that, anyway.

'What's going on outside?' Karel asked.

'There are a few lights on. The man with the baby's there. Jigging him up and down.'

'He's too rough with that boy,' Karel said. 'Every night too rough.'

'The child's got wind. Even I can see that.'

'He's too rough with him.'

'Since when did you think that?'

'I've always thought that,' Karel said.

Karel sat at the card table peeling his first orange. His hands were large and powerful, his fingers nimble and dextrous. He took no time or pride in peeling the orange. He ate a quarter in one, then a half. Then peeled another.

Outside an *ocabasi* a woman with tightly pulled-back hair was smoking a cigarette. Eugene watched her take a phone from her handbag and press a button. Karel's phone rang. He answered it, licking his fingers. Eugene watched the woman speak. He heard her talk into Karel's ear. He heard the frustration in Karel's English. His manic corrections. He heard him say no three times; say no three ways. Eugene watched the woman end the call. She looked to the window where he was smoking. He waved and she walked away, up the hill.

'Are you not seeing her, then?' Eugene said.

'Not tonight, no,' Karel said in Russian.

'You go and see her, don't worry about me. Don't let me ruin your fun.'

'You wanted to watch the football together. I told her that's what I was doing.'

'But —'

'No,' Karel said. 'We watch the football.'

Karel had a laptop and when Eugene was in they watched American cop shows, Russian soap operas, British football. It was a nothing match that night, but they sat on their beds, the laptop propped up on an orange crate, and drank a few bottles of Budweiser. At the end of the game, Karel's phone rang. He answered with apologies, but moved on to anger. The call ended and Karel ate the last of the orange.

'Trouble in paradise?' Eugene said.

'I'm going to bed,' Karel said. 'A long day tomorrow.'

'Every day is long,' Eugene said.

'She's a beautiful girl, that Nina,' he said. 'But the most beautiful women are from Minsk. I remember the first —'

'I must sleep. Please, Gen, let me sleep now.'

'It's not even eleven.'

'I know, Gen. I know.'

Karel sat at the card table peeling an orange. His hands were large and powerful, his fingers nimble and dextrous. By the time he'd finished, the flesh of the orange was scuffed with pith and odd spots of rind. He left it in the middle of his plate.

'Were you always in love with my mother?' Karel said. It was a Saturday and so there was vodka. Eugene was looking out of the window, the windows opposite empty save for nets and curtains.

'Yes, always. Everyone knew that. Your father used to make jokes. When I was a young man they called me lapdog. I didn't care.'

Eugene was by the window, smoking the last of his cigarette, a can of beer in his hand. Outside there were three women hailing a taxi, a kid in a baseball cap talking loudly to another boy.

'Does she ever talk of me?' Eugene asked.

'She says you're the kindest man she's ever known.'

'Ah!' he said. 'Well you know what that means.'

Karel took a sip of his vodka and his phone wriggled in his pocket.

'Maybe in another life you could have been my father.'

Eugene wanted to strike him. To get up from the bed and cuff the boy around the ear. So stupid a reaction; this man, his not-son, was the size of a bear, had arm muscles to make boxers seem girlish. He could never hit him. The anger passed.

'I wouldn't have made much of a father,' Eugene said and sat down at the card table. 'You were lucky there. Your mother was lucky too.'

It had changed nothing: his story, his confession. He'd hoped the boy would understand. That men who wander fall in love easily. That Karel's mother was just the first and therefore most pungent of memories. That Eugene knew best. Karel peeled another orange and Eugene went to the window, opened the sash.

'What's going on outside?' Karel asked.

'The man and the woman and the child are there. They —'

Eugene looked over his shoulder and Karel was talking on his phone in a low voice. As he listened to Nina, Karel mouthed sorry in Russian.

Eugene plotted his route again on the small map, though he already knew exactly where he was heading, how long it would take and where to get off the bus. Karel's laptop was useful now he knew how to use it. He had used GoogleEarth and had seen the road on which Karel lived. There were no shops, no bedsits and studios running like a mezzanine above them; just blocks and blocks of flats, trees outside on the pavement, cars double parked in white-lined bays.

Despite the planning, Eugene was a half-hour early. There was a bar around the corner and he drank an expensive bottle of Budweiser while a large crowd watched the rugby. He ordered vodka and the bar staff, as accented as him but better dressed, served him his drink. The customers were eating roast dinners, drinking wine and beers and Bloody Marys. The pitch of the referee's whistle cut through the loudness of their voices. Some of them looked at him. He downed his drink and headed out the door.

There were forty-seven buzzers outside Karel's block. He pressed number 22 and Karel answered as quickly as peeling an orange. He was buzzed through and Eugene took the stairs two at a time. Concrete grey. A smell that made him hold his breath. At the top of the stairs he saw a long corridor with a single door open. Karel appeared, wide smile on wide mouth, wiping his hands on a dishcloth.

'Gen!' he called out down the corridor. 'So good to see you!'

'Karel, my boy, speak Russian,' Eugene said. 'It's Sunday; don't you know to speak Russian on a Sunday?'

'Come on in, Gen,' he said after they embraced. 'Come see my new place.'

The flat was ferociously tidy, three rooms – kitchen/living room, bedroom, bathroom – with laminate flooring and the cheapest kind of furniture. There were two bowls of nuts on the coffee table and the small dining table was set for three. Nina was stirring a large pot on the stove. She looked like she had been stirring the pot for a hundred years.

'I brought some things for you,' Eugene said and took out some beers from his shoulder bag.

'Thanks,' Nina said. 'Good to see you, Gen,' She kissed him on the cheeks.

'You're looking well,' he said tapping her stomach. 'It must agree with you.'

She nodded and Karel put his arms around her. She pushed him away and went back to stirring the pot.

'We have a balcony too,' Karel said and opened the fridge, poured beer for them both. 'Let's go outside, yes?'

They opened the door onto the smallest balcony Eugene had ever seen. It was just about big enough for them to stand side by side. There was an ashtray set on a very small wooden card table.

'So how are you?' Karel asked.

'Fine. You?'

'Fine,' he said. 'Excited.'

'You have a lot to be excited about.'

Eugene smoked a cigarette and they both drank their beer and both agreed how good it was to see each other at last. Then Nina called Karel inside to help with serving lunch.

Nina was a fine cook and Eugene had three helpings of stew.
'You can come any time, Gen,' she said.

'Thank you, Nina,' he said. 'I would be honoured.'

After they had cleared the plates, the two men went outside again. The wind had got up and there were teeth in it. They agreed the food was good, that Nina was a fine cook.

'I have something for you,' Eugene said as they went back inside. Out of his shoulder bag he took a plastic sack and handed it to Eugene.

'Here,' he said. 'I thought you must be missing them.'

'Thanks, Gen,' he said. 'Look, Nina, Gen has brought us oranges!'

'Oranges?'

'Yes, look, from the shop I used to live above. Best oranges I ever tasted.'

'They were nice, yes,' she said and shrugged everyone back to the table.

Karel sat at the table peeling an orange. His hands were large and powerful, his fingers nimble and dextrous. By the time he'd finished, the flesh of the orange was clean, pithless and perfectly round. He passed the plate with the orange to Nina. She split open the orange and quickly ate it. He peeled another, split it, and quickly ate. Eugene watched the two of them, the juice on their chins, the way they licked the juice from their fingers. He watched them smile and, with his right hand, Eugene took an orange from the plastic sack. He dug his thumbnail into its flesh and began to peel.

ELIZABETH BAINES

TIDES

OR
HOW STORIES DO OR DON'T GET TOLD

THERE'S A SCENE that keeps coming back to me: the two of us standing at a wall by the sea one evening in Wales, me and him. It was dusk, the tide was out and just beginning to come in. It feels to me as if this moment is the focus of a story, our story, the point from which the tale could go backwards to all that happened before, and forwards, beyond that night. I see us from outside, silhouetted against the sea and the sky, me in my leather jacket, he in his waterproof – we'd been walking in the mountains – two figures in a tableau, the hero and the heroine of the narrative to be told.

But the light was fading, and as I stare into the memory the thing we were watching then is taking my attention now: the slip of sea coming in between the black and slick-shiny mud flats. The sky is fading, but this little river is paradoxically brightening, as if pulling all the light down into itself. It glistens like mercury, and even as we watch it's coming nearer and growing, because there on the straits the sea comes in quietly but fast from different directions at once.

And I can't yet see how to tell the story, or where to go from

that moment, just the two of us together there at that wall by
the sea.

I could pick the time he betrayed me, which would make the
story a Gothic drama. It was autumn. The smell of rot was in
the air and berries outside the window dripped like darkening blood. I wanted to lock him out for his betrayal, though
his footstep on the path was like the footstep of the vampire
to whom no door could be barred . . .

But I'm distracted from our story. Other stories are crowding me, the ones I was thinking of then by the sea, stories misty
with legend and others concrete and linear with the building
stones of history. My eye – then, and now in my memory – is
drawn to the island across the water, black against the sky,
plump with trees and the tales of the people who regarded
them as sacred and there on that shore fought the Romans
with hair and robes flying and torches flailing and blood-
curdling cries. And nearer, drawn on the tide of that growing
river, are the stories of the other invaders and travellers, the
Celtic monks pulling onto the once-wooded shore where we
stand, the Norman king who cut the trees down and built the
castle looming behind us, setting the contours of Constanti-
nople in the blue-green light of this north-western land.

Our figures, mine and his, are becoming indistinct to me
in the dark.

And I'm thinking now, as I was thinking then, of the time
in my childhood when I lived nearby, an English-speaking
invader myself: my own story, which ended long before I
met him, featuring custard made from powder and canings
at school, and which can be a jovial realist tale or a misery
memoir, depending on my mood.

It leads me on – stream-of-consciousness – to remember
now that earlier that day we'd been shopping. He whizzed
around with the trolley and I went straggling behind, side-

tracked by the fact that the supermarket assistants spoke mostly in North-West English accents, not Welsh. Later on we made an inquiry in a shop that hadn't yet opened for business and was still being stocked with huge ugly soft toys by three Asian-looking guys. They were from our own town in England, I commented, but, surprised, they said no, they were locals, and when I asked them where they got their accents they said they had no idea.

And I stood in the pedestrianized High Street while he went to the bank machine, and watched a giant-seeming seagull drop onto a toy-town-seeming chimney, while a young mother, like my own mother here once, struggled by with a pushchair and kids, and I couldn't decide if it was a bad end to a story – a culture and a language swamped, in spite of the educational and heritage initiatives, by the Englishness sweeping down the new roads and the TV channels – or actually a good one, riddance of the differences that created old enmities.

Or maybe – more like – there's just no end to the story.

He came from the bank machine towards me, took my arm, waved back at the guys through the glass; we waved together, him and me: that's how we are now, a companionable couple, we went off for a companionable walk in the hills, it's not the heart-stopping thing it once was.

I could tell that story, the time I ended it between us. I could make it a feminist re-telling of a fairy tale: the waking princess (me) kicking the prince away from the glass coffin, ie my house which I had to myself again at last. I could end it there and people would be glad of a satisfying ending and none would be any the wiser, leaving out the way the house then filled with shadows, the fact that I stopped eating, that I longed for the sound of his step on the path again, and when it came, like a stroke on skin, rushed to the door and the light flooded in . . . And then I wouldn't be able to mention those years we spent together with the children – years like a TV sitcom – or indeed the two of us standing by the castle and the straits all that time later, side by side, not quite touching, watching the day dying, this image which just now seems central to it all.

The dark came down, the island was lost to us; the only thing to be seen was that river, still brightening and growing, and we turned into the pub under the castle wall just behind.

We'd bought a paper and tried to read it, but it was Saturday night and the pub was noisy and full. In spite of the bitter weather young women were wearing the briefest, most glittery fashions and they shrieked with a confident abandon which within easy living memory would never have been allowed in this town. Young men bellowed. A lad nearby pulled his shirt from his trousers and kept showing off his belly and every now and then staggered like a toddler up to a fortyish guy sitting nearby and performed a low drunken bow.

Twenty today, that older chap explained, and then engaged him, my companionable man, in conversation. I turned to the paper and read that the terrible summer had been caused by storms in the Arctic, which in turn had been caused by the warming of the seas elsewhere in the world. And then I looked back up and here in the pub it seemed the wrong story: the flowing drink, the skimpy clothes and bare flesh were the real and concrete components of a better-known, more comforting one, the certain progression of the familiar seasons.

My eye was caught by a teenage girl in the doorway, in a little-girl dress with puff sleeves and high princess waist, and I was swamped by nostalgia, which of course is what such fashions are designed to do to you, and I thought of myself in the time before I made all my choices, when all the narratives were open, when I couldn't have imagined I'd be sitting here one day with a man I almost lost, once because I nearly gave him up and once because he nearly died.

I could tell that last too, as a complete and rounded story, a grim, realist tale: the symbolic slam of the ambulance door, the ice-rink of the hospital corridor, his skull pushing up through his skin, the emergency operation. Would I mention my sense then that nothing had meaning and that my life after all was no story, or would I lie, since he recovered, and make those symbols fit a narrative arc with a happy ending?

I looked beyond him, and framed in the pub window was that channel of sea, now hugely swollen, still lit with a light that seemed to come from nowhere.

The other guy was still talking to him, in an accent part Welsh and part something else. He came from Liverpool, he was saying, and when he had kids here he vowed he'd bring them up properly Welsh. His son was the friend of that lad whose birthday it was; they were in the Welsh Guards, and the reason they were making hay this weekend was that the following week they were off to Afghanistan.

Outside the window the river broke an invisible barrier and poured across the mud flats.

The chap saw where I was looking. He said, did we know that the council sold the land on the harbour for a single penny to developers, to be rid of the responsibility of protecting the town when the sea level rises?

It was time to go. We picked up the paper.

Outside the sea had drowned the mud flats altogether and was lapping blackly, high against the wall.

The light was all gone.

We joined hands in the dark, in the oncoming rush of all the possible stories.

THE SEA IN BIRMINGHAM

CYRIL'S EYES ARE extraordinary. Every time I shave him, I say that to myself. A rare blue. So clear. All the secrets of the world there. Not watery. Not glazed. Just clear blue. Sometimes, in the sitting room, he will beckon me over. I have to crouch down because he wants to whisper. 'I was a sailor, you know, in the navy.'

'Would that be with Nelson, Cyril?' I ask.

'No.' He chuckles. 'The war.'

'The Great War?'

'They're all great, son.'

Now I can't get him into his room. 'There is a woman in the mirror,' he says. 'She lives there.'

'I don't think so, Cyril.'

'There is, son. A woman – in the mirror.'

Matron Judy comes into the corridor. 'Lucky you, Cyril,' Matron Judy says, and, taking Cyril's shoulder, she walks him firmly into the room. 'She'll probably come out tonight and you can have lots of fun.'

Matron Judy positions Cyril in front of his bed and starts to undress him. He tries to protest, raising his hand, but she has his belt. She pushes his hand away and his trousers fall. 'Sit, Cyril.' A small shove and he is sitting on the bed. His neck cranes backwards, towards the mirror.

'Cyril. Cyril love. Look at me.' His head returns. His lip quivers, a sob takes him, and Matron Judy softens. 'Come on, Cyril, there's nobody there, in the mirror or anywhere else. Pass me his pyjamas, Stu.' Her hand glides down the side of Cyril's face. 'It's your imagination, sweetheart.' She strokes his head. 'You're a silly boy, aren't you? What are you?'

Cyril says nothing. Matron Judy wipes away the tears on his cheek. 'You're a silly boy, that's what you are.' I hand her his pyjama trousers.

'Up. Up. Stand. Put your hands on my shoulders. That's it. Now I'm going to get you all nicely tucked up in bed. Then you'll be all right, won't you?' She turns. 'Okay, Stu. I'll see to him.'

Later she catches me in the domestic corridor. 'I thought I told you to get rid of Cyril's fucking mirror.' It's under her arm. 'Here. Put it behind the wardrobe in Muriel's room.'

I take the mirror. Hold it up. Look at it. 'Bloody hell, Jude, there's a woman in here.' Matron Judy kicks me in the arse.

Tomorrow I am going to strangle Cyril. I shall strangle all of them, starting with Matron Judy, who I will do slowly – in the main lounge, before the cinema-sized television screen, in front of which a horseshoe of the D residents sits. Some glance up at it now and then, some never take their eyes off it, some of course hardly ever open their eyes – but no one watches the television. My nan died while watching TV: *Good Morning with Anne and Nick*.

And when Matron Judy is a lifeless heap, lying like an offering before the screen, I will go round the circle of the sleeping. The circle of the faded, the jaded; the circle of the tired, the deranged. The useless. The dreaming. I will go round snapping necks. Briskly.

Symbolism is important in acts of mass murder. It ensures the perpetrator – the murderer, if you must – will be remembered, he or she taken seriously, considered, written about, the subject of films, the inspiration for fiction. The mystery of symbolism is more climactic, more resonant, more important than the killings themselves. The camera closes in on the teddy bear beside the bloodied knife; the author takes the reader beyond the splayed bodies to the votive candle burning in the corner of the room.

Cyril hardly ever sleeps in the daytime. Not like the others. Often the snoring is louder than the television. Matron Judy stands in the doorway, smiles. 'Ah, just look at them, Stu. So peaceful. A shame to disturb them. We'll skip teatime.' She turns to Chris. 'Make Cyril a cup of tea, though, will you, love?'

'I was a sailor, you know. Once.'

'I know you were, Cyril, and you'll be going down with the bloody ship if you don't take a nap. Only one sugar, Chris. His weight was up again last week.'

'You are mad. Mad, mad, mad,' Vladimir says. 'Crazy.' He is making Yorkshire pudding. Holding an enamel bowl aloft. The mixture, like Hokusai's *Great Wave*, rolls from the bowl down into the oblong baking tin beneath. It is a joy to watch. The mixture finds its level and Vladimir shakes it smooth. 'I think you should see some doctors. It is easy. Moseley has many good doctors. I think you should take Sertraline.'

I have been describing my murderous plans to Vladimir for weeks now, but it is only recently, as his English has improved, that he understands what I am saying.

'Judy will be the first,' I say. 'I'm going to wire her up to the toaster. She'll come in here, first thing as usual, pop in a slice as usual, flick the switch – as usual – and then pop, she'll light up! She'll glow, her earrings will –'

'What is *glow*?' Vladimir is placing the mixing bowl in the sink, turning the tap.

'Glow?' I think about the word. 'It's, like, red hot. The tip of a cigarette glows. Anything really hot will glow.'

'You will make Judy glow?' There is a lascivious smile on his face that isn't nice. There is a rumour that Vladimir fucks Judy sometimes when dinners are over, up in Edna's room on the top floor. 'I thought you were going to drown her. You said yesterday you would drown her in Joan's bath –'

'Win's bath. I said I would drown her in *Win*'s bath. I'd need to use the hoist.'

It is you. I've been watching you. All the time. Watching. And I'd know you anywhere. What you did to me. How could I forget you? It is you – it is, isn't it? If I'd bitten your bloody tongue off, I'd know. Not much to say for yourself now, have you? Kissing – you call that kissing? I was drowning under you, I was.

'How many times have I told you, Sonia? Don't let Bill out of the summer room in the afternoons.' Matron Judy is standing in front of Cyril, holding his hand. With his other hand Cyril tries to undo his belt.

Sonia tuts. Or clicks. Some noise with her tongue while simultaneously widening her eyes to Matron Judy then casting them away; she always does this when anyone has a go at her. 'I didn't see him go nowhere.' Sonia speaks to the floor.

'Then you weren't looking. He's gone into the small sitting room and arrested Cyril again. Got him on the floor. Frightened him. Look, he's pissed himself.' Matron Judy lifts her and Cyril's clasped hands, forming a bridge to expose the sodden front of Cyril's trousers. 'Look!'

Sonia turns her head slowly, sullenly, tuts again.

Cyril whimpers.

'Don't worry, love, it's all right. Well, you can change him.' Matron Judy gives Cyril's hand to Sonia. 'I don't think he's got any clean trousers at the moment. Put him in a pair of Fred's tracksuit bottoms.'

'He don't like tracksuit bottoms,' Sonia says, taking Cyril's hand.

'It's only for today. You'd better pad him; I know, he doesn't like that either. He drinks too much bloody tea. God knows why Bill always goes for Cyril.'

'He must remind him of some villain he's arrested in the past,' I say.

'He arrests every bloke in the place. But it's only Cyril he gets nasty with.'

Joan comes into the corridor laughing, carrying her knitting.

'Joan!' Matron Judy says. 'What are you doing out of the sitting room, love? You're supposed to be watching the film.'

'Bill, he's arrested Cyril. Sailor boy. Done for him proper. Tell the black girl she let him get away and he arrested Cyril. Good job, too. He should swing for what he's done.'

'Joan, love. That's not very nice. Bill was a copper so many years, he gets mixed up. Old habits die hard. Cyril's never done anything.'

'That's what you think. I'm a witness, I am. I know. He shouldn't be here. Not in Birmingham. Not a sailor. I know –' As Joan raises a finger to point at Matron Judy her knitting falls. The needles stick up like daggers in the carpet. The ball of beige wool rolls along the corridor, the knitting unravels. Joan, surprised, stares at it.

'Stu, get that, will you, and take Joan back to the film, there's a love.'

'It's over,' Joan says. 'It's snooker now.'

Bernie, the night deputy, clocks on at eight o'clock. I've just finished the cocoa run. She's in the office going through the record sheets. She looks at me, asks, 'What you doing here?'

'Apollonia phoned in. Her kid's sick. Judy blagged me into an extra shift.'

Bernie taps the logbook. 'How did Bill get out?'

'Sonia was on her own.'

There's a shout. Then another. A cry really.

'*Cyril!*' We both head down the corridor to his room. He is outside the closed door in his pyjamas, holding the handle.

'There's a woman in there,' he says. 'Hiding. She's in the wardrobe.'

Bernie's good with him. 'Oh dear, Cyril.' She puts her arm around him. 'Her again. I know all about her. She's a real pest she is, but I'll sort her out.' Bernie goes into Cyril's room, shouts, 'Out you. Out. I've had enough of you. Right, there you go, m'lady. And don't come back.'

Cyril is pissing himself. Realising what's happening, he grabs his balls. 'Oh. Oh. Oh.' He starts to cry.

'It's all right, my darlin'.' Bernie takes his hand, kisses it. Kisses his forehead. 'She scared you, that's all. But I've got rid of her now. She won't be back.'

'She's in the wardrobe.'

'Not any more she's not. I promise you, my love, she's gone, and she won't be back. Stu will clean you up. Put you back to bed. All safe and sound, pet.' She kisses him again. 'All safe and sound.'

'When I shoot them all, I might let Cyril off. It's the eyes. I could only shoot him if he closed his eyes. Or if I blindfolded him. Bill would blindfold him for me. He'd like that.'

Bernie and I are standing in the open doorway of the conservatory having a cigarette. You can hear the hum of evening traffic from the Moseley Road. Nesma, the night housekeeper, has collected the day's wet cushions from the lounge and put them against the radiators to dry. Next, she starts sorting out the ironing. St Anne's clock strikes the hour: ten o'clock.

'Amazing, aren't they?' says Bernie. 'Greeny-blue.'

'No, just blue. Clear blue. That's what's so rare about them. The clearest blue.'

'Whatever, I bet they broke a few hearts. Anyway I thought you were going to use poison.'

Nesma laughs.

'I said that to Vladimir, and now he never takes his eyes off me in the kitchen. Thinks I'm going to put bromethalin in the cocoa. No, it's definitely going to be a gun. Judy first, *p-bang*, then I've decided Sonia will be next – she won't look me in the eyes; I might have to get Bill to blindfold her too – then the residents. Well, all the D residents anyway.'

Behind us Nesma turns on the radio. Indian music plays very softly.

'How's Cyril now?' Bernie asks.

'All right, I think. Clean. Dry. Not entirely convinced you got rid of his visitor.'

'He's still upset about Bill having a go at him. I wish he'd stop picking on Cyril like that.'

From her ironing at the back of the conservatory Nesma joins the conversation: 'Bill will arrest anyone when he gets aggressive.'

'Judy should talk to the doctor about his medication,' Bernie says. 'Something stronger. It's happening too often. He's arrested me a couple of times. Called me an IRA bitch once. Wanted to know where the bomb was.'

'Did you tell him?'

'Told him I'd stick it up his arse if he didn't behave himself.'

'You didn't, did you?'

'Course not.'

'Judy would have.'

'Then she'd have forgotten the first line of the handbook: *Respect for the dignity of every individual resident is the basis of our care.* I just took Bill's hand, called him love and said it was a case of mistaken identity.'

'You're good with them. Bags of patience. Me, I just –' The door opens. It's Betty. In her nightdress. Holding a pair of shoes. 'Hello, what are you doing down here? You should be upstairs.'

'Should I?'

'Yes, you should, young lady.' I take her hand. 'Come –'

'But I've got an appointment with Maureen. I can't go out with my hair like this. Maureen's got me in for an appointment. I'm going somewhere. A dance, I think. At the West End Ballroom probably. In Paradise Street. I like it there.'

I look at Bill sleeping. A shuddering sleep, the snores like small sneezes. On his door is a picture of him in uniform. A peaked cap, so I suppose he was a senior cop of some sort. Taken in central Birmingham. The Rotunda in the background. His leg jerks suddenly. I wonder what he's dreaming about. Chasing some villain? He jerks again. There's a framed photograph of him and his late wife beside the bed, suntanned and smiling on a cruise, the ocean blue behind them.

Betty's asleep now, too. I've put a couple of armchairs at the side of the bed in case she tries to get out again. It's Matron Judy's rule that women do the night checks in pairs – there's always the chance you'll find somebody dead – but she says it's okay for men to do them on their own.

'Cyril, what are you like, mate?'

He's out of bed on his hands and knees, looking underneath it. 'There's a woman under the bed.'

'Come on now, Cyril. It's the middle of the night – well gone ten, anyway – and I want to go home.'

'She's there. Under the bed.'

'She's harmless, Cyril. She'll be as good as gold. You won't even know she's there, mate. That's it. Good chap. In you get now.'

'I've sailed, you know. Years ago. I've been all over.'

'I know you have. I know you have, mate. Now come on.'

'I've seen action.'

His palm cups my chin – her chin – pushing back, pushing up. His fingers are splayed over my face. My nose through his fingers like the beak of a bird through a cage. Her face? My face? Am I watching? Or is it me? He is kissing me. Kissing me through his fingers. Kissing – you can't call it kissing. His other hand is up my skirt, in my knickers, at me. Now both hands hold my head. He is pushing his face all over mine. Pushing me under. Mouth. Holding her under. Mouth. All over hers. All over mine. Close my eyes and I won't see what's happening to her. Close my eyes.

Why didn't I bite the bugger's tongue off? Why didn't I bite?

I see you.

I see you there. I'm watching. And I know it's you.

I'm in the office, filling in my timesheet.

Matron Judy and Chris are trying to solve the problem of space. It is Tuesday. Maureen is hairdressing in downstairs bathroom 1 – all day – and the chiropodist is using downstairs bathroom 2 until at least three. The comp volunteers are in this afternoon doing Living History projects with some of C's residents and they need somewhere to go to talk to them. Usually they use the C dining room, but Father James will be in there giving communion to the Catholics, while the Active Hands lady will be using the smaller D dining room for her exercise class.

Maureen pops her head round the office door. 'Stu, have you got a minute?' She is taking Betty back to the big sitting room.

'That looks nice, Betty,' I say.

'Do you think it's all right?' Betty touches her perm.

'Beautiful. If I was forty years older . . .'

Betty laughs.

'You'll have to watch him,' Maureen tells her. She turns to me. 'Cyril's just gone into the visitors' lounge and I've got to bring Bill through for a haircut. He's already going on about not being first. Says he's giving evidence in court this morning.'

'Oh, blimey. Okay. Give me a minute.' I head for the lounge.

Cyril is on his knees beside the coffee table, peering into the dark sheen of its polished surface. I crouch down beside him.

'She's in there. See. She's there.'

I see his reflection staring back at us, his face framed by flowers in a vase on the table. What does he see? I wonder? *She's in there.* The face of a beautiful woman, floating like John Everett Millais' *Ophelia*, just below the surface of the wood? And I feel like crying. 'Come on, Cyril. She's all right. Don't disturb her.'

He turns to me; old blue eyes, old blue blue eyes, except these eyes aren't old. 'Is she all right?'

'I think so. Come on, mate. They're laying the tables for lunch. Shall we go and watch them? Or shall we look at the aquarium?'

'The fish.'

But the three armchairs in front of the aquarium are all filled by sleeping residents. 'It's so peaceful watching those fish,' Matron Judy always says. 'Makes me want to drop off myself.'

'I can hear music, Cyril. Can you? That's Kathy Kirby, that is. *Secret Love.* Let's go and see who's listening to Kathy Kirby.'

I know who you are, mate. I've got your number.

What you did to me. Kissing in a cage. A bird with a broken beak. What's kissing got to do with it? Banging my head against the floor – and kissing. Uniform means nowt to me. Soldier, sailor,

rich man, poor man. Thief, you old bastard – thief. You know what
you took from me.

But I've got you now.

I've got you now.

We're all crowded into the kitchen, Matron Judy leaning
against the fridge.

'God knows what the comp are going to think now. They'll
never let their kids anywhere near the place. Vladimir, cut that
coconut sponge up into fingers. Chris, make up some squash,
will you, love? And some tea for the police. A few biscuits as
well. Stu, go and see what's happening, will you?'

'I can't. She told me to stay here – the policewoman in
charge. You know she did. *Stay in the kitchen.* She said it to all
of us. They've put Sonia in the lounge.'

'That's so they can question her,' Chris explains. 'They're
going to talk to us all.'

I jump up onto the draining board and kneel on the window
ledge. Open a window.

'Stu,' Matron Judy squeals. 'You can't get out that way.
You've got to stay here.'

I'm leaning out of the window. Half in, half out. 'I'm not
going anywhere. I've got to have a fag, that's all.'

'You can't do that. Not in the kitchen.'

'Fuck off, Judy.'

'Leave him, Jude,' Chris says. 'He's upset. He's had a nasty
experience.'

'We're all upset, Chris. We've all had a nasty experience. I
am still having one.'

Vladimir reaches for my leg. I pull away, tumbling to the
ground outside. 'He's escaping,' Vladimir shouts. Matron Judy
shrieks.

Chris is at the window. 'Are you okay, Stu?'

'Yeah. I'll just have a fag then I'll climb back in.' Pressed against the kitchen wall, I light a cigarette. Inhale. The smoke burns, the smoke calms. A miracle. And in the smoke I see the shape of Cyril, under a white sheet. Lying as he does in bed sometimes, on his side, one leg drawn up so that a foot rests on the knee of his other leg. Under the sheet he looks like a seahorse, carved in plaster of Paris.

*

What colour would describe these walls? the police officer wonders. Pea green would probably do it. She is aware of beads of sweat breaking on her back; a trickle running down her spine. They keep these places so warm, she thinks, no wonder the old folk sleep all the time. 'Let's open a window, shall we?' she says to the man before her. 'Let some air in.' She moves past him to do it.

It's a good move. The young man – youngish, he's probably thirty – is visibly disconcerted by the sight of his sketchpad on the table she's been using as a desk. *Prominent silent display*: her old boss Sean Dowd's tip. Just let it sit there. Get on with other things. You'll soon find out if it has any evidential value. *Evidential value*, that's what it's all about at this stage. *Initial questioning*. Almost informal. Just her with each staff member in turn; her colleague WPC Morris sitting quietly beside the door, almost invisible.

The police officer breathes in the cool air: 'That's better.' She turns back to the room, leans against the sill. Another old Dowd technique: speak to the suspect's back. 'Tell me exactly what happened, Mr Hibbs. Stuart. Exactly as you remember it.'

The man's head turns a little as he shuffles round in his chair.

'Just stay where you are, Stuart,' she says. After what the chef has told her she needs to go in fairly hard with this one.

'I was in the lounge. On my own –'

'On your own?' Cooler now, she returns to her seat.

132

'Sorry. I was the only *member of staff* in there. Just me and the residents. They were watching television. Well, it was on. Most of them were asleep. Not Cyril, though.'

'This is Mr Turvey?' She places a hand on the sketchbook. Mr Hibbs notices. Blinks. She thinks again of the chef's peculiar smile as he handed her the book: *In here, I think, you will find things you should see.* His hand deliberately brushing hers. Unpleasant. You get some odd characters in places like this.

'That's right. We call them by their first names. To create a family atmosphere.'

'Go on.'

'He wasn't asleep. Then Joan comes into the room –'
'That's – Miss Walters?' She looks down to her notes. So many names . . .

'That's right. She's a B resident, but she sometimes comes into the small lounge. She goes over to Cyril and looks at him, really hard, and she starts to laugh. "It's you," she says. "I knew it was. I'd know you anywhere." Then she called him a bastard. She does swear sometimes, Joan. She said, "I knew you'd surface one day, come bobbing up – and I'd be ready for you." Cyril was upset by this and he started to get up. I called to her to leave him alone. I went over, took his arm and was saying something like, "Come on, Cyril, let's have a little walk," when I saw her behind us. She'd got Brenda's walking stick, the one with an ivory handle, up above her head, and before I can say or do anything she brought it down on Cyril's head. He went straight down. Without a sound. Just crumpled. Joan tried to hit him again. "There, you bastard," she was saying. "Down you go. I knew I'd get you one day."'

The police officer waits. Lets her finger tap the sketchpad. 'And that was it?'

'Yes. Then I went for help.'

He is watching her finger on the sketchpad. Now still; now

tapping. She tries to forget the chef's smile, his sticky hand. 'What was Mr Turvey like?'

Hibbs smiles. 'Oh, Cyril was a lovely man. Gentle. Quiet. Easily scared of stuff. A bit troubled. He had beautiful blue eyes.'

There's a pause. The police officer opens the sketchpad, turns two or three pages until she finds what she's looking for. 'Yes, you seem to have been quite taken by Mr Turvey's eyes, Stuart. You have drawn them several times.' She watches him swallow. 'On this page, just the eyes, drawn twice. Labelled *Cyril's Eyes*, and then –' She flicks on through the sketchbook. '– here they are again, but this time with wings. And here, curiously, in what looks like a goldfish bowl.'

'Surreal –'

'They certainly are.'

She looks at him and he looks back. He's sweating. Forehead. Nose. He swallows again. Indicators? Dowd would say so. Not evidence, but strong indicators. 'These are very peculiar drawings if you don't mind me saying, Stuart. Some people might use the word *disturbing*. This one that's labelled *Edna Asleep*. Why have –'

'That's in the style of Modigliani. That's why the neck is elongated.'

'All her features seem distorted to me. And here we have another of Mr Turvey. At least that's what the caption says – *Cyril*. But unrecognisable. Broken up, one might say. Mutilated.'

'A sort of Picasso rip-off. Cubism. Breaking down an object into its visual components. I was thinking of his portrait by Juan Gris when I did it.'

'I see.'

He swallows again. Hard. Like he's got a fucking bird fluttering about in his throat. The police officer watches. There's a slick of sweat like varnish across his face, despite the room being cooler now. She watches, and waits. Dowd would be proud of her. Then, 'I have to say there is something very brutal about these sketches, Stuart, something that doesn't seem to be entirely compatible with what one would expect from a paid carer of the elderly.'

'Where did you get that?' Hibbs nods to the sketchpad. 'Did Vladimir give it to you?'

'Mr Karpin, yes he did. He also told me something that is supported by some of your other colleagues, something quite repellent really.' Her fingers dance across the Cubist portrait of Mr Turvey. 'It seems that you spend a lot of time threatening to kill the residents.'

It's a difficult investigation. All the residents who had been in the small lounge at the time of the attack are suffering from some form of dementia, and pretty advanced they are too. Both a doctor and the manager had been with her when she had painstakingly gone round to each, crouching beside their armchairs, trying to talk to them. Nothing. Gaga, all of them. Joan Walters, the woman Stuart Hibbs claimed hit Mr Turvey, had clapped her hands like a child, singing *Who's sorry now?* and blowing kisses.

And now she has a man sitting in front of her who believes he is leading an investigation into the bombing of a pub in the city centre and wants to start making arrests. 'Now. Now. Get the buggers in custody,' he barks. 'If they're Irish, arrest the bastards. Get them down to Edward Road. We'll sort them out there.' Bernadette Ryan, one of the senior carers, sits beside him, stroking his hand, but he's oblivious. He's on the case.

The police officer moves away from him back to the window where she takes a breath of cool air, looks out at an empty garden. A fruit tree in blossom. A bench beneath it covered in the stuff. It's ten years since she's had a cigarette, but by God she could do with one now. A long smooth Dunhill and a glass of cold Chardonnay. She turns back to the pea-green room. The man's ranting has ceased. He's looking around. Trying to work out where she's gone, probably. She hopes someone will put a bag over her head before she ever gets to that stage.

There is always a motive, she tells herself, if you know where to look. But that's in the real world. Here it is different. She looks across to the medication trolley standing in the corner, thinks about people like Dr Shipman, people like Beverly Allitt, Vanessa George. Cruelty. Madness. Power. Easy to see it all here. Another world. Locked away.

The man at the table has moved on from the IRA and is talking about a cruise. The Ionian sea. The blue blue sea. She won't get any sense out of him. Perhaps she should take Hibbs in for further questioning. Or maybe let things lie, go away for a day or so and think it through. Cyril Turvey has no family, so there'll be no one banging the door down for action. Perhaps she'll have a chat with Dowd, too.

She could probably pin it on Hibbs. Circumstantial, but even so. He's obviously a weirdo, the sketchbook shows that. And he's made threats. All the time, apparently. Fantasy? Possibly. But then she knows serial killers often fantasise about killing, long before their first murder. If he gets away with this one, who knows how many he might do in before they catch up with him again?

There was no wedding ring on Hibbs's finger. She wonders if he has a partner. If not, if he's a loner, that would strengthen the case. After all, why would an old lady, however dippy, suddenly attack Mr Turvey? It didn't make any sense. The manager has assured her that Joan Walters has never displayed any violence or serious aggression, other than poking people with her knitting needles, and the doctor confirmed this. *Sweet* was a word the staff used. *Funny*. Why would a sweet old lady attack Mr Turvey? No motive, nothing a coroner would see in her background as an explanation. Whereas Hibbs. He was the only one there at the time of the killing. Or, at least, he was as good as the only one. And she sees the faces – Shipman, Allitt, George – like a hand of cards before her. Yes, she'll take Hibbs in. See how he holds up to questioning at the station. Get everything on record.

The man at the table turns. 'The sea in Birmingham,' he says. 'It's much deeper than it looks. Not many people know that.' He taps the side of his nose; he is telling her a secret.

AILSA COX

HOPE FADES FOR THE HOSTAGES

EVERY NIGHT AND every morning. Two red zeros staring straight back at you. Exactly three a.m. A surprise. Not a surprise. The scent of a sleeping body lying by your side in the darkness. The steady puff and blow of breathing. Gentle, slowly now, do not disturb. The dead grate in the living room. The carpet threaded by silver trails. The house feels abandoned and hollow, and you yourself are its wandering ghost, pouring a whiskey, reading last week's papers while you're waiting for tomorrow. *Hope fades for the hostages*. Won't be up long. But this time it's different. A noise. Not just the wind sawing the trees, or the hum of the fridge, or a car swishing by. Something else, a dripping sound. Something dripping. Hold your breath and listen. You almost think it's stopped. But there it is again, a little louder, gentle, insistent. Upstairs the sleeper dreams on, unaware.

It's three in the morning. I'm writing this letter thirty thousand feet above the surface of the planet, the cabin lights down and the passengers snoozing, their bodies strapped in, slumped under the blankets, their faces gone slack and their mouths hanging open. You know I can't sleep with this weird congregation of strangers, hate making these trips to the ends of the earth. When it's three in the morning, back home in England, it'll be 3 p.m. in Eastern Siberia. Dream of me while I'm talking landfalls and terminals with Mr Kim in the Chukotka Suite at the Hotel Anadyr.

They pull in at the motorway services, a constellation of low roofs floating somewhere in the void between departure and arrival. Frank has stopped here before, or his shadow has lingered, waiting for change from the fat man at the till. 'Can I interest you . . .?' pointing at the giant Aeros, mint and orange flavour, hurrying back to the van, coffee spilling on his sleeve, the muddy verges sucking at his shoes. He didn't want to stop, if it wasn't for the rain he would have kept on driving, but he can't see the road for the mist and the spray of the lorries. Beneath the duvet, Linda's breathing seems to be slower and hoarser, but she's okay, she's just sleeping. 'We're fine,' he says out loud, 'we'll make it.' She knows that he would never let her down.

A tiny drop of water in the corner of the bay, how could you have not ever seen that before, and the cracks, new cracks everywhere, and the old ones spreading inexorably, and what have you done about it, nothing, not a thing, to stop that inevitable progress, until the whole place splits apart like the House of Usher. Bed down on the sofa. There will be no more sleeping. Your brain's reeled in and yanked to the surface, and the small plangent sound of the drip punctuates the long hours like an irregular pulse, and it's all the fault of the sleeper upstairs who said the house was solid, and he could do the work himself, and the only bucket you can find to catch the leak has got a hole in the bottom, why would you keep a bucket with a hole, and why are there so many chairs in this house . . .?

On the world map, England's tiny, the British Isles just an outcrop, crumbled from the jagged edge of Europe. Flip the page round, and what do you get? On either side, the great mass of North America and Russia, and in between them a white patch, the Arctic, a white patch which is shrinking, and it is because the ice is melting that Mr Kim plans to send ships through to sink a cable which will cut the London-Tokyo latency by sixty milliseconds. Not much to you and me, but if you're an algorithmic trader you get very excited by this kind of thing. Imagine a great snake nipping the toe of Cornwall, dipping down to the ocean floor, plunging across the Atlantic, hundreds of feet below the surface, amongst those deep sea creatures barely glimpsed by human eye, heading through the North West Passage and on to Murmansk, looping over the roof of Russia en route for Japan.

She's so frail, there's nothing to her, when he lifts her she might float away, but she begged him, begged him, to drive her to Truro. Another week or two, and they could have brought the baby to see her, but the worse she became the harder it was to say an outright no. So an if became a maybe and then a probability, and before he could stop himself he was bedding her down on a mattress in the back of the camper van, which was not something you really should be doing, but the van was running like clockwork, and there was no reason they should be pulled over, and she was no less comfortable there than she'd be anywhere else. More comfortable in some ways – it reminded her of when they used to go all over the place, parked up by rivers and roadsides. If they set off in the evening when the roads were so much quieter, they could be at their daughter's in five or six hours. That was before the weather came down. But not to worry, they can still make it. He sends a quick text to his daughter, telling her not to wait up, and she sends something long and angry back to him within seconds. Can't do right for doing wrong. Isn't that always the case? When he starts the ignition, it makes a rasping sound, and they've hardly left the services behind before he's on the hard shoulder, rain trickling down his neck, desperately trying to bring the engine back to life.

. . . and what does he do all day, what does he do, he goes round junk shops buying chairs that need fixing and comparing the prices they might fetch on eBay, and if you call someone in to give you an estimate for the plastering it'll be a slur on his manhood, and besides those are cracks that can't be skimmed over, fissures and canyons running deep inside the brickwork, and even as you lie there the drip is getting louder and he just won't care, say it's *par for the course*, an old house, decrepit, same as you and me, and he'll make a show of senility, sounding a bass note on the solar plexus, and screwing his face into a caricature, winding you up, like when he talks about growing his hair and it looks awful. He spends money buying you beautiful things, an emerald necklace or an old lithograph, but you don't want anything, you don't want any things, and it comes to you that what you want for your birthday – what you'd really like – is for him to just get a hair cut.

Of course this is all on paper. It might not ever happen. If you check the Bude and Stratton Post, the news is still the falling quality of the local bathing water and the impact of bad weather on the tourist season – not a word about any trans-Arctic project starting on the beach. And yet somewhere on the globe they're talking billions of dollars. Deals are being brokered, torn up and rewritten between cartels and oligarchs, speculators and major providers – every spin of the wheel setting smaller cogs in motion, sending PR men and security consultants and engineers like me, boarding planes in the hope of securing a contract, keeping an eye on those other passengers in blue shirts staring shifty-eyed at their smart phones shortly after the safety lights switch off. My job is simple.

I do the drawings. Whether it happens or not, that doesn't matter to me.

What a fucking moron. Putting petrol in the tank instead of diesel – he's seen plenty of other fucking idiots do it – what else could it be – and what in Christ's name has he done, bringing her straight to the hour of her death? That's what he keeps thinking, as he works in the driving rain by torchlight, keeps thinking and remembering something that's stuck in his mind – three o'clock, they say that's the turning point, if he doesn't get her safe by three she won't survive. There's no help, never was, not the carrot juice or the vitamin pills or the positive thinking, just the hope of a miracle, the faint possibility that he's wrong and it's no more than a faulty connection. The phone buzzes in his pocket, but he can't bear to answer because that'll be Dawn again, and she won't leave it to him, she'll want to call an ambulance, and that's something Frank can't do. He cannot send Linda to hospital.

So now you've decided. Everything's clear. Tomorrow you'll have that conversation which will mark the first step towards a new beginning. Not even the drip seems so bad after all. Not even the cracks in the wall. You're ready to creep back up to bed, and curl up beside the sleeper, rehearsing what you're going to say when morning comes. Squeezing past a set of dining chairs stashed in the hallway, you set foot on the stairs, listening for the steady puff of his breathing, and suddenly it seems that you're stepping on a gangplank and the house is swaying with the motion of the sea. He's standing there waiting to help you aboard, but what kind of ship this is, and where you're sailing, is something that is yet to be explained.

The only thing that keeps me sane, cooped up in this vacuum, is the thought of sealing the envelope, and somehow finding a stamp and a postbox in a wasteland of snow and barbed wire. Of course it won't really be like that. The town will be pretty much the same as any other – a grid of office blocks between the mountains and the harbour, the last trace of snow just a passing reminder. In the Chukotka Suite, I'll pause to take off my watch for rewinding, just as I always do at the start of presentations. 'Yes,' I'll say, if there's any reaction, 'it's hand made, an anniversary present, as a matter of fact. My wife knows I like old-fashioned things.' Ah, wives – a small murmur of laughter. By then this letter will be on its way. One day I'll come back from work to read your name on the envelope, and I'll keep it with all the others in case you decide to come home.

But in the end there's no alternative. That's what he tells Linda. The van's fucked. So some one's going to have to come and get them. Just too bad. But at least they're nearly there, and she can see the baby tomorrow. A few more miles, that's all. He hates the sound of his own cheery voice. Everything he's saying sounds like a lie, even the things that are true. But she seems no worse. She's even taking a mouthful of soup from the flask. 'Do you remember,' she keeps saying. 'Do you remember when we . . .?' He can't make out what she's saying and there's no time to ask before he hears the sound of the ambulance screeching like an owl.

CHRISTOPHER PRIEST

UNFINISHED BUSINESS

HE WAS STANDING at an open window and he was naked.
He was pressing binoculars to his eyes and he was pointing
them at me.

It was a shock reversal of voyeurism. I was the woman being
watched, peered at through binoculars, privacy invaded, possibly at risk. But *he* was naked, exposed, vulnerable. I turned
away in embarrassment, but as soon as I did I realized how
irrational it was, so I looked again.

I was on my morning commute, an ordinary weekday in
early summer, the train slowing down as always – there is a
junction of three main lines outside London Bridge Station
and during the rush hour it is always congested. The train was
full but because I live close to the beginning of the line I could
always get a seat. The same one every day, by the window. Most
days I read or listened to music, but that morning I was staring
out of the window instead, watching the London suburbs go
by.

He was still there when I looked back but now he was
leaning forward to follow me with his glasses, angling out as
the train bore me on past and around a shallow bend. He was
soon lost to sight.

I knew I was blushing and I felt the palms of my hands
sweating. I glanced around at the other passengers, feeling

irrationally guilty, but they were commuters busy with their newspapers, magazines, smart phones, e-readers and books. I was unnoticed.

I leaned back against the hard head-rest, closing my eyes, trying to calm myself. The man had been in one of the houses in a street where the terraces backed on to the track. Surely it was only a weird accident that he should seem to be looking at me? I could just about comprehend why a certain kind of man would expose himself as a train went by, but why should he pick me out, stare so intently?

The train continued its slow journey through the complex points and signals, halted briefly at London Bridge Station, then rattled on, eventually crossing the steel bridge above the Thames and into Charing Cross Station on the northern side.

I left the train and went through the crowded concourse. Collecting a large cup of coffee I took the familiar walk to my office. I was shaken up by what I had seen but I needed to collect my wits for the day ahead. My first appointment was with the people who represent Yuri Maximov, an arms trader and holder of Siberian oil shale rights and our most important Russian client. I had been working on this presentation for two months. After that I had to see my line manager Kersey and report on the meeting. I always dreaded being in his office, because Kersey liked to mix business with pleasure. An ongoing problem, but I had it under control. Then a lunch with one of the agency heads. In the afternoon, more of the same.

I put the incident of the naked man out of my mind. On the way home that evening the train trundled past the same row of houses, but my thoughts were running through the events of the day and I was catching up with incoming text messages. I forgot to look.

That time.

The next day was Friday. I tried to act as if it was just another day. I gulped my organically sound breakfast, hurried to the station. The train arrived on time and I took my window seat. I nonchalantly read my copy of *The Times*, solved a few crossword clues. I listened to the BBC news on my mobile radio, then afterwards I sat back to watch the London suburbs go by.

As the train slowed on the approach to London Bridge I was craning my neck to see ahead. It was a sunny day – I saw reflected light glinting from binocular lenses.

He was already pointing them at the train, at my carriage, at my seat by the window. Again I felt the impact of that cold, unexplained regard, the sense that he had picked me out.

But there was nothing he could do but look! So I stared back frankly, feeling brazen, daring. At first it was just the same as the day before: the blatant, intrusive stare, the disguising blackness of the binoculars across his eyes. Then he slowly raised his free hand and waved.

The train was moving more slowly than the day before. I thought, I will have to report this! I must try to remember details!

As the train carried me on past I tried to see objectively, so if necessary I could give a clear description. He was of medium height, had a paunch. He was white-skinned. Bald, or his head was shaved. He had some kind of beard or moustache about his mouth, but because his arm threw a shadow it was difficult to see exactly. And he was hairy – his chest was matted and everywhere else I could see was smudged with hair.

Soon the moving train dragged us away from each other. Again, the man leaned out to keep me in view for as long as possible.

Other than his behaviour there was nothing about his appearance that was in any way unusual. There must be a million men in London like him: roughly middle-aged, bald or shaven, stocky of build. A million, but only one of them was doing what he did. And was doing it to me.

I worked through the day and when I caught the train home in the evening I made sure I was sitting in a different carriage, further forward, a seat where I hoped to get a good view of the house. The train went along, accelerating away from the junction, and as it went past the houses I leaned forward to look. All the windows were dark, though, and because it was early evening the sky was bright behind the houses. There was nothing to see.

Kersey was coming to dinner over the weekend, with four other non-work friends to help keep him off me. It meant going to the supermarket and preparing and cooking, but I still had time to think. I had to be logical.

Who was the binoculars man and why was he naked? The answer: I did not know. I did not want to know and most of all I did not care. Big cities are full of perverts and wackos and the discovery of one more was not my problem.

But harder questions remained. Starting with this: why did I imagine he was looking at *me*? Couldn't it just be chance? Maybe he stood at the window all day looking at women on trains.

It had happened twice. Once might have been chance, but twice? Coincidence? No, not chance on two consecutive days. He was looking at me, and it was deliberate.

So why me? Had he picked me at random? Perhaps he had spotted me on the same train, every day, always in the same seat, felt curious . . .

No, that did not make sense either. When a train goes by you can barely see the people on board, let alone pick any one of them out, and never mind noticing them again and again. Trains in London are not reliable: they are often late, sometimes early, occasionally cancelled, and the operators change the rolling stock unpredictably. From the track-side it's difficult to identify any individual train.

So not random. Then had he chosen me for some reason? Had he followed me home? Was he a stalker?

Again, no, not possible. How could he know where I lived? He was in an inner London suburb, while I lived in a middle-class dormitory town more than forty miles from the centre of the city. There was no way he could have found my house or located me in some other way, figured out which train I would be on, in which seat . . . No way in a sane or comprehensible universe.

It left only one possibility. He was someone I knew, or had once known.

Oh no.

A thought to spoil a weekend. Not long after, Kersey arrived at the house with a bottle of champagne, a wet kiss and greedy hands, and the weekend went from spoiled to difficult.

I am a woman of what is sometimes called, out of courtesy, a certain age. I am in general well and contented. I look after my health, I work out once a week, I eat sensibly and walk as often as possible. I believe I have kept most of my youthful good looks, but there is no denying the calendar and I do not try.

My name is Janine, a conventional name and my friends call me Jan. I am an independent woman, a successful businesswoman, junior executive in a graphics imaging firm that specializes in conceptual drawings for large engineering or mining companies. I enjoy my work. I pay my bills and taxes, obey the law, vote in elections, have an African child I support through a charity, clean my house, care for my friends, and much more besides. I am in short an honest, decent, kind, hard-working citizen.

Twenty years ago, though, things were different.

Yes, different. The world was different. *I* was different.

For a period of five or six years, from when I was about nineteen, I lived more or less entirely for the promiscuous pleasures of the flesh and the chemical distractions of the mind. I was young, single, living alone in London, free to do whatever I wanted and with whomever I wished. There were many places I could go, and many friends from which to choose. I observed no boundaries. Recklessly, I drank a great deal of alcohol, I experimented with many substances, I tried out a range of positions.

I slept with an awful lot of men – I suspect I also slept with a lot of awful men.

Now, today, do I regret that period? Do I look back on it as a kind of golden age? Do I miss that lifestyle and secretly yearn to go back to it? Was I damaged by it all? Would I recommend it to others?

Yes, No, Yes, Maybe and No.

Or then again: No, Maybe, No, Yes and Yes.

Or yet again: well, you understand.

The point is that I survived, that eventually I matured a little and cleaned up my life and found new friends and took a proper job and bought an apartment I love to live in. And became someone who pays her taxes, gives to charity, is kind to others . . .

There is no denying that past, though. Once I had eliminated other options about the man, I began to wonder if I did after all know him, and what I knew of him and, worryingly, what I might have forgotten about him.

All through that weekend, and while my guests sat around the dinner table, I thought back and back: old boyfriends, former lovers, brief encounters, all the emotional and sexual detritus left around by a paid-up member of the permissive society. When I thought about those men I remembered them, some with fond or happy or unhappy or indifferent memories. Others I recalled more vaguely, all feelings dimmed by time. I still remembered them, though.

But I did not remember every man. Somewhere in the

deeper recesses of the past there was a succession of befuddled or blanked-out or forgotten one-night stands, casual pick-ups in pubs or nightclubs, chance encounters at raves or parties. There were likely to be some good memories there, but many more dark ones, some guilty, some irrelevant. Who was to know now? Everything was in the past, over and gone. I cast the forgotten to the night.

I survived, I survived, I did no harm, I hurt no one, I survived.

If I had ever been afraid that something or someone from this past would return to haunt me, that was long gone. I felt immunized by the passage of time.

It was only later, after the dinner guests had left, that my thoughts returned to my naked phantom. What if there really was someone out there who held a grudge against me? For a moment, a memory flickered at the edge of my consciousness, the ghost of a face, something I had tried to bury. I realized my heart was racing, but before I could identify the source of my fear the image had vanished.

Vanished too was Kersey, cast homeward into the night with the others, but only after a silent but determined struggle. Perhaps I should not have let his hand rest so long on my knee beneath the table, but my mind had been on other things.

The man was at the window again on Monday morning but I afforded him barely a glance. This time I wanted to identify the road in which the house was situated and I was clutching a detailed street-map of London for that purpose. Before the train had rolled slowly around the bend I had positively identified the street: Ennert Road, London SE16.

The day after that, while the man watched me I ignored him and counted the houses. He was in the fifth along.

Wednesday he was there again and I went on to work. The day after that I called in sick but I went to the station and caught my usual train. Took the window seat. Waited, read for a while, then watched the London suburbs go by. He was at his window again. After a quick glance to be sure he was there I looked away.

The train slowed down and entered London Bridge Station. No one lives in London Bridge – they just change trains there. On normal days I would sit tight as what felt like half the population of London climbed off my train and the other half piled back in, but that Thursday I joined the crowd who left the train. I walked down to street level and consulted my map.

Distances can be deceptive when you clatter by on a train – it turned out to be a long way back to Ennert Road. I had rarely walked through this part of London before. After the metropolitan bustle and noise around London Bridge, within a few streets I was passing through a less populous commercial area where former warehouses had been turned into office spaces. Beyond these was a warren of narrow residential streets, some lined with the sort of old terraced houses I had seen from the train, but in many places post-war apartment blocks rose on both sides. Cars were parked everywhere. Street signs were hard to see and even with the map I made a couple of wrong turns.

I took a break at a café. There was a taxi driver at the next table, and using my street map he gave me exact directions to Ennert Road.

Twenty minutes later I found it. Ennert Road was fairly long, but the part of the street running parallel to the rail tracks was a short section. As I arrived I heard trains going by noisily beyond the houses. I walked the length of that stretch to gain some sort of idea about the neighbourhood – many of the houses had racks of multiple bell pushes, indicating they had been partitioned into apartments. Most of them were in poor condition: the curtains looked shabby, the windows needed cleaning and the paintwork on the doors was dulled by exposure to the weather.

The fifth house along was different.

Without being conspicuously so, it was cleaner than the others, more recently attended to, the windows had ornaments and there were small potted plants on the sills. There was a single bell push by the door.

I stepped back, counted the houses again to be sure. Then I pressed the bell.

The door opened almost at once. The man who stood there was fully dressed, in baggy denim shorts and a T-shirt. He looked clean as if he had recently stepped out of a shower. He was wearing round spectacles that glittered in the daylight. For a moment I thought I was in the wrong place, but then I realized it must be him. He was staring steadily, appraisingly at me. I suppressed an impulse to stammer out an excuse, back off, run away to safety down the street.

Then he said, in a level tone, 'You took longer to find me than I expected. Come in, Jan.'

I followed him up a short flight of carpeted stairs. Behind him wafted the scent of bath oil or shower gel, but underlying that was something stronger, more animal, more of the body. For a couple of seconds, as I watched his sandalled feet climbing the steps in front of me, I was disoriented by the smell, taken back by an associative memory. I said nothing, but something deep stirred inside me: connection to him, identification of him, memory of him? I had prepared myself for anything when I called at the house, but these recollections took me by surprise.

He led me into a room with a large, uncurtained window. Sunshine flooded in. Cushions were scattered across the floor, a stack of books lined one wall, rows of music and video discs another. The pages of a newspaper were spread across the carpet. The screen of an iPad glowed mutely from beside one of the cushions.

I went to the window where there was a close view of the railway line. He stood somewhere close behind me as I glanced across the tracks. My heart was racing, my fists were clenched. There was a pair of binoculars on the sill.

Then he said, 'Do you remember me, Jan?'

'I think so. I can't remember your –'

'It's Theo. I wasn't using that name, back then.'

I turned to face him, and he was close to me. Too close. Again, the faint odour wafted across the space between us. Theo? Theo?

'OK, Theo – what is it you want?'

'You took my money. I want it back.'

'Money?' I was astonished. This was about money?

'Fifteen thousand pounds. You took it and I want it now. I'll have it in cash, and you can have a week to bring it to me.'

I wasn't thinking about money. Associations with the man's body smell were spreading around me, almost shocking in their unexpected clarity. I remembered a closed van in the dark of a freezing cold night, some stolen goods and money stuffed into a bag, an ancient stinking mattress laid across the compartment at the back. The vehicle was parked somewhere close to the side of a busy highway, a stream of traffic roaring by, the trucks shaking us with the violence of their close passage, brilliant beams of headlights shafting in, and this man, Theo, and me, lying on the dirty mattress, naked from the waist down, greedily going for it in that sordid dark, thinking of nothing but a carnal need for each other.

It made me catch my breath to recall it. In spite of everything, I wanted it again.

'Money? What money?' I said again, dazed by the powerful physical sensations rising in me.

'I took the rap, Jan. I served eight years for armed robbery, and you took the money to look after until I came out.'

'I don't remember,' I said weakly, but in the same moment I thought I probably might. 'I need to sit down.'

I sank down to one of the big cushions on the floor. He squatted on his haunches in front of me, trying, I think, to be threatening, but instead once again blurring my senses with the smell of him. He leaned towards me and I could see a resemblance to the young man I had briefly known. He had not been called Theo then – we agreed on that. He had had a headful of greasy hair, long and falling across his eyes, no moustache. He was lean, angry with the world, out for what he could get. What he actually got, he said now, jabbing a hand at me, was a long jail sentence. After release he went to find me, needing the stash of money. No one knew where I was so he went abroad – Sweden, Russia, then Thailand, Australia, back through India and eventually to Europe, always on the move and burning with the injustice of losing the money to me.

Now he had found me somehow and he wanted the fifteen thousand pounds. Cash, he said. This week.

'I can't just find fifteen thousand pounds,' I said.

'It was a lot then, but not any more. I want what is mine, what was mine all along. Fifteen grand is nothing to someone like you, a middle-class bitch with a job and a place out of London and fancy friends.'

'Don't call me that.'

'You used to like being called a bitch. Jan the bitch.'

'You don't need money,' I said, glancing around at the stuff he had in his room, the general ambience of the house, which if not prosperous was certainly comfortable. 'How do you afford this place?'

'Mind your own business. Let's say you're not the only bitch who owes me.'

I was trembling – with fear, but also with a irresistible

impulse to have him. He terrified me, but he was reawakening familiar old urges.

'Theo, don't,' I said.

'Jan, don't,' he said, mocking me. 'A good-looking woman like you always has a way of raising money.'

'All right.'

I believed I knew what he wanted, that the solution was swift and sure. Inexplicably, I wanted it too. Staring into his cold grey eyes, the light from outside glancing off the shiny dome of his shaved head, I stood up, undid my skirt, allowed it to slip down my legs. We did it then, roughly and noisily across the cushions, with the sunlight on us and the trains rattling past the open window, again and again, slowing down for the points.

Afterwards, he pushed himself away and stood there over me as I sprawled on the floor, a close-up image of the man I saw at the window, his face and chest shiny with sweat, and even after what we had just done he remained threatening. It was not because of what he might do, but for what I might want him to do.

He kicked my clothes back to me across the carpet.

'Good try, lady, but you don't pay me off that way. You still owe me fifteen grand.'

It took me three hours to travel home after this. His last words as I left the house: 'One week.'

It had happened the night I was in the van with him. Theo, or whatever he called himself then, had made me drive him to an office building he knew, took a gun, pulled a balaclava over his face and ran inside. A minute later he ran out again, fired the gun in the air, swung into the passenger seat and yelled at me to get the hell out of there. I drove fast for half an hour, into the gathering night. Theo eventually decided we had got away with it so I parked the van on the side of the highway and we scrambled to the back where the filthy old mattress was. We celebrated.

Later that night I drove him to the place he was staying, and took the money to the place I was staying. (Where were those places? Probably best forgotten.) I never saw Theo again, because a snatch squad of a dozen cops smashed down the door while he was still asleep and the law took its course.

What happened to the stolen money? I know I held on to it, determined never to spend it. I knew that the man was not one to mess with and I was frightened of him.

But the months went by and turned into years. My life, as I said, started to change for the better. I made new friends, found places to live that weren't either falling down or deep in filth, took on a few jobs, and in general detoxed myself. That period is almost as much a blur to me as the dark days preceding it, but at the end of it some matters were certain. I had a permanent place to live, I had a job, I was no longer living on the razor's edge of my dangerous old life.

And I had no idea what had happened to the stolen money. Somewhere along the line I had spent it, lost it, given it away – whatever, I no longer possessed it or the shabby old bag that it was contained in. I did not waste too much time worrying about it. The years slipped by and I heard nothing of Theo.

Well, now it seemed he wanted his money back.

As he and I more or less agreed, fifteen thousand pounds in the present day was not an impossible sum to find, or raise, or borrow, or even earn. I had savings accounts, a few shares, I had equity in my apartment, my credit rating meant a loan would be simple. I could even draw the money on credit cards.

Somehow, though, I did not feel like doing any of those. Everything around me, my home, my possessions, my savings, all were symbols of the moderately successful woman I had become. I simply would not give any of it to Theo.

It was not even his money. It was stolen, so it belonged to

the people from whom he had stolen it – or, more likely, to the insurance company that would have covered the loss.

The weekend came, then on the Monday morning I caught my usual train and went to work. The train duly passed Ennert Road and there was Theo, naked again at his window. He waved to me.

Later that day I thought of our Russian client, Yuri Maximov.

Maximov is in the top fifty of the Forbes List, and is one of the three richest oligarchs in Russia. Part of his wealth is based on arms deals with despots in the Middle East, but most of it comes from an area of Siberian tundra several thousand square kilometres in size, where oil shale can be found not far beneath the permafrost. The dirtily obtained oil helps keep the Russian economy working, it creates atmospheric and groundwater pollution on a scale so horrific that it cannot be imagined let alone measured, and it keeps Yuri Maximov supplied with all the palaces, luxury yachts and private jets that he and his family seem to need.

My own glimpse into the Maximov fortune was through a client deposit account his distant organization kept open in our firm's accounts. This was used for many unspecified transactions, nearly all of which involved numbered bank accounts.

The interest alone on this client account came to more than twenty thousand pounds a week, credited in irregular, uneven amounts every few weeks. As a trusted executive I had managed Maximov's client account for several years.

It had never occurred to me that I could steal any of it, but once the notion came to me it was irresistible. It was suddenly not a question of whether I should or should not, but more practical concerns: how to do it, how to conceal it, how to get away with it.

That afternoon I made a deliberate error on Maximov's account, and 'accidentally' transferred a hundred dollars to one of his numbered accounts in the USA. I waited to see if the internal audit software would show up the anomaly, or if Kersey or anyone else on the network would notice, but by the time I went home there was not a stirring of awareness anywhere.

The next morning at the office (as the train passed his window Theo waved to me again and this time I waved back) the 'error' was still unnoticed and definitely unchallenged. Without further ado I transferred fifteen thousand pounds to a small internet account of my own. I had the jitters for the rest of the day, but all was well. On the train home that evening I tried to spot Theo at his window, but he was not in sight. I waved towards him anyway, my fist clenched.

Because I failed to see how Theo could force me to pass the money over, I sat on it for a while. Even a small amount like fifteen thousand makes up an impressive pile of banknotes, and I liked having them around me. One evening I spread them over my floor and ran my fingers across them. The theft was unnoticed and I was fifteen thousand better off. Theo had no hold over me – he had only the vaguest idea where I lived.

I soon discovered how wrong I was. He must have searched my purse for my address when I was at his house. One morning he was outside my apartment block as I left to go to work. He fell in beside me, matching my stride.

'It's thirty thousand you owe me now,' he said.

'Theo –' My heart was thumping in fright. 'You said fifteen.'

'That was then. This is now. Let's call it a penalty for late delivery. Thirty grand, within a week.'

'I was going to hand it over at the weekend!'

He halted. I paused beside him.

'You've got the fifteen?'

'Well, yes.'

'Where is it?'

'Back there,' I said. 'In my apartment.'

We turned around. I made him wait outside the building while I went in to collect the cash. I had stuffed it into a large canvas bag, so I took this down and handed it over.

'I want the rest in a week,' he said. 'Another fifteen grand, in cash.'

'Aren't you going to count it?'

'You're not crazy enough to cheat me,' Theo said. 'Just get the next fifteen. You've done it once, so you know how. Bring it to the house next week.'

'Will that be the end of it?' I said, but he was already striding away. I called after him, 'Is this the last time?'

'Just do it.'

He was gone, but I noticed he was not walking towards the station. I waited until he was out of sight, then hurried on my usual way. I caught the train with seconds to spare.

Theo was of course not at his window when the train went by, but I could not resist looking.

Alone in my office I stared at the monitor, with Maximov's account details up. I ran the usual checks but there was no sign anyone had spotted the theft. Kersey, indeed, had attached a routine note to the account, saying Maximov had once again renewed our contract. Another great slug of interest had been credited that morning. It made me think, the kind of thinking I found irresistible.

I had the power to clean Maximov out, or at least the minuscule part of the financial empire represented by his client account. Inevitably I would be caught if I did that, but there was just a chance if I was swift and clever –

But I did not want to be caught.

Another fifteen thousand pounds was an unnoticeable drop in Maximov's ocean.

I thought and thought. I set up the transfer, ready to go.

I could do it – should I? Wasn't theft in itself wrong, no matter how abhorrent the victim might be? Was this going to be Theo's final demand? Did I have the guts to try again? Was I tempted beyond endurance?

Yes, Yes, No, Maybe and *Yes*.

Maybe, Yes, No, No and *Yes*.

No, No, No, Yes and *Yes*.

The *Yes* was at the end of the line. Every time. My index finger twitched on the mouse button.

Continue Y/N?

Kersey had entered my office without my hearing. He walked up behind me, reached forward and cupped a hand around my breast. I went tense and my finger clicked the mouse. The transfer went through.

'Let's celebrate this evening, Janine,' Kersey said.

JOANNA WALSH

FEMME MAISON

YOU WANTED TO look different for him. You wanted a change of a dress. You wanted a new dress you had never seen before. You wanted to be someone else, someone neither of you knew.

But then you have not met Him yet.

He will take you away from all this. As things are, you can't go on in any way: everything is missing. If you were somewhere else, you would already be wearing the different dress, a summer dress. You would be comfortable. But the dress you have is too big. You can't wear your dress if you can't alter it, and you don't have sewing machine needles. You broke the last one and the shop didn't have any more.

You were typing on your laptop: something important, you can't remember, but you began to search for sewing machine needles.

It's the same all over the house. You go to look for things but they are always in the wrong room. Where are they? They might have been left outside in the rain. They might have been put on a high shelf so the children would not get them.

No sooner is there something to do than it requires something else to do it with. The piece of information needed is always at one remove: scribbled on an envelope already in the recycling; printed on an old bank statement, perhaps shredded; written in a letter filed in the cabinet you don't open any more.

It's question of systems. Go upstairs and you'll notice a tea towel that should be in the kitchen. Bring it down and there are the books that should be by your bed. How did they change places? Why didn't you notice the books before you went upstairs for the tea towel? Then you could have taken them up and put them by the bed and picked up the tea towel and taken it down. Except it wasn't the tea towel you went to look for, was it? It was something else, but exactly what you can't remember.

Sewing machine needles.

You should have established some kind of process.

There *is* a process to the day. You eat at established times though it's such a bother to make. Always afterwards you find a wrapper without a name snaking across the kitchen surface. What is it from? If it is vacant, why was it not cleared? How did you miss it? On tables small things migrate according to the season: the seals from plastic milk cartons, beer bottle lids (though it was He who drank beer whereas you drink wine). How did they get there? Why were they not removed? There must be a way to get rid of them.

You forget to wash your hands before re-opening your laptop. Its keys are slick with butter. At least not with jam but this is because the jam is still in the shop where you forgot to buy it. You came away with 250g of cherries and a pint of milk. The milk you needed, undoubtedly. You needed cocoa but they did not have cocoa. The queue was long and you were distracted by the labels of the wine bottles behind the counter, not the bottles with graphics and fancy typography but the bottles with pictures of chateaux, sea bays, farmhouses. You walked into each of these landscapes, as if you were visiting. If you were in those places, any of those places, you could wear the dress instead of tight urban

162

jeans, the dress that needs altering. You could have been comfortable.

You go into the post office in case there is something else you need. Each time you go in you look at the magazines and consider buying *Vogue*. You do not buy it. Next time you shop you will do the same thing.

All your life you've been asked to choose: to be the woman who didn't drink canned sodas, who didn't watch American television programmes, who would never, even in fun, decorate her home with Anaglypta wallpaper. Some of these injunctions you have overturned, but there are always fresh ones. You choose not to choose any more.

It's not only your fault. After the children left, bit by bit you and He abandoned the house, eating takeaways, spending evenings in cafes. At one point you had been able to afford to eat out every weekend. But the house missed you. The fresh flowers you bought were, it knew, an insult, a sop. That's why you knew He had to go.

But how did your keyboard get so dirty? The dust builds all over the house, always on a different surface. You chase it with a corner of the dress's sleeve. The dirt is still there, grey and furry. It has merely transferred. You are now part of it.

After He was gone, things altered. You expanded into the areas of the house you hadn't previously used: the study, the front room. You felt, for the first time, that they were yours. You also felt you owed it to them.

But the house is still not a perfect fit. Still things surprise you. When you try to get to the cupboard holding the dusters, there is something in the way: a stand of washing, a tall stool from the counter. Who put them there?

You turn, you remember – the laptop. You had forgotten. You remember. You had got up. You had wanted to clean the keyboard. You had gone to find a duster.

Something was altered. What was it?

Wait. You remember.

You had cut but you had not pasted.

Your words hover in vacant space. You turn. You run. You will save them.

You paste. They are still there.

How could you have left them? How could you have forgotten? How did you manage to leave your thought at its waist to search for the duster? How did you fail to get the duster but return to the laptop?

What you had written might have been lost for ever. The words are still there. But so is the dust.

You thought it would be OK after He was gone. You thought you'd have more time for work, for fusslessness. But the house is relentless.

The fridge must occasionally be defrosted. Something knocks in the icebox. Frost has grown on the walls of the cool section as moss does on a tomb but inverse, its fingers reaching down towards the salad drawer. An afternoon hacking though the ice forest may reach a single embryonically suspended fish finger.

You still attempt to generate one bag of rubbish each week: the bin demands it. The dishwasher is completely redundant. The washing machine begs to be used but your piles of laundry are dwindling, pathetic. They barely skim the bottom of the drum: they are hardly dirty.

Vines slap agains the window. On the patio the barbecue is rotting, the lawnmower is rusting. How are you meant to attack the overgrowing jasmine? With the blunted shears? With the kitchen scissors?

Some things used to matter so much: the exact shade of green of the garden chairs, which did not match the exact shade of green of the garden table. Now both are sun-bleached, flaking. 'A Generous Family House.' That's what the estate agent said when he came to value it, 'Generous.' For a few weeks he sent you emails: would you sell? But that was years ago.

The machines wait patiently. They must wait. In the daily round, certain chairs must be sat in.

You put the dress into the washing machine. It will be clean before it is altered. You add detergent, switch it on. The drum goes round and round. The dress is not dirty but perhaps dusty. The dust travels from the dress to the inside of the washing machine, then out through the tubes. The house senses an exchange. It is satisfied.

IT

THEY DIDN'T KNOW what to do about it. Nothing seemed to fit. She had suggested they bury it; he said it should be burned.

I hear they let off this nasty smell when they burn up, he said. She lamented that there was no earth anywhere *to* dig up even if they *were* to bury it. There's concrete over everywhere nowadays. There's no trees.

I remember when there used to be trees.

They went to dinner with it and shared awkward glances across the table; they swapped little iris messages. Little ocular murmurs. She wore that nice red skirt he loved, and the black blouse she had worn on their second date (remember that?). He had taken especial care of his beard that night – spending close to half an hour absent-mindedly plucking and preening in front of the bathroom mirror. All the while trying his utmost hardest not to look at the corner of the looking-glass where he knew it could be seen in the corner of the panel, a dark stain spread across the surface.

Initially, many of the other diners were disconcerted by the presence of it; they shuffled largely in their wooden seats and smiled apologetically at each other. Someone made a joke to his party about it and watched with delight as they exploded in calculated mirth. Someone else discretely asked the head waiter if he could possibly do something about it.

The waiter floated over and gravely addressed the embarrassed couple.

I know, I know, the man said, but what are we meant to do? Just tell us that.

We've tried everything, she implored.

The waiter spent a while shrugging and pulling faces then just slunk off, defeated, leaving them alone – a course of action which the particular gentleman who had made the initial complaint clearly disapproved of. His wife assured him that he was powerless to do anything; that some people don't understand; some people are selfish; the waiter was incompetent at his job. They wouldn't come here again. After some time, the room settled down and the undulating waves of interest ebbed towards more familiar attractions. Wine was poured, food was relished. Lips were smacked.

They settled the bill and left.

This was one of many incidents. Of course there were good days; sometimes it didn't matter that it was there – after all, they reasoned, who hasn't known it? Friends would come round and no-one would notice anything – their laughter would pour under doors and sweep against the skirting boards and everything would be okay.

She would say to him, I love you.

I love you, he would say back to her.

Everyone would smile and be happy. But then it would enter the room and sit down and look; it would envelop the room with its gaze. Not with its eyes (it didn't have eyes – how could it?); but with the *idea* of eyes. It wore a carved remembrance of a smile and beamed cavernously at them. It didn't smile with a mouth (it didn't have any mouth – how did it eat? I don't know, she had once replied); but with the *idea* of a smile, of a mouth. Regardless, they would gather themselves together and embrace each other as if it wasn't there. They were all friends here after all.

167

After a time it insinuated itself into their favourite music, over-seasoned their favourite meals. It cropped up in old photographs, standing ominously in the dog-eared corners, eating air. He took to taking long bracing walks all by himself, whistling familiar tunes and keeping the beat with the slap-dash shuffle of his feet. This gave him time to think and a space to himself. When he came back he would lift the heavy key up to the big, red door and enter the house, putting on a face of studied nonchalance and peace, pushing past the disused pram and the rain jackets in the hallway and striding confidently into the front room.

Nice walk?

It was okay. I went by the old park, it's still lovely in there.

I'm sure it is, she smiled, looking up from her work smeared out across the furniture.

Listen, when are we going to get rid of that buggy in the hall? I damn near break my neck every time I come in.

She hardened. Not yet, she said.

It began to stir in the corner. She went back to her work and he went through into the kitchen to make some tea.

It was becoming too hard to ignore now – they soon learned that the restaurant fiasco had been but the tip of the iceberg. What had once drawn curious gazes from strangers had now evolved into a tempestuous adolescent which drew the attentions of both frightened spectators and concerned family members alike. They tried to cover it, to hide it. She would daub it with gaudy make-up in an attempt to make it presentable. To normalise it.

No-one will notice, she assured herself.

He dressed it in extravagant swathes of cloth; desperately tightening cords, tying knots, fastening buckles. Staring into the ever more inconceivable depths of its new-found bulk, he pulled and tugged more and more desperately each time. Unwittingly, he had discovered an accelerated unknown urgency and his frayed fingers struggled to keep up with the frantic desires of his diseased mind.

More, more, more, he mumbled.

More.

Soon the local news caught wind of what was happening. A frothing editor waved his arms madly and commanded his photographers and journalists to camp outside the couple's front door. He gave them strict orders to report anything that they saw and photograph anything which seemed of interest to the general public. Out of the kitchen window, she could see the camera lenses scattered amongst the privets like so many shining marbles – whenever it walked past there would be a frenzy of clicking followed by the confused murmur of the reporters.

What is it?

What happened to it?

What's it doing?

Why won't they leave us alone? she asked him.

They're not interested in us, he sighed, they're only interested in it.

They tried to trick it into staying outside, into getting lost. They would drive it to seaports, parks, supermarkets and leave it there, where someone else might find it – but it always found its way back. Driving back from the docks where they had left it one time, they would be nearly weightless with relief – they could even afford to share smiles – until they arrived back at the house to find it standing serenely amongst the pale leaves crowding the garden, with the reporters huddled around it, impotently asking unanswered questions. The couple just sat there in the car and watched it.

We should have burnt it when we had the chance.

Maybe you're right.

I *am* right.

Maybe you are.

Every night now it would come into their room and wait listlessly at the foot of their bed. It was too big now, too big. It occupied space like an obsession and swallowed up moods whole. With a growing stench of regret, it wallowed in its own actuality – a void too despairing to be looked into, a maniac sun which would scar the eyes.

We should do something, before it's too late.

She rested in her silence for a time.

Okay. Tomorrow night, she whispered.

The next evening, they tied it up and covered it in sheets. It didn't resist, but its chilly touch sent the clean knowledge of emptiness straight through to their cores. The crowds of spectators and hustling reporters had made it difficult to enter their house when they returned from work that afternoon – as usual – but tomorrow, they told themselves, there would be no more problems of this ilk. This was the final step. To be safe they strapped belts around the inert bundle; then to be extra safe they taped it up securely as well.

Let's put it in the trunk. Come on, help me lift.

They stumbled clumsily to the garage having had to take several stops along the way and then gingerly placed it in the back of the car with the sort of reverence one might reserve for a child.

There, he said with finality.

She puffed out her cheeks and nodded.

They drove out past the scattered remains of the crowd – those photographers still ravenous enough to set up camp on the lawn – and sped out of town with a festering urgency, leaving the winking bright eyes of the cameras in their wake. They used to take trips out to the country all the time; they would pack their suitcases full of new clothes and optimism and just head out, making bookings by phone on the way. She would laugh with her pretty little laugh and point out all the beautiful things she saw and he would marvel at her trained eye, at her innate elegance. Like those nights of old, the stars were all the way out again tonight and the planets blistered in the sky with a familiar and intimate power. They stopped some way out west near the coast and parked the car in a forgotten field, painted a thin hue of silver in the light of a dead and indifferent moon.

After the gasoline had been poured over the grim, still bundle, she lit a match and let it drop. They stood and observed the wreckage from a reasonable distance, the flames flaring and teasing their way across the couple's motionless faces.

Maybe we'll miss it, she mused.

How can you miss something that isn't there?

A pause, then: You can.

The house rose triumphantly from the glistening, dew-sodden lawn on their approach. All the news crews, the photographers, the journalists had scattered by now, off to pursue fresh stories. No doubt they had found newer, unspoiled gardens to bustle about on. He reached out and grasped her hand, passing on a look of trepidation in the process. Nodding grimly towards one another they anxiously stepped towards the big, red front door like tongue-tied young newly-weds who blush beautifully on their wedding night.

Something moved, in the front room. The half-drawn curtain recoiled and shuddered. His hand, holding the key half raised to the lock, froze. Their eyes met and they shared a sense of dreadful lightness. Trembling slightly, he continued in his mission to open the door but now all the weight in the universe seemed to rest in that key, all the unknowable, terrible secrets of the world resided right there in that hushed and sudden moment, each groove and its intricate spacing along the calculating metal seemed to hold the terrible knowledge of the ancients – the key sang of barriers in its own language; it told of the slow lift and then the release, of doors opened throughout time through all the world to lead two lovers to this very instant, this very place.

Click, said the key as it opened the door.

Thud, said the door, as it hurled itself against the wall.

She said she would go in first.

Sure, okay, he replied.

Stepping across the threshold, she pushed past the detritus in the darkened hall and edged her way gingerly to the doorway of the front room. The door was open and on its sure, wooden bulk the dappled shadows of the night outside were in riot. He hung back as she positioned herself resolutely in the frame, body receptive to the room, alert and determined.

Well? Is something there? What's happening?

Nothing. Silence. He waited for her to speak but the tendrils of moonlight which reached for her features through the shrubbery in the garden carried a strange mood with them. Her eyes gleamed emptily under flickering anaemic spurts of illumination and her expression became ossified and unknowable.

Again: What's up? Can you see anything?

Light and not-light took turns to caress her pale and delicate face, death-tones reflected from a dead rock which spoke sullenly of absence and its immutable stillness.

Well? he rasped urgently. What *is* it?

I don't know, she said. I don't know.

CLAIRE DEAN

GLASS, BRICKS, DUST

AT THE TOP of the mound he was king. The broken-brick, gravel and glass mountain had stood for over a year in a deserted street not far from the boy's house. When the excavators and bulldozers had come to demolish the old mill, a high metal fence had barricaded the site. But when the men in high-vis vests and hard hats disappeared with their machines, they took the fences with them. They left polystyrene cups balanced on top of the gateposts, where they filled with rainwater. They left the building's ribs – inner walls and doorways without doors. They left lumps of concrete, lengths of pipe, metal girders and fire exit signs. And they left the mound. As the days passed, rubble and red-brick dust spread onto the pavement and gathered in the gutters of the road.

On summer evenings he crept around the edge of the mound, toeing shards of glass and empty cider cans. He circled his kingdom, noting newly burnt lumps of wood and scrunched-up cigarette packets, but he never caught sight of the grown-up intruders who'd left them. There were lazy red butterflies on the tangle of flowering weeds that had pushed through the building's remains. Black birds gathered on the street's only lamppost before darting off overhead. He clambered up the mound, which looked like an enormous sand dune against the bright blue sky. From up there he could see the whole town: rows of terraced roofs, two church steeples, the town hall clock, and the last mill chimney with its luminous supermarket sign. At his back were the moors and the wind.

One evening, the boy was crouched on the top of the mound making a new town out of a heap of broken glass. He liked this time of day best – after tea, before bed. The air seemed to get grainy as its colour changed from vinegary yellow to candyfloss blue. He could rub it between his fingers like dust and slow time down. At the top of the mound he was in charge and he didn't want to go home to bed. He collected green glass shards and broken brown bottle necks. He tumbled fragments of old window in his hands like shattered marbles. He pushed the glass into the mound, making houses, balancing roofs on them, building towers. The last of the sunlight caught and glinted in the tiny glass walls.

More of the black birds than he'd ever seen before rushed overhead and gathered on the lamppost. The orange light hadn't yet switched on but the shadows were growing. He heard nine chimes of the town hall clock. For a moment, the lamppost looked like a tall thin man wearing a large black hat. When the man turned towards him, he looked like a lamppost. The man had a greyish-green coat speckled with rust and a black hat that quivered with beaks and feathers. The man didn't need to climb the mound; he was face to face with the boy with his feet still planted in the pavement.

'What are you making?' asked the man.

The boy didn't answer.

'It would be better to tell me. I could help. Every child is always making something. Cut them open and shake them out and they're full of dust and dreams.'

The boy squirmed at the mention of cutting. He stood up, ready to run, but then he remembered that at the top of the mound he was king. He dug his heels into the rubble. 'I'm making a new town, better than this one. The sun can shine in through the walls. The buildings look grander. It'll be a great glass city.'

'All it needs is people,' said the man.

'Yes, it needs people,' said the boy. And when he looked down, tiny creatures were scuttling beneath the glass roofs. They looked like ants or spiders, but the sky was darkening and the creatures were moving too fast to be sure. He looked to the man but there was only the lamppost and as its orange light snapped on, the birds launched into the sky.

The boy plunged down the mound and ran, hoping he wouldn't get told off for being late home. Before he reached the end of the street he knew something was wrong. The world was too quiet. Where were the sounds of cars? Of footballs being kicked against walls? Of smokers chatting outside the pub? There were no shouts from parents calling everyone in.

'Mum?' He pushed open their front door. The house was in darkness but the telly was switched on. His mum wasn't in any of the rooms. A half-drunk cup of tea had been left on the arm of the settee.

The boy thundered back along the silent streets. He stood in the orange light beneath the lamppost. 'Give them back,' he shouted.

Nothing happened, although he could hear the rustle of feathers coming from the darkness above the light.

The boy ran to the top of the mound. 'Give them back!'

'But I haven't got them.' The man's face glowed. 'You have.'

In the gloom, it was hard to make out the tiny creatures beneath the glass roofs. They were no longer moving. The boy couldn't be sure what was a particle of rubble and what was a person sleeping in their broken-glass house. 'How do I get them back?' he asked.

But the man was a lamppost again.

The boy crouched at the top of the mound and looked out

at the night-dark shapes of the town. If he made the town as it really was, an exact replica, maybe that would bring everyone back.

He worked all night, building with bits of old brick. The clouds overhead moved slowly and their bellies were orange. Every time he looked up and caught a glimpse of a star, a bird flew from the lamppost to blot it out.

When the dawn came, it was damp and grey and the boy's fingers were stained red with brick dust. He looked proudly at his miniature town, with its rows of roofs, two steeples and the last mill chimney. He peered into the glass town beside it and saw it was empty.

The boy skidded down the mound and ran home. The streets were still silent, but they would be so early in the morning. In the living room the telly was still on, the cup still on the settee arm. The boy pounded up the stairs, not caring if he woke his mum and got into trouble. But she wasn't there. Her bed was empty.

The boy raced back to the mound. There were an impossible number of birds gathered on top of the lamppost watching him. The light had switched off, ready for a new day. At the top of the mound, he peered into the little broken-brick houses. The gaps he'd left for windows were too small to let in much light; he couldn't separate any tiny people from the darkness. He pressed his fingers into the grit and dust. He had to try again. He gathered small mounds of dust and emptied rainwater from the old polystyrene cups onto them. He moulded houses and steeples and the chimney and the tower for the town hall clock. The buildings were misshapen and muddy.

'Aren't you going to ask me to give you the people back?'

The boy looked up at the lamppost. The creak of its voice had disturbed its hat, and wings were thrust out here and there.

'No,' said the boy. 'I'm going to go and get them.' As his

words touched the air it thickened with dust and as he rubbed it between his fingers he knew he could make himself small.

The boy was no longer at the top the mound, but standing in the dusty street outside his house. He looked up at the sky, trying to see the edges of the bigger town where there was a mound of rubble on top of which he'd built this town. But the sky was too wide. He walked through the doorway without a door to his house and found his mum, dust collected in the lines round her eyes, sitting in front of the greyish lump of the telly. 'Mum.'

She didn't look up. 'Don't interrupt, love,' she said, 'this is a good bit.' So he took a deep breath, and blew. He blew at the telly and at the walls and at the clouds of dust that surrounded him. He ran out into the street, climbed to the top of a mound of dust and he blew and he blew and he blew the town away.

At the top of the mound he was king. The ruins of the three small towns lay scattered at his feet. He could hear cars and footsteps and voices and the nine chimes of the town hall clock.

When the boy turned away from the mound and the lamp-post, he found the streets were coated in dust. Soft greyish-brown snow. He felt the gritty air between his fingers and knew that if he rubbed it he could slow time down. But he didn't want to be in charge again, at least not for a while. He wanted to go home to bed.

JOANNE RUSH

GUESTS

THEY SAY FEBRUARY is the best month to step on a mine. If it is under enough snow it may not detonate. The snow begins in December, like the first gospel; by February it is several feet deep. It is a matter of record that, on Candlemas night in 1994, a group of women from the village of Lisac, in flight from Mladić's army, crossed the mined snowfields to safety. They did not speak, or they spoke only in whispers. They held the barbed wire apart for each other. Then did they run or crawl or dance, knowing that at any moment the solid ground might buck them into quick oblivion, the snow convert to flames?

It is the first of June, 2011. My husband will be glad the snow is gone, despite the increased risk of being blown up: he found the Bosnian winter very cold. He said so last Christmas, in a rare phone call. He didn't mention Bosnia openly, of course, because the British government has no official presence there. Each time he phones he tells me not to worry. He says he's not in danger, but I know this to be untrue. There are no exact maps of the minefields in Bosnia. Even now, sixteen years after the war ended, a donkey sometimes loses its life; or a child, or a spy.

I met my husband when I was nineteen years old. I had come up to Cambridge from a village in Warwickshire to study

Computer Sciences. He had come up from Victoria City, Hong Kong, for the same reason. In Cambridge it is called coming up even if you come down. We were called compscis. Only students of unfashionable subjects were given abbreviations: as well as compscis, there were natscis (Natural Scientists) and asnacs (an acronym for Anglo-Saxon, Norse, and Celtic). When I got to know my husband, he would say these all sounded like animals that hadn't made it onto the ark.

Getting to know him didn't happen at once. There were lots of other compscis, most of them dishearteningly loud, and for a while we hovered shyly on opposite edges of this crowd. We finally met on the last Tuesday of Michaelmas term, in the café of the William Gates building. I often ate lunch there; he rarely did, but the kitchen on his college staircase had been declared unsafe. I found this out because he was behind me in the queue for jacket potatoes. One of the first things I noticed about him was that he breathed in, almost inaudibly, before each sentence: a slight inverted gasp which gave a feeling of urgency to his utterances. I also noticed that his elbows stuck out slightly, and that he had very fine black hair, like a mole.

He asked permission to sit beside me, and conscientiously tucked his elbows in. Then, impelled by the dual forces of hunger and loneliness, he plunged into his potato and his life story. His name was Jon. His mother was English, his father Chinese; he had arrived in Cambridge – which was very beautiful, but the cyclists were suicidal and everyone was on drugs – after a twelve hour flight to Heathrow, eight weeks ago, and he was still living out of a single suitcase; he had sent his other possessions ahead 'by sheep', and they were yet to turn up, though he had called the lost property line 'a tousand times'.

In the weeks to come, I would grow to love the crisp Cantonese consonants that occasionally snuck into his English sentences, and his unsteady phonemes. Already I was entranced by his suitcases, voyaging from Hong Kong to Cambridge by sheep.

What followed our first, word- and potato-filled encounter, was an almost entirely non-verbal companionship. Then as now, Jon preferred computer languages to human ones, and most of the time I found this restful, but it did make things harder when we were apart. He particularly disliked telephones. So what stands out most brightly in my memory of the summer at the end of our first year, when I returned unwillingly to my parents in Warwickshire, and he went home to Hong Kong, is the day he sent me a postcard of Victoria Harbour with two lists on the back:

Things we like
  1. *Quiet*
  2. *King's College Chapel*
  3. *Different sides of the bed*

Things we dislike
  1. *Bicycles on pavements*
  2. *Weed*
  3. *Crowds*

Beside the second list was a pencil sketch of an ark, in which were two blobs. In case I should mistake these for his still lost suitcases, or even the miscreant sheep, he had printed below them: COMPSCIS.

'What do you feel about mmharriage?' Jon asked me, at the beginning of our fourth year in Cambridge. (He doesn't stutter, but with certain English words he sometimes fumbles a catch.)

We planned a very modest ceremony. His parents couldn't come – they didn't like flying – but mine were there: my father gruff, my mother querulous. She had already made plain her feelings about my mmharriage to 'a half yellow man'.

'Of course I'm not racist, dear,' she said, a number of times. 'It just that he's so quiet. Don't you want someone more like us?'

1. Quiet, I thought. *2. King's College Chapel. 3. Different sides of the bed.*

Things did get more complicated later on, but I never doubted the soundness of this basis for love.

Jon's supervisor took him aside a few weeks before we graduated. She had been asked to recommend someone for a job at GCHQ. 'Legalised hacking,' she called it: exactly the sort of thing he'd be good at. I was already planning to set up as a freelance web designer, and neither of us wanted to face London. So we moved to Cheltenham Spa.

Our shabby third-storey flat was not a castle, unless of the air. It had white stuccoed ceilings, quietly peeling, and few comforts at first beyond a second-hand dinner table and a very low futon bed. Nevertheless we were happy there.

For two years Jon was deskbound in Cheltenham. But twelve months ago he was invited to a meeting about an important operation, co-run with the Americans, which needed someone in precisely his field of expertise. If he agreed, he'd be stationed at an old British military base in Bosnia. They couldn't say exactly how long for. My husband is a man of principle: he does things he doesn't want to do because he feels he should. I've got fewer principles: I just hoped it wouldn't take long.

Jon left for Bosnia in June 2010. That summer I kept myself busy, working from home. My job meant I spent a lot of time on the phone, explaining to clients the difference between mythology and technology, turning their dreams and visions into navigable sites – I'm not an imaginative person, but I'm good at detail. I got through one day at a time.

At the end of our street was a coffee shop, which was Polish and sold astonishing cakes. When the flat felt too empty I worked there instead. The waitress wore a black panelled apron with DONT ASK written across it in wobbly white velcro letters, or sometimes ASK ME L8R. 'Wait one minute,' she said. '*Sernik* arrives from kitchen.' This was often the closest I got to a real conversation all day.

When I wasn't working, I went for long walks. Sometimes I walked past GCHQ, that vast blister of glass and concrete on the edge of the A40. I'd been told it had a street inside, and a computer room the size of the Royal Albert Hall. Jon's face appeared in there each day, pixelated, on a plasma screen. 'Good morning, Cheltenham,' he said. 'See and hear you fine.' Then he vanished, replaced by a man in Beirut or Kabul.

Autumn came, then winter. The waitress in the Polish café said I was looking peaky, a word she'd recently learnt. I stopped going there so often: I didn't like people fretting. But I still took long walks, sometimes right up into the Cotswolds. On these walks I allowed myself to picture Jon. I did this cautiously, small bits at a time. His hands. The blurred edge of his jaw. Never whole.

I spent Christmas alone, after some deliberation. In the morning I ate half a croissant and started crying. The tears took a long time to stop. At four o'clock Jon phoned. 'Happy Christmas,' he said. He sounded far away. He asked me how I was, and I told him I was fine. 'It's very cold here,' he said. We talked for a stilted quarter of an hour. He said, 'Take care of yourself. I love you.' Then he added quickly, 'Listen, I may be onto something. I can't explain on the phone, but it might mean I'm back soon.'

'I hope so,' I said. I put the receiver down, expecting to feel happy. But instead I felt more sad. My husband didn't know that leaving someone could not be put right simply by coming back to them. Delicacy, filaments, were beyond him. He had strong hands, but that meant his forte was lifting heavy objects: small things slipped through his fingers, fragile things cracked in his grip.

When Christmas was over, I had a stroke of luck. A maritime museum in the south of England commissioned me to design a website. Charles, the man I spoke to on the phone, said they didn't want to use templates: everything must be bespoke. It was a challenging project; it would take three or four months to complete. I was anxious to begin.

A few days after that I ran out of milk, and popped into town for more. When I got back, there was a diminutive old lady in a headscarf standing in my kitchen, grinding coffee in a brass mill. At her elbow was a small copper jug. *'Dobro jutro,'* she said. Her smile was animated, but she was clearly dead.

Over the weeks that followed, unaccommodated ghosts filled the flat. The oldest arrived first, shapeless, clutching suitcases. They came from Mostar, Sarajevo, Banjaluka, from eighteen years ago. They had walked past engines blown out of vehicles and the half-cremated remains of other human beings, they had fallen over cliffs, stepped on mines, and been shot with guns – in the eye neatly once or the back many times. They had borne most, without a doubt, so it was not up to me to question where they chose to put it down.

It was a busy time for me. Charles phoned several times a week to discuss my progress, which was never fast enough for his taste. But it was nice to have company when I finished work in the evenings, and mostly the ghosts were no bother, though sometimes they moved things and it took me a while to find them. When I walked past they reached out to touch me.

Their hands grazed my shoulder, tugged on my hair. None of this was malicious: all they wanted was my attention.

At first their conversations were unintelligible to me, like the lyrics of music that is playing in another room. But over time the words separated out and acquired meaning.

When they perceived this, the *gosti* – ghosts, guests – became more demanding. They needed paprika, they needed clean towels. They needed someone to listen to them, and who else was there?

In spring more ghosts arrived: mostly men. They appeared to be waiting for something, and to ease this process they got hold of my husband's single malt whisky. They also smoked constantly, dropping the butts on the carpet. I don't mean to be rude, but it wouldn't have killed them to use an ash tray.

As the flat filled up, it was the living room that attracted the greatest number of ghosts. The fumes from home-grown Bosnian tobacco mixed with the earthy smell of American cigarettes accepted as bribes or bought on the black market: Smokin Joes and Camel Reds were passed across my coffee table by card-playing Muslim soldiers whose fingers were stained pollen-yellow with nicotine. '*Čmaru jedan*,' they muttered. '*Baja pojela ti jaja*.' You arsehole. I hope a bug eats your balls. When they were winning, they switched to old battle songs. 'The scent of lilies fills the meadow,' they hummed under their breath. On the other side of the room a dead Serb glared.

One of the ghosts, a young boy, stood apart by the TV. My attention was drawn to him because of his wing-like elbows, which reminded me of Jon. He was clutching a bass guitar, although his hands had been destroyed by a shell.

'That one is my grandson.'

It was the old woman with the coffee pot, the one from the

first day; she'd walked through the wall beside me. I wished they wouldn't do that: it left marks.

'He's a good boy, but I don't like his music – all that banging and shouting. You want a little coffee? Yes you have time. Sit here next to me.

'Tchk! Look at this. My doctor calls them liver spots. I said to him Doctor, it looks to me like I'm going mouldy. He gives me cream for them but I don't like to use it, Allah never meant for us to cure old age.

'Now Tarik, that grandson of mine, he's a Muslim but you wouldn't know it. I've seen him drinking šlivovica, he even eats sausage rolls. Well like his daddy he was raised in Sarajevo so it's not surprising. Young people there just glue their eyes to the West, it's always been that way. Tarik's in a rock band with three older boys I don't like much. They call themselves *Histerija*, and worship some London noiseniks by name of Led Zep Lin. The only time I went to one of their concerts I had to put my hands over my ears. "*Ja sam budućnost*," they kept on shouting. Such nonsense. I think all the jiggling about was meant to be dancing, but it looked more like some kind of fit.

'Just a few weeks after that the siege started. You know, every morning of my life I'd woken up to the tram bells, but on that day they stopped dead and didn't ring again for three years. It seemed like everything stopped, even gravity. Snipers were killing people in the streets, and by the time anyone dared go out for the bodies they'd got stiff. I'll never forget how the arms stuck out and the heads twisted sideways instead of flopping. Or the shelling either: it was like that rock concert all over again.

'My husband, may Allah rest him, left the house each evening to stand on the street with other Sarajevan men and talk. Those poor men looked worse than the dead and no wonder: they'd eaten bread made of oats, then of the stalks of hazel bushes, then of ground apple skins. They said the West had forgotten us, but it's my opinion the West never knew we existed. Of course Tarik listened to them. He knew he was a Muslim by then, surely enough: he thought he'd grow up into arms. But I sent him out to buy beans the day the mortar hit Markale market in February '94, and sixty-eight people died. That shell blew off both his poor hands, though what killed him was the fragment that got buried in his skull.'

Tarik stood in the corner of my living room, clutching his guitar. 'I am the future,' he whispered. Angry chords curled around him. '*Ja sam budućnost.*'

'Motherfucking Chetnik!'

'Sisterfucking Turk!'

The coffee table across the room from us collapsed, and playing cards swooped through the air like startled birds. Two red-faced men in black leather jackets squared up to each other: the glaring Serb had tripped over a card player's foot. I thought they were going to fight, but the card player's friends grabbed him by the shoulders and the Serb allowed himself to be shunted back to our side of the room, grumbling loudly and cracking his knuckle-tattoos into his palms.

Such eruptions were frequent, especially at first. 'You did this,' the ghosts accused each other. 'You did that.' But their voices were tired: it was hard for them to remember which flag to kiss and which to burn. The elderly ghosts were happier recalling their vegetable gardens than their disputes; they sat together to drink šlivovica and reminisce. And the soldiers from different armies exchanged cigarettes more often than blows. So in my living room Bosnian Muslims, Catholics, Orthodox Christians and Sephardic Jews gathered and pooled like drops of water.

In March or April – I'm not sure which – Charles began to call more persistently, wanting to know when the website would be finished. 'Is something wrong?' he said. Eventually I took the phone off the hook.

I barely left the flat, even to buy food. Instead I ate what the ghosts cooked. They filled my kitchen with the smell of lamb frying in garlic and paprika; then they got distracted, by an argument about politics or ingredients, and burnt the bottoms of my pans. I did sometimes go out, to get things they had forgotten: tomatoes, an egg. But those times were getting rarer. The light was too bright, the people too solid; their voices reached me from a long way away, like sounds heard underwater. I preferred to devote myself to the ghosts: their recipes and whims, their stories.

So I was there when Lejla walked in. Though barely more than a child, she was visibly pregnant. She leant against the living room wall, just inside the threshold, holding her heavy belly in her hands.

'Pass that cushion, dear? *Ouf*, that's better. At my age a body has too many bones and they all get closer to the surface.'

It was Tarik's grandmother again, clutching her eternal coffee pot. 'That poor child,' she said. 'She's a Croat, see the dinky gold cross? It's a wonder she held onto it. I've just this minute been chatting to a woman who was locked up with her in Banjaluka. She's making chicken liver pilaf if you want some later.'

This was Lejla's story, as told to me by Tarik's grandmother, who heard it from the ghost in my kitchen, who saw it with her own eyes.

She was a nice girl from a good Croat family, who didn't decide to get out of the newly declared Republic of Serbia quickly enough. So she was separated from them and held in a makeshift prison camp next to the police station.

At night there were rapes. Guards with flashlights, or just torches made of lighted paper, searched for anyone who was young and female.

They used a knife to cut her dress open. Then they raped her many times in one night. She was thirteen years old. When she became pregnant they continued to rape her nightly.

Eventually they put her in a train waggon meant for cattle but crowded with Croat women and girls. The train travelled south to the foot of Vlašić mountain. When it ran out of track, buses took them the rest of the way up. Lejla joined an interminable line of people: heads down, shuffling, sometimes stumbling, but moving slowly towards free Bosnia, or so they hoped. The road cut into the side of the mountain was narrow, and there were corpses on the rocks below. At some point in the night she tripped and joined them.

In my living room, she – Lejla – listened shyly to the music that came from Tarik, the handless guitar-playing boy. She moved towards him so slowly she did not seem to be moving at all. But she was.

'Jimmy Page,' she said quietly.

He frowned. 'John Paul Jones.' He had a memorable voice for a boy: gravelly, smoke-scarred.

'Is he better?'

'I prefer bass guitar.'

'I do too.'

It wasn't long before the Muslim boy with the shell-broken hands was deep in conversation with the raped Croat girl.

She did tell him some of what had happened to her. Shutting her eyes, touching the raised bumps of the wallpaper with one hand. But mostly they talked about rock music. He was enthusiastic about the electric guitar of Plavi Orkestar; she giggled. 'They dance like chickens,' she said. 'They hug turkeys in their videos.' She mentioned the plangent music of Crvena Jabuka; he thought it was wet. 'You may discord,' he said politely. But she did not discord with him, not at all.

I watched her a lot, I admit. She was so young. I worried

about how she would cope with motherhood: how could a child look after a child? Sometimes I forgot that they were both already dead.

I stopped work on the maritime museum's website. When I was not watching Lejla and Tarik, I went into the kitchen and helped the older ghosts cook: I peeled their potatoes, I rubbed flour and lard together to make pastry. Or I sat at the breakfast bar and listened to them talk. All the ghosts were keenly interested in the search for General Mladić, the Bosnian-born Serb who had led an army through their country; most of them were angry at how long it was taking.

'He's in Serbia.'

'He's not in Serbia at all, he's in Montenegro.'

'He's escaped Europe altogether by now.'

'That butchering peasant.'

'What occupies him these days?'

'He used to keep bees.'

'No doubt he still jeers at his goats.'

'The ones he named Major and Mitterand and Kohl?'

'Yes, after those Western politicians he so despised.'

'His health too must be much on his mind.'

'He's old by now.'

'So would I be, but for him.'

'So would we all be.'

At first the ghosts were easily distracted from the manhunt. They compared the size of their gardens, or the size of the peppers they had grown in their gardens. They had aimed to sit on a porch swing through summer evenings, but into their modest ambitions had blundered Mladić. He had shelled their houses and mined their vegetable patches. He had said: 'I shall be vindicated by history.' They were his dead.

Then, last Thursday, I came downstairs to find all the ghosts clustered round the television, jostling each other for the best view. As I watched, the screen fizzed and spat, and my husband appeared. It was definitely him: his pointy elbows, moley hair. The ghosts nudged me slyly, but then the picture flickered and Jon was replaced by a man with a polka-dot tie and greased-back hair. 'Kruno Standeker, the journalist,' Tarik's grandmother whispered to me. 'He was killed by a road mine near Mostar seventeen years ago.'

'Ratko Mladić,' intoned Standeker, 'was born in Bosnia in 1942. He went to military school in Serbia and entered the Yugoslav army, rising to the rank of Colonel General. When Bosnia declared independence in 1992, he blockaded the city of Sarajevo and shelled it for four years. In 1994, he allegedly ordered the genocide of over eight thousand Muslims in Srebrenica.'

The screen filled with soundless black-and-white footage. The war was over, and Mladić – ears sticking out beneath his peaked cap – was retreating to Serbia, where he lived in army barracks, going openly to football matches and horse races. Then the political atmosphere turned against him and he was on the run in Han Pijesak and New Belgrade, moving every two or three weeks between housing estates whose walls were covered with spray-paint vampires and signatures like coils of barbed wire. Serbia put a price on his head; international arrest warrants were drawn up. He left the overpopulated cities and went to live in the country, in a village of plum tree orchards and pepper fields, in a farmhouse made from clay bricks. He had mistaken boredom for safety; he thought no one would look for him there. Even so, he went out only at night. It was as if he had become one of the graffiti vampires from the housing estate walls, as if light petrified him.

For as long as he could remember, Mladić had been a skilful chess player, winning games across the length and breadth of Bosnia: in prison camps, at military headquarters, on the front lines. Now he sat before the chessboard, hour after hour, while an invisible foreigner, a man with electronic eyes and ears, chased his pieces across the black and white squares.

Mladić lived, fortified by obscurity, with cousin Branko, his Glorious Defender: his castle, of course. But most of his pawns – the army, the police, the secret services – had already been taken, the treacherous bastards, they'd gone over to the other side. And now his queen was under threat, his wife Bosiljka suddenly detained and questioned; harassed, beset, while he, helpless, fumed. Even his son – his slick-wheeled, Dacia-driving knight – was closely watched: it was too dangerous to see him much.

The screen spurted into Technicolor, revealing a woman sitting upright at a virtual desk. 'DAWN RAID,' she reported, and the ghosts inhaled a collective gasp. They'd been channel-surfing since the news broke – they knew the story off by heart, in all its permutations – but this was their favourite part. 'MEN IN MASKS MOVE IN,' they mouthed in perfect synchronicity with the woman on the screen, working their mandibles hard. Ten plain-clothed policemen or twenty special officers, armed or unarmed, depending which broadcaster you picked. Mladić was on his way to the garden for a pre-dawn stroll, or he was sitting in his front room wearing a tracksuit. He was hand-cuffed or he was not handcuffed; he was made to sit in the yard or he was taken into the house. He definitely offered his captors some home-made plum brandy. 'Checkmate,' he conceded politely. 'Which one of you is the foreigner?'

I started to understand.

'High-tech surveillance and tracking techniques were behind this operation,' the reporter was saying primly. 'The British and American intelligence services have been formally thanked for their assistance. Also Bakir Izetbegović, the Muslim member of Bosnia's tripartite presidency, has announced that the arrest was completed with the support of Bosnian security agencies.'

Was *that* what my husband had been doing? Hunting down the butcher of Srebrenica, bringing the man who called himself God to justice for crimes against humanity? Of course – it must be. Why else would the ghosts have come here?

All day long my guests were jubilant: they twittered and squeaked. They wanted a banquet, a celebration: they wanted, when it came down to it, a wake. Most of them also wanted to keep watching television, so although I'd have liked to see if Jon reappeared, I offered to help in the kitchen.

The first thing we made was *bosanski lonac*, as this would take five hours to cook. We layered chunks of lamb and potato with vegetables including cabbage and peppers, added garlic cloves and chopped parsley, seasoned it generously, and poured white wine and stock over the top. I turned on the gas and brought the oven up to temperature, then placed the stew carefully on the bottom shelf.

The ghosts showed me how to make *sarmas* while the stew was cooking, rolling grape leaves around tiny portions of rice and meat. Once or twice someone opened the oven, and the kitchen filled with the warm, heavy smell of lamb and the floury sourness of half-cooked potatoes. Whenever that happened, cigarette-smoking soldiers appeared in the kitchen to ask how long it would be. The cooks shooed them out. They made *baklava* ahead of time: spreading honey onto filo pastry and adding rosewater to crushed pistachio nuts. The air filled with a back-of-the-throat sweetness and another smell I couldn't identify, which made me uneasy.

I went into the living room to get away from this smell, and also to check what was happening on the news. It's a good thing I did, because soon after that there was an almighty crack as the oven exploded in the kitchen. I remember being lifted off the ground by the force of the explosion, and the sound of glass smashing; then nothing until the siren-scream and epileptic blue lights of the ambulance.

So that's it. I am in bed in a private room in Gloucestershire Royal Hospital. I have concussion and two broken ribs, and the doctors put me on a drip when I first came in because I was badly emaciated. They said that firemen had been over the wreckage of my kitchen and found nothing but a few pieces of an empty pot in the oven; they suggested I had barely eaten for weeks or months. I know they wanted me to concede that I let the gas build up to dangerous levels on purpose, triggering the explosion in a cry for help. But I survived because I was in the living room not the kitchen, and gas doesn't explode by itself. It must have been a spark from one of the soldiers' cigarettes: they kept looking in the oven to see if the stew was done.

When I pointed this out to the doctors, they said it might help if I wrote down what I remembered of the last few months. I've been happy while doing this. The ghosts were always telling me their stories, so I think it is what they would have wanted, too.

And now I'm told my husband will be coming back from Bosnia soon. One thing is certain: Jon won't see the funny side of me being the one to get blown up. When he goes away he says *be safe*, by which he means *safer than normal*, because if something happens to me he won't be here.

PHILIP LANGESKOV

BARCELONA

FOR THEIR TENTH wedding anniversary Daniel had arranged for them to spend a weekend in Barcelona, hoping to surprise Isla both with the fact that he had remembered at all and with a reminder of their honeymoon, which had also been spent in Barcelona. The idea struck him a few weeks before the actual date and it immediately felt like an important thing to do. In order to arrange accommodation at such short notice – it was the weekend of a crucial Barça v Real derby game and the hotels were full – it had been necessary to contact an old friend of Isla's, Josep, who lived in the city, and who Daniel had met once or twice in London, and who had, on those one or two occasions, said that if they ever wanted to visit they should let him know and they could stay in his apartment, which was near the centre, while he would vacate and stay with friends for the duration of their trip. Daniel would rather not have done this – Josep and Isla had had a fling once, years ago, when they were students, long before he and Isla had met – but he could think of no alternative if the trip was to come off as he had imagined it.

Planning everything out in his head brought Daniel a great deal of satisfaction. He could not wait to see Isla's reaction, both to the whole event and to the little things he had lined up for when they were there: small things mostly, like coming upon a certain view at a certain time of day, or appearing to end up by accident at a bar they had got drunk in on their last visit. It would be such a surprise for her, all of it. And such a boost for them, as a couple. They hadn't done anything like this for years. Of course, Daniel swore Josep to secrecy and had no reason to suspect anything until, when he told Isla, one evening after work, the two of them drinking in the kitchen, that he had booked a trip for the coming weekend, the weekend of their wedding anniversary, she reacted not with shock or delight, but with calm assurance.

'Oh darling,' she said. 'I can't.'

'What do you mean?'

'I mean I can't. I have something on. I'm sorry. You should have said.'

'What do you have on? There's nothing on the calendar.' As he said this, Daniel gestured to the back of the kitchen door. He was sure he had checked, sure he had looked closely; he remembered doing it, as if it were yesterday.

'Yes there is,' she said. 'Look.'

Sure enough, when he looked again, there was something – the scrawl of Isla's tiny handwriting – in one of the little boxes. He had to peer closely to make out the words: Conference (Warwick).

'When did you put this in?' he said.

'Weeks ago,' she said. 'I'm sure I mentioned it.'

'Weeks ago? But I checked.'

'You can't have done, honey,' she said.

Daniel didn't quite know what to make of it, this apparent blindness on his part, and could only blurt out: 'But it's our wedding anniversary.'

'I know. I know. And it's important.' Isla spoke slowly, in what Daniel recognised as her serious voice. She really wanted him to know that this was as important to her as it was to him. She ran her hand along his sleeve. 'Love,' she said.

He didn't respond.

'Love,' she said again, looking directly into his eyes. 'We could do something another time, couldn't we?'

Daniel was conscious that he was on the verge of sulking. It was a struggle to decide whether it could be justified or not, whether a case could be made. The importance of the weekend, the value that he had attached to it in his mind, swirled around him. From his perspective, he knew, its significance had become outlandishly inflated. It was, after all, only a couple of days, but to Daniel those days had come to seem possessed of a precipitous, life-altering power. And all that thinking he had done, all that imagining: places to go, restaurants, moments to remember. It was, now he came to think of it, a reaffirmation of his commitment to Isla and he wanted it to be recognised as such. He hadn't even considered that it might go wrong, or, if he had, he had done so in a minor key: a bad meal in a supposedly good restaurant, being ripped off by a taxi driver, losing something. In the end, he decided not to speak. He just folded his arms and looked at his feet.

'Love,' Isla said again. She had moved round to stand in front of him. 'We can talk about it later, but I have to get ready. I'm meeting Grace, remember?'

This might be the limit, he thought, not for the fact, but for the timing, the moment when sulking becomes inevitable. 'Where are you going?'

'Just for a drink.'

'But.' He was about to gesture once more towards the calendar, then realised that it would be ridiculous. He knew everything about this drink with Grace. Isla had told him, had invited him, even implored him to come. 'We'll talk about it later?' He hadn't intended to make it sound like a question, but that's how it came out.

'I'm sorry,' she said, taking her glass upstairs. 'We will talk about it later. Promise.'

After Isla had gone out, Daniel spent the evening mooching round the flat. He couldn't settle on a single spot. He lay on the couch, on the bed, he sprawled in the armchair in the study. As he did so, he mused over everything that had transpired. Josep must have told her, he thought. The dirty bastard. He had half a mind to ring him up and ask him, but decided against it. What did it matter, really? Josep was Isla's friend, not his; there should be no surprise as to where his loyalty might lie. At the kitchen table, on his laptop, Daniel looked into the possibility of changing flights. There was a fee, but it could, as far as he understood the website, be accomplished. Fine, he thought. They could simply go another time. It wasn't a big deal, nothing to get upset about. He opened a bottle of beer and congratulated himself on his equanimity. In fact, the more he thought about it the more he became convinced that another weekend would be better. They could stay in a proper hotel, for one thing.

When Isla returned, however, she was in a different mood. Daniel was already in bed, reading. When he heard the door go, he pretended to be asleep. He listened to the sound of Isla dropping her bag in the hall, easing off her shoes. When she entered the bedroom, she sat alongside him and began to stroke his hair. He could smell the wine on her breath.

'You're awake, aren't you?' she said.

Daniel smiled, but kept his eyes closed.

'I'm sorry about earlier,' she said. 'It was just a surprise. I didn't react very well.'

'It's all right,' he said, opening his eyes. 'I should have asked. We can change the dates. I've looked into it.'

'No. You were right. We should go at the weekend. It's our wedding anniversary.' She smiled.

'Are you sure?' Daniel wondered what role Grace might have played in getting Isla to change her mind, what level of sacrifice this whole new mood implied. 'I mean, we could go another time. I really don't mind.'

'I'm quite sure,' she said.

'What about Warwick, the conference?'

'Balls to Warwick. You're my husband. It's not as if I'm giving a paper or anything.' Then she added, as what seemed an afterthought, but which could just as well have been a theatrical diversion to conceal the fact that she already knew the answer to her question: 'Where are we going?'

'Don't you know?' he said. 'I thought you knew.'

'What do you mean? Of course I don't know. How would I know?'

'Just wondered if a little bird had told you.'

'No. No little bird. Where are we going?'

'You'll see.'

'This is intriguing. Which little bird? Do you mean Grace? Does Grace know?'

Suddenly Daniel felt much better, as if a weight had been lifted. Perhaps Josep was reliable after all.

On the Friday, as they were leaving the apartment for the airport, Daniel grabbed, at the very last moment, on a whim, the copy of Graham Greene's collected stories from the table in the hall. A colleague, Steve, had lent it to him months ago, after Daniel and Isla had watched *The Third Man* and liked it. Daniel hadn't got round to looking at it and thought that maybe the flight would be an opportunity. Then he could give the book back to Steve, lifting another weight from his conscience.

Isla was in a chirpy mood as the taxi weaved through the streets around Paddington Station. She kept looking at Daniel, touching his arm, and asking: 'Where are we going?' To which he replied with a smile and by raising a finger to his lips: 'It's a secret.' Of course, at the airport, he would have to reveal their destination, but he maintained the suspense for as long as he could, watching her as she tried to work it out, the expression on her face changing. When it finally dawned on her, as they neared the departure gate, she broke into a grin.

'Barcelona!' she said.

Daniel opened the book on the plane, shortly after they had levelled out. Isla was already asleep next to him, which he didn't think anything of at the time. He browsed the contents page, looking for the shortest story he could find. He wanted a quick fix, a hit, something that he could get into and out of in the least time possible; something that he could race through and get to the end.

The shortest story was called 'The Overnight Bag'. It concerns a man, Henry Cooper, travelling by plane from Nice to London, carrying an overnight bag. At the information desk he is given a telegram. It is from his mother. She wishes him a safe journey and looks forward to seeing him on his return. So far, so normal. As he read the story, Daniel felt a pleasant flash of recognition. On the one hand, this was because he knew the airport at Nice, could imagine its location, and, on the other, because he and Isla had just passed through an airport of their own and, although neither he nor Isla were carrying what could be called an overnight bag, they both had hand luggage and had, on boarding the plane, been faced with the dilemma of what to do with it, whether to place it on the seat, under the seat, or in the overhead locker.

In the case of the story, Henry Cooper is very particular about his overnight bag. He places it 'tenderly on the ledge of the information desk as though it contained something precious and fragile like an electric razor'. Later, on the plane, he sets it down on the empty seat next to him and secures it with a seatbelt. When a woman, sitting alongside the seat on which he placed the overnight bag, asks him why he is being so particular, he replies that he doesn't want it shaken about. When she places her own bag on top of his, he reacts testily: 'I don't want it squashed,' he says. 'It's a matter of respect.'

As Daniel read, Isla shifted in her sleep, so that her face was turned towards him, rather than towards the aisle. Her head was back, her straight brown hair half covering one of her eyes. She had a vague, almost apologetic smile on her face, as if, in a dream, she was having an experience that was both pleasant and troubling at the same time. Daniel looked at her for some moments thinking this, trying to penetrate her consciousness, to glean her thoughts, before brushing his fingers down her cheek and returning to his book.

The woman reacts angrily to Cooper's concern regarding the bag: 'What have you got in your precious bag?' she asks. To which Cooper evenly replies: 'A dead baby. I thought I had told you.' This, as Daniel could well understand, sends the woman into paroxysms of bewilderment. She splutters that he shouldn't be doing this, that the baby should be in a coffin and not an overnight bag, that there must be regulations for this kind of thing. Although Daniel smirked, picturing what he imagined was a rather pompous old woman, he was forced to consider what kind of regulations there might be for the event of transferring a dead baby from one country to another. He was sure there would be several forms to fill in. From this, he found himself contemplating a possible sequence of events that might lead to him, Daniel, having to conceal a dead baby in his own hand luggage.

Cooper explains to the woman that his wife didn't trust a foreign coffin. 'Then it's your baby,' the woman says. 'My wife's baby,' Henry Cooper corrects her. 'What's the difference?' 'There could well be a difference,' he says, sadly.

Daniel paused. He didn't quite know what to make of things. Cooper didn't seem a trustworthy character, not that

Daniel thought that mattered particularly, but his language seemed at odds with the reality it claimed and the effect was distracting. Well. He would carry on, to see if things would work themselves out. There was a bottle of water in the seat pocket in front of him and Daniel took it out and drank from it, rolling the water around in his mouth as if to extract maximum benefit. He felt an itch in his side and, having scratched it, lifted his shirt to examine the surface of his skin. Nothing there but a small red mark, as if he had been bitten by a tick.

He read what remained of the story. There was a rather bizarre and comic episode with a taxi driver, who drives Cooper home. Although it is a cold day, Cooper asks the cabbie to turn off the heating, out of concern for the dead baby. 'Dead baby?' the cabbie says. 'He won't feel the heat then, will he?' Boom, boom. When Cooper reaches home, his mother is waiting for him. He places the overnight bag in the hall. She has laid out his slippers. They talk a little about his trip and he relates a peculiar tale about a severed human toe being found in a jar of marmalade. When his mother goes to put on the shepherd's pie, Cooper goes through to the hall. 'Time to unpack,' he thinks. He has a tidy mind, we are told. And there the story ends. There is no further mention of a wife, a baby, and the true contents of the bag are left unresolved at the end of the story.

Daniel sat there with the book in his lap staring at the half-page of white space at the end of the story, where someone, Steve perhaps, had written, in pencil: yes, well? Daniel knew how this mystery annotator felt, or, rather, he knew how he felt and assumed the annotator felt the same. He turned back a few pages and began to read again, in case he had missed something, some clue. As he did so, however, the pilot announced their descent into Barcelona. Daniel didn't like landing. In preparation, he slid the book into the seat pocket in front and turned to Isla. She was still sleeping and when he tried to rouse her she responded slowly.

'Is,' he said, shaking her. 'We're landing.'

She opened her eyes and looked at him, bewildered, as if she were returning from another realm of consciousness in which she had not been herself. 'Already?' She glanced quickly to either side, and then put her hand to her chest. 'My god, what a dream,' she said. 'It was like.' She paused. 'I don't know what it was like. Have you got any water?'

Daniel passed her the bottle and then sat back, watching, as she drank from it.

'Have I really slept through the whole flight?'

'Yup.'

'Completely ridiculous. I'm not even tired.'

Daniel reached for her hand and then closed his eyes. The plane shook as it passed through some turbulence. He thought about the story. It troubled him, made him uneasy. He couldn't have said precisely why it troubled him, even to himself, but already, as they made their descent into Barcelona, swinging wide over the city lit against the dusk, it preoccupied him to an unusual degree. He squeezed Isla's hand. She squeezed back.

Daniel was still thinking about the story as they went through passport control. The queue moved slowly. What was it that upset him so? The obvious thing to think would be that it was the suggestion of the dead baby, that this in some way hinted to an unspoken sense of loss within him regarding the decision he and Isla had taken – long ago, before they were married – not to have children. They just couldn't be arsed, or so they told themselves. They were either working too hard or having too much fun. Although subsequently they talked it over from time to time, wondering about the difference it might have made to their lives and whether they had changed their minds, Daniel was clear that they had never regretted it. Yes, they had friends whose children they liked, spent time with, but they never wanted the same for themselves, they never felt a lack. It wasn't that. It couldn't be that.

In the baggage hall there was a further wait. Isla was still drowsy from sleeping on the flight and she leaned against Daniel, one arm around his neck, as he stood there staring at the unmoving carousel, occasionally and distractedly kissing her hair.

The more he thought about it, the more Daniel began to think that the story was actually unpleasant, offensive even. Some coldness at its heart had made him shiver and he was not grateful for the effect. He wished he had never read the story, wished he had never picked the book up from the table in the hall, wished Steve had never loaned it to him.

There was quite a wait before the carousel got going and the people waiting – an assortment of families, couples, groups, people on their own, whispering into mobile phones – gave all the signs of growing impatient. As he waited, Daniel came to think that his problem with the story centred entirely on the character of Cooper. He didn't like him, it was simple: didn't like the way he behaved, the way he turned so felicitously from one situation to the next, switching personas, fazed, it seemed, by nothing. Of course, Daniel, in thinking, had realised that there was no baby in the story in the first place, nor was there a wife. This made it worse, Daniel thought, grasping for a rationale for his distaste. They were all constructs of Cooper's imagination; versions of his life that he chose to wear in public like clothes, sending out a false message. Really it was this that Daniel didn't like, this duplicity. He couldn't think why it bothered him particularly now, except to say that it was suddenly as if he had been introduced to a certain quality in himself that either he had not known about or had chosen to ignore or worked hard to suppress.

Around him, groups of people made comments about

Catalan efficiency, looked at their watches, harrumphed. The delay frustrated Daniel too. It was, for the time being, as if they were in an in-between state, both there, in Barcelona, and not there, held back, in some way restrained, kept in England, or on the plane. As a consequence, with the story occupying a considerable part of his brain, Daniel didn't feel able to concentrate on his actual thoughts; nor could he commit himself fully to the act of imagining the anniversary weekend to come.

Finally, a half-hearted cheer went up. The luggage carousel had started to move.

With Isla cross-legged on the floor and Daniel standing with his arms folded, they waited as bag after bag passed before their eyes. Other passengers came forward to collect their belongings, hoisted them onto their shoulders or onto trolleys and headed out through the automatic doors to the arrivals hall. Beyond it, Daniel could glimpse the darkening Barcelona night, its palm trees and taxis. Only once in his life had he had the experience of his bags not coming out onto the carousel. It soon became apparent that he was about to have the experience for a second time and it was as if he knew it before it had even happened.

Daniel looked at his watch. They would be late for Josep, for one thing. More than that, they would be late to bed, which would mean they wouldn't want to get up early, which, in the normal run of things would be fine, but as things stood, Daniel had plans for the morning, things he wanted them to do, not booked exactly, but certainly mapped out in his mind. They could be flexible, of course, but still. As the time passed and the number of people left waiting dwindled, Daniel began to develop a competitive streak, cultivating a sense of enmity towards the other people waiting, making judgements on their respective predicaments, weighing up whether they deserved the arrival of their bags more than he and Isla deserved the arrival of theirs.

'It's no good,' he whispered to Isla. 'Just you wait and see. They've lost it. They've lost the fucking bag.'

'Wankers,' Isla whispered back, each time someone else went to collect a bag.

In the end, it was just the two of them and a man of roughly Daniel's age, with close-cropped blond hair, a blue suit and an open-necked floral shirt. He had first noticed the man back in England, at the departure gate, in the queue, and now here he was again. The carousel squeaked emptily along. Rather than looking at the man, Daniel concentrated his attention on the mouth of the carousel, looking for every advantage, willing their bag to arrive, while at the same time knowing, deep down, that it would not. In the game of his imagination, the question of whose bag emerged next had become a matter of life and death.

Eventually, a bag did emerge. From a distance, it looked like theirs, but just as Daniel was thinking this, the man moved forward, with a glance across at them, as if he were fully conversant with the rules of the game, understood the gravity of the situation.

'That's our bag,' Isla said, whispering into Daniel's neck.

'Are you sure?'

'Yes.'

'Wait a minute,' Daniel said, not quite loudly enough.

At the carousel, the man, having lifted the bag off, paused. He examined the bag closely. He opened one of the compartments and peered inside, rummaging around with his hand. Eventually, he looked up at Daniel, one arm still in the bag. 'Actually, this isn't mine,' he said. 'It must be yours. Sorry.'

'I wondered,' Daniel said.

'Same type of bag,' the man said, calmly, before handing it to Daniel. 'Same colour and everything.'

'Well,' Daniel said. Now he looked at the bag, just to be sure. It was theirs. 'Thank you,' Daniel said. 'It is ours. Perhaps someone has taken yours by mistake.' He had meant to say it generously, but in the circumstances he feared that it sounded sarcastic, a little bitter even.

When he returned to Isla she squeezed his arm. 'Well done, darling, saving our bag from the nasty man.'

'I'm sure it was a genuine mistake,' Daniel said.

'Nonsense. He would have nicked it if you hadn't said something.'

After they had cleared customs, they stood outside the terminal waiting for the bus. The air was hot, oppressive. Daniel rifled through his hand luggage.

'Shit,' he said.

'What is it?'

'I left that bloody book on the plane.'

'Oh, love,' Isla said. 'Do you want to go back?'

'No. It's not worth it. We're late enough as it is. Maybe I'll call tomorrow. Only it's Steve's.' He was about to say something else, something about the story, about how it was probably a good thing he had left the book on the plane, when it became apparent that Isla's attention had been caught by something over his shoulder.

'Look,' she said. 'It's that man. The one from the carousel.'

Daniel turned and looked. It was him. He strode out of the arrivals hall. It appeared his bag hadn't arrived; he wasn't carrying one at any rate. He walked straight across the pedestrian crossing, causing taxis to stop, and got into a car that was waiting for him at the side of the road. A woman was in the driver's seat but she didn't turn to look at him as he got in. As soon as his door closed, the car moved off, the man's gaze meeting Daniel's as they drove past.

'Was he English?' Isla said.

'I think so. He sounded it, didn't he?'

Suddenly, Isla doubled over and yelped in pain.

'What is it?'

She gathered herself quite quickly, standing up fully and taking a deep breath, in the way that somebody does when encountering a challenge. 'I don't know.' She put her hand against her stomach. 'This sudden pain.'

'Where?'

'Where I'm touching,' she said. 'Where do you think?'

'Sorry,' Daniel said. 'Do you mean here?' He moved his hand to cover the spot.

'Yes, there. I'm sure it's nothing.'

'It didn't seem like nothing,' he said, taking her head in his hands.

She nodded. 'It's nothing. I'm fine. Just a cramp, or something. It's passed.'

Daniel took her in his arms and held her close, kissing her head and smelling her hair.

When the bus arrived, they got on. Daniel looked out of the window as they moved through the outskirts of the city, past car dealerships, warehousing, industrial estates. In the story, Cooper never got the comeuppance he deserved. This was the thing, this was why he was annoyed. He invented this line about the baby, creating, in the minds of both the woman on the plane and the taxi driver, the experience of a trauma that in fact had not taken place. Cooper's just desserts, Daniel realised, would have been to find himself suffering precisely the traumatic experience he had called into being for others.

'What's on your mind?' It was Isla. She reached for his hand. 'Are you all right?'

'I'm fine,' he said. 'Just thinking about the bloody story I read on the plane.'

Soon enough, they were at Plaça de Catalunya. It was alive with people. They decided to walk to Josep's apartment on Calle Valencia. They had a map and it didn't seem far. It was about 11 o'clock. They strolled arm in arm through the evening crowds and Daniel at last felt the pleasant lassitude of heat and travel. This was what he had wanted from the outset: to be walking these streets, at this hour, with Isla at his side. The feeling washed over him at first, but then went deeper, as they caught sight of familiar things, half-forgotten, but no less powerful for that. There were restaurants they had eaten in, shops they had shopped in, buildings they had wondered at.

'It's good to be back,' Isla said.

'It is.'

As they left Passeig de Gràcia, the crowds thinned and they entered that region of Barcelona in which they had spent so much time wandering on their last visit, their honeymoon, ten years previously. Here, again, they saw the elegant apartment buildings, with their wrought-iron balconies, the intricate designs in the plaster. They felt, or at least Daniel felt, an immediate familiarity in that atmosphere of dusty night, the warm air, the shuttered shops, the little cafés still open, their tables set out on the street.

'Do you remember all this?' Isla said.

He smiled.

'Why are you smiling?'

'Because I was remembering all this just as you asked me.'

She squeezed his shoulder and they walked on, under the shadows of trees cast by the streetlamps, past the all-night florist, a chemist.

'We were so convinced we would live here,' Isla said. 'Do you remember? I was going to get a job at the university.'

'There's still time,' he said. 'We still could.'

Isla didn't say anything for a few paces and then squeezed his arm again. 'Yes,' she said. 'We still could. Anything's possible.'

As arranged, Josep was at his apartment to meet them. Daniel could hear his voice, crackly, through the intercom, as he buzzed them into the building. In the tiny elevator, so small that the two of them with their luggage could only just fit inside, Isla held her hand in front of her stomach and winced.

'Is it that thing again?'

'Yes. Just a little, you know.'

'I know. Are you sure you're all right?'

In the light of the elevator, her face was pale. He lifted her hair out of her eyes and felt her forehead.

'There's no fever.'

Josep met them at the door. Although Daniel had only met him on those one or two occasions in London he remembered him well, as if, although he hadn't been conscious of it, Josep had occupied a considerable part of his subconscious mind. He didn't appear to have changed. In fact, it's possible he was even wearing then the same suit he had been wearing on the previous occasions Daniel had met him, a narrow blue two-piece, elegantly cut, and a crisp white shirt. His dark hair was, as it had been, cropped close, revealing a little bit of thinning at the forehead.

Josep embraced them both, Isla first and Daniel second, and then returned his attention to Isla, holding her face, cupping it in his hands.

'Isla,' he said. 'You are here.' When he said her name, his accent had the curious effect of making Daniel think that he was talking to someone else, someone who was not his wife but someone else's, someone who he had not in fact met until that moment.

Suddenly, Isla buckled over in pain once again.

'Isla!' Josep said, stretching the second syllable. 'What is it?'

Isla flicked her eyes in Daniel's direction, before looking at Josep. 'It's nothing. Just a cramp.'

'Are you sure, darling?' Daniel said. He turned to Josep. 'There was another one, at the airport.'

'Then we should call a doctor,' he said. 'Of course.' He spoke English very quickly, the words running into each other.

'No,' Isla said. 'It's not that bad. I just need a painkiller.'

'Come on,' Josep said, 'follow me.' He ushered her through to the bedroom, turning to Daniel to say that he could drop the bags there, where they stood, before taking Isla into what Daniel presumed was a bathroom. Daniel stood there for a moment, before following them through to the bedroom, where he put the bags on the bed. He stood and listened at the door of the bathroom, but beyond a vague murmuring of a male voice and then a female voice, he could make out little above the sound of the extractor fan.

Daniel went through to the main body of the apartment. It was extensive, stretching across the whole top floor of the building, a large living area at the front, a pair of chaises longues to one side, set at an angle to each other, and bookcases lining every wall. There were two balconies, with their shutter doors folded back. Daniel went over and stepped onto the balcony to the left. Across from where he was standing, there was another apartment building, more or less the same, the same shuttered windows, the same wrought-iron balconies, the same intricate detailing in the fascia. Again, he thought of their first trip, of how they had then aspired to live in just such an apartment block. He lit a cigarette. Perhaps because of the heat, the night, the street sounds and the familiar smells, it was easy to remember the pleasure they had felt on their honeymoon, the lightness and the gladness in their hearts – a kind of bursting sensation that had threatened to leave both of them in hysterics for no reason other than their happiness.

Daniel was thinking about this when Josep came to join him on the balcony. 'I'm sure it is nothing serious, but I have called the doctor. Just to be safe. He lives quite close by. He will not be long.' As Daniel motioned to go back into the apartment, he held up his hand. 'No. Stay. Finish your cigarette. She is resting. I have given her an aspirin.'

'What do you think it is?'

Josep smiled. 'I don't know. I'm not a doctor.'

'But what do you think?'

'I think it is nothing serious. Something with her stomach perhaps. She will be better after rest. The doctor will know. Maybe she's pregnant.'

'I think that's unlikely,' Daniel said, smiling.

'Yes, of course. Would you like a drink?'

Josep returned with two tumblers of whisky. They stood on the balcony and drank.

'Ten years,' Josep said, raising his glass. 'Amazing.'

'Yes. It is.'

'You know, when I first met you, I didn't think you were good enough for her, for my Isla.'

'But now?'

'Now, I think you'll do.' Josep smiled. 'You care for her very well. She tells me things. And this trip. It is obvious.'

'I know how lucky I am,' Daniel said. 'Don't think I don't.'

Daniel turned away and leaned on the balcony edge, looking out at the apartment block opposite. Beneath them, despite the hour, traffic roared down the avenue. 'I love it here,' he said. 'These apartment buildings.'

'Yes. It's not the same in London, I think. Here we can see right into people's lives.'

Of all the windows in the building across from them, only two were lit. It was, after all, a Friday night and Daniel supposed that most of the occupants were either out, having dinner or drinks, or away from the city for the weekend. One of these windows, in the top right-hand corner of the building, gave on to a room that appeared to be lined from floor to ceiling with books, more like a library than an apartment. There was a man, or what Daniel thought to be a man, sitting at a desk, with a brass lamp, writing, or reading, or in some other way engaged in an activity for which sitting at a desk was necessary. In the other, lower down, two floors below, partially obscured by the half-open shutter door, a man lay on a sofa in his underpants watching a football match on a large television fixed to the wall.

'You would like her, I think,' Josep said.

'Who?'

'The woman at the desk.'

'I thought it was a man.'

'No. Woman. She is a professor. German. Quite well known in Spain. She has led a glamorous life. Her husband is an antiquarian book dealer from Colombia. You can visit his shop. It is just around the corner. I know him a little.'

'And what about him?' Daniel said, referring to the man in his underpants. 'He is a man, isn't he?'

'Yes. He is.'

'What can you tell me about him?'

'Nothing. I don't think I've ever seen him before.'

Standing there together, sipping their drinks, smoking, Daniel allowed himself to become engrossed in watching the young man. Really, he did very little. He watched the game, occasionally scratched himself.

At that moment, a buzzer rang.

'That will be the doctor,' Josep said, looking over the balcony, directly below. 'Yes, it is him.'

Daniel looked over the balcony too. Beneath them, fifty or sixty or seventy feet down, there was a man in a black suit. He held in his hand a briefcase. At the kerb, a black car, quite large, old. A Jaguar, Daniel thought, or a Daimler. Josep shouted down and waved, before taking a last drag on his cigarette, flicking it over the balcony and turning back into the apartment.

They waited and listened as the lift hauled the doctor up

to their level. He was a short man, glasses, beard, grey hair, which was slicked back over a well-tanned scalp. Daniel was introduced. The doctor and Josep spoke. Daniel thought that there were certain words that he recognised, like husband and London perhaps. The three of them went through to the bedroom. It was dark and Daniel stood leaning against the doorframe.

'How are you darling?' he said, as Isla raised her head.

'Okay, I think. I'm sure it's nothing serious. It's ridiculous all this fuss.'

Josep then spoke to the doctor in Spanish. The doctor lifted Isla's T-shirt and poked at her stomach, his small hands like paddles. Isla murmured when he reached a certain point. The doctor said something to Josep.

'Can you describe what it feels like, Isla?'

'Like a swelling, like there's a ball in there or something.'

The doctor looked up towards Josep and nodded, after which Josep turned to Daniel and said that they should leave them – the Doctor and Isla – to it. The two of them then made their way back through to the living room.

'It is okay,' Josep said. 'He thinks it is nothing serious. An inflammation, perhaps, something like that.'

'Good.'

'Another drink?'

'Why not,' he said.

Josep settled himself on one of the chaises longues and invited Daniel to sit on the other. As if understanding Daniel's thoughts, he said: 'It won't be long.'

'It's all right,' he said. 'I'm just a little anxious.'

'Of course,' he said.

There was silence between them for a minute as they both sipped their drinks. Daniel cast his eyes around the apartment. He was about to say something about it – about how nice it was, or how he liked it – when Josep spoke first.

'What plans did you have for your trip?'

'Well. We'll have to see. It depends on Isla, but there were certain things I wanted us to do, repetitions of what we did on our honeymoon, or things we didn't have time for. There was a place we visited last time we were here – over by the harbour, in Barcelonetta, hidden away down a back street, but I can't remember the name. I think I could find it, if it's still open. I think I have it in mind for us just to stumble over it and it to be the same as last time.'

At that point, Josep looked up. 'Ah, the doctor.'

Daniel turned around and saw him standing on the threshold to the room. He stood with his feet together and his arms in front of him, the fingers of both hands meeting. Josep went over to him, but the old man beckoned him into the hall. Daniel strained to listen, but not only were they speaking a foreign language, they were also whispering.

'Well,' Josep said. 'He thinks it is possible it might be an ulcer, but it is not serious. Isla should have it checked out when she gets home, but for now the doctor has given her something to help her sleep. She should be fine in the morning with rest, although rich foods won't be a good idea if that's what you had in mind.'

The doctor gathered his things. Daniel rose, went over to him and thanked him in Spanish. The doctor nodded, curtly, first to Daniel and then to Josep, before leaving. Again they stood for a moment listening to the workings of the lift.

'Strange little man,' Daniel said.

'He is,' Josep said. 'But very good, reliable.'

Eventually, Josep started moving around the room, gathering various things, car keys, a wallet.

'I would stay and keep you company,' he said. 'But I have to go to my friend, to Katya's. I am late and she has work early in the morning. You understand what I mean.'

Daniel nodded.

'There is food in the fridge, if you are hungry, or' – he walked past Daniel and out on to the balcony and pointed back down Valencia towards the centre of town – 'there is a little place two blocks away, open late. It's quite good. Steak and such.'

'Thank you,' Daniel said.

'Here are the keys and, here, I'll write down my number in case you should need to contact me.'

They shook hands near the door. 'She'll be fine tomorrow. Just you wait and see.'

Daniel thanked him and held the door open, casting light into the hallway, as Josep waited for the lift.

After Josep had gone, Daniel went through to the bedroom. Isla was already in bed, under a cotton sheet, curled, with her legs brought up to her chest. She looked up at him, the light from the hallway causing her to squint.

'I'm sorry,' she said.

'What for?'

'You know.'

'There's nothing to be sorry for.'

'I was sick.'

'You were sick?'

'In the bathroom. I was sick.'

'My poor baby,' he said and rubbed her back. 'And how do you feel now?'

'I really don't know. A bit zonked. I suppose I just need to give the pills time to work.'

In this position they remained, looking at one another in the half-light, not speaking.

'What will you do?' she said.

'I don't know. I might read. I might go out for a bite to eat.'

There was a pause. 'You don't mind?'

'Mind what?'

'You're not angry, I mean?'

'Angry? God no.'

'About this. About me being like this.'

'I mind that you are like this, because I don't want you to be ill, but I'm not angry. Not at all.'

'In the morning I'll be fine.'

'You will. Now put your head down and get some sleep. I'll keep watch.'

She put her head down on the pillow and he kissed her. He went through to the bathroom, splashed some water on his face, then sat on the toilet seat. His own head was throbbing from the heat. In a cabinet under the sink, there were some pills, he took the last two and put the empty packet in the bin.

He went back through to the bedroom and knelt by the bed. He intended to speak to Isla, to tell her that he loved her and that he would be there, in the next room, if she needed him. His arm was on her shoulder, which was bare above the cotton sheet. Her eyes were closed and she didn't move.

'Are you awake?' he said.

She didn't respond.

Daniel stayed there for some minutes, looking at her face. In the end he didn't do anything. He didn't wake her or speak to her or anything. He just watched her sleep, the rise and fall of her body.

After a little while, he got up and left the room, taking the bag he had used as hand luggage with him. He remembered that he had left his book on the plane, then he remembered the story. He would have liked to read it again, if only to work out why it was stuck in his head. He thought about how ridiculous this was as he went to the fridge to see what food there was. There was some cured ham, some Manchego and some quince jelly. He put some of the ham and cheese on a plate along with a spoon of the jelly and carried it to the dining room table, where he sat with his back to the open doors of the balcony. Just as he was about to raise the first morsel of ham and cheese to his mouth, he caught sight of an open bottle of wine on the counter, next to the sink, and went back into the kitchen to fetch the wine and a glass, before returning to the table. He poured the wine. The food was good, just what he needed. After he had eaten, he carried the plate back through to the sink and rinsed it.

He was tired, but not sleepy. Not wishing to lie in bed, awake, with the danger that he might disturb Isla, he sat for a little while in the only armchair and drank the rest of the wine. He felt the oddness of unfamiliar territory – the late hour, Isla asleep and him awake. He couldn't bring himself to read any of the books that lined the shelves of the apartment, most of which were in Spanish in any case. He went back out to the balcony.

He wondered about Isla, about how she was. Wondered what the doctor meant by an ulcer. How serious it was. He had heard of ulcers bursting, but that wouldn't happen. It couldn't. He was fantasising. Worse than that, he was catastrophising.

From where he was standing, it was possible to look down, at an angle, on the hexagonal junction of Valencia and one of the cross streets. Periodically, a little clump of taxis streamed past, the odd car, a motorcycle swerving at pace down the road. A gaggle of people stood on the street, smoking, fanned out around the doorway to a bar. Not far from them, Daniel's attention was caught by an old woman and an old man walking up the cross street and round onto Valencia. They were beneath him, but on the opposite side of the road. The woman was bent nearly double and carrying plastic bags with what Daniel presumed to be food inside. Certainly, he thought he could see a baguette sticking up, perhaps the outline of a bottle of wine. The old man was pulling what appeared to be a trolley behind him. It was only by looking closely that Daniel could see that it was an oxygen tank; from there he was able to follow the tubes that led from the cylinder to the man's nose. Every few paces the couple stopped, the woman putting down her bags, the man, drawing level with her, putting out a shaking arm and grasping her by the hand. After a time, a young woman broke away from the group outside the bar and came over to the couple. Although Daniel was high up, he could hear the sound of her voice. She took the bags from the old lady, who touched her arm. Then they walked across the road and disappeared from view.

As he looked at the empty space that they had left, Daniel felt like the world was a very remarkable place indeed. It wasn't specifically because of the good act he had just witnessed, although it certainly helped. Even the couple by themselves would have been enough: the great sense of life that they hauled in their wake seemed to verge on the miraculous. Was it easier, he wondered, in a city like Barcelona – in a country like Spain, for that matter – to romanticise the lives of the old? Their history seemed more transparent, the lines more clear: you were either on this side or you were on the other side, or so it appeared. Did he even think like this at home, or was it only here, or abroad in general, that he came upon thoughts of such a character?

He went through into the bedroom and got undressed in the dark. After brushing his teeth, he got into bed. Isla turned towards him in her sleep and mumbled something that he couldn't make out. He put his arm around her and pulled her to him. Whether it was the sight of the old couple, or Barcelona itself, or what, Daniel renewed the vow that he would do whatever he could to protect her, even to the extent of sacrificing himself. The reasons didn't matter, but such things were easy to forget, with all the ins and outs of normal life. They had a chance of being different, however. Nothing was yet set in stone. He lay there for a little while in the dark, feeling both optimistic for the future and completely terrified by it. Just as he was on the point of falling asleep, an image drifted into his mind: Cooper, in the near-silence of his room, unpacking the overnight bag, his mother in the kitchen, dealing with the shepherd's pie.

The following morning, Daniel woke to find the bed next to him empty. He could smell the familiar scent of Isla's shampoo. The bedroom door was open and through it he could see all the way to the front of the apartment. The shutters were open and the sun streamed in. He called Isla's name, but there was no reply. He got up and pulled on a pair of shorts and walked through. He could see her on the other side of the window, sitting on the balcony in the sun.

'Morning,' he said.

'Morning, darling. You slept well.'

He kissed her head. Her hair was wet. 'What time is it?'

'Almost ten.'

'Ten! How did that happen?'

'I didn't want to wake you, not after all the palaver last night.'

'How about you. How did you sleep?'

'Not so well. I've been up for hours, just sitting here. The sun's lovely,' she said, stretching her arms above her head.

'What do you think you can cope with today?'

'I'm not sure. Not too much, perhaps, but maybe we could go out and get breakfast somewhere. I'm starving. Did you have any ideas?'

'I did, but we don't have to do any of them.'

When Daniel had showered, they left the apartment and rode the elevator down to the lobby, before stepping out into the sunlight of a Barcelona Saturday. It was fiercely hot – hotter than he had expected; it was only May. As they walked, Daniel's anxieties of the night before seemed to slip away. Everything was going to be fine; nothing was going to happen. They wandered for quite a time, eyeing up possible places to stop, feeling the heat on their backs and the pleasant sensation of being far from home. When they found that they were nearing the Sagrada Familia, they turned back. In the end, having almost done a complete loop, they sat down at a table on the pavement, a place just a couple of blocks away from where they were staying. They garbled their order apologetically in half-Spanish, half-English, but the waitress was sympathetic and brought them coffees and a selection of pastries. There were a handful of people sitting at other tables, reading newspapers, consulting travel guides.

'How's the pastry?' Daniel said.

'Not sure yet. It's a bit sweet. There's apricot in it or something.'

'I hate that,' he said. His own pastry was very dry, more of a cake.

When they had finished, Daniel lit a cigarette and offered one to Isla.

'That's better,' she said, once it was alight, puffing the smoke out with real satisfaction.

'What shall we do tonight, do you think? It is our actual anniversary after all. Do you think you'll be up to something? A meal, maybe? We could go back to that restaurant from last time.'

'Let me see how this goes down,' Isla said.

At that moment, her phone went. She answered it. It was Josep. Once Daniel knew that, he allowed their conversation to fade into the background. He watched the traffic, the play of the light through the trees.

When Isla finished the call, she related its contents. Josep had suggested that he take Daniel for lunch, allowing Isla to rest a little more, giving her the opportunity to be fully restored for the rest of their weekend.

'Is that what you want?' Daniel asked.

'I wouldn't mind a little more rest,' she said. 'What about you? Would you mind?'

'If you'd like me to go, I'll go,' he said. 'I never say no to lunch.'

'No, you don't,' Isla said and smiled. 'And it will be okay with Josep? He won't get on your nerves.'

'Not at all. We had a nice chat last night.'

She phoned Josep back and it was all arranged. Daniel had another coffee, they both had another cigarette. It was pleasant out there on the street and he was able to bat away all negative thoughts.

When they were done, they strolled back to the apartment. For the next couple of hours, they lazed on the balcony. Isla read some essays she had to mark and Daniel attempted a crossword in a newspaper he found in the bottom of his bag. Not long before two, Josep texted. He was outside. Daniel kissed Isla and went down.

Josep was parked by the kerb, in a convertible BMW. He had sunglasses on, shorts, his legs enviably brown and hairy. Daniel jumped in and they roared off into the traffic.

'How is Isla?' he asked.

'All right, I think. It's good of you to take me for lunch.'

'It's nothing. There's a little place I think you'll like. It's not special. In any case, you must save your energy for tonight.' He turned and looked at Daniel, a smile on his lips and, Daniel imagined, in his eyes behind his sunglasses.

Daniel smiled back. 'Now, now.'

'You know what I mean,' he said. 'Tonight's the night, no?'

'You mean our actual anniversary?'

'Yes.'

'Yes it is,' Daniel said.

They drove down a wide avenue, a grand arch ahead of them, set back in a park that Daniel remembered visiting before. There had been buskers underneath and he and Isla had danced, a little drunkenly, and had their photograph taken by a procession of strangers. Josep had his eyes on the road. They were driving towards the sea and soon it came into view, glinting, the sails of boats peaking the horizon. Daniel thought of Isla back at the apartment, the cool tiles beneath her feet. He hoped she was reading, or sleeping, or doing whatever it was that made her comfortable.

'She'll be okay, won't she?' he said, leaning over to make himself heard above the traffic. 'I don't have to worry.'

'She'll be fine,' Josep said. 'Relax. We're nearly there.' He swung the car to the left and they drove down a road lined with restaurants, their tables spilling out onto the wide pavement. The vista seemed familiar. Away to the right was a large, low, sandy-coloured building. Daniel had seen it before. It was the maritime museum. 'We're not going here,' Josep said, nodding to the restaurants over to the left. 'This is for the tourists.'

He turned the car left again and drove slowly down a side street, white and terracotta buildings on either side. It was less grand than the area in which Josep lived and the smaller balconies in this part of the city were draped in flags, pledging allegiance to a bewildering array of what Daniel presumed to be football clubs. Again, it all seemed familiar. Then, as Josep pulled into a space on the left, it became apparent why. It was the very place that he and Isla had been to on their honeymoon, the one he had been talking about the preceding night as he and Josep stood on the balcony.

'But this is the place I was talking about last night,' he said.

'Really?' Josep said. 'I had no idea. This is a place I always visit.'

'And you had no idea?'

'None.'

He had no way of telling if Josep was in earnest or not. Perhaps Daniel had told him, or Isla had, long ago, after their honeymoon, and subsequently forgotten. Whatever the reason, as he walked along the pavement, Daniel telephoned Isla. He wanted to tell her about the extraordinary coincidence. You won't believe this, he was going to say, but the phone rang and rang, the unfamiliar ring tone of a foreign exchange, then it went to voicemail. Assuming she was sleeping, Daniel left a message, telling her not only about the restaurant, but also that she needn't feel any pressure about going out that evening; he would, he told her, be more than happy just to stay in and curl up with a book.

The restaurant was much as Daniel remembered it, only busier. The previous time, with Isla, had been a weekday and they had had a pick of tables. With Josep, however, they had to share a table with an older couple, a man and a woman, their faces worn from exposure to the sun. It was clear that Josep was a familiar presence, as he nodded to the waiting staff – all men, wearing dirty white T-shirts and blue jeans. A counter separated the tables from the kitchen, which stretched to the back of the building, maybe five chefs working away on various types of grill or surface. The counter itself was covered in open dishes, already prepared and ready to be picked up by the waiters and carried to the tables.

'Everything is good,' Josep said, raising one of two cold beer bottles, which had appeared in front of them. Around him, the room was alive with voices.

'I know,' Daniel said. 'I've been here before.'

'Of course,' Josep said, smiling and chinking Daniel's bottle once again.

The beer went down smoothly. It was precisely what Daniel wanted, cold, sharp. Josep shouted out an order to a passing waiter, who returned with more beer. Daniel had a thirst on, it was clear. He found himself wanting to convey to Josep the strength of his feeling for Isla, how fortunate he was. Josep seemed to understand, both what he was saying and why he was saying it.

With the heat and the beer, things became distinctly heady as they tore at the little plates of food that were brought out in rapid succession, the waiter dropping the rattling dishes on the table as he rushed by carrying any number of other dishes for other tables: grilled prawns, aubergines, some kind of fried mashed potato.

Josep knew about the food, how it was prepared, why it was good, what its origin was, and Daniel – two, three, then four beers down – was happy to hear him talk about it. His knowledge was impressive, as was the speed with which he spoke English, his fluency; it was as if, Daniel imagined, with just the two of them in freely flowing conversation, the language which Josep had learned all those years ago, when, as a young student in London, he had first known Isla, was properly coming back to him.

The dishes of food came and went. There were desserts: burnt custard, raspberries, an almond rice, all in little terracotta ramekins, each containing no more than three or four spoonfuls' worth. Josep did all the ordering. Daniel didn't have to do anything, other than eat and drink. In the bathroom, he looked at himself in a cracked mirror. His face was flushed with the heat and his clothes were damp. When he returned, a fresh glass of beer was on the table. He looked at Josep and smiled.

'Last one,' he said.

'There's no rush,' Josep said. 'Let her rest.'

'I know. You're right,' Daniel said. 'But I can't help worrying.'

'It does you great credit,' Josep said, nodding and at the same moment raising his beer. 'To you and Isla.'

For the first time, it dawned on Daniel, that Josep had been drinking as much as he had, and that he was similarly affected. 'Yes,' he said. 'To me and Isla. I'm sorry she's not here. She would have loved it.'

'I'm sorry, too. Although, if she was here, I suppose I would be somewhere else.'

'Where would that somewhere else be?'

'At Katya's.' He smiled.

'And who is this Katya?'

'Oh, a friend. More than a friend. I don't know. We have known each other for a long time and the situation remains the same.'

'And you'd like it to change?'

'Maybe. I don't know. I think so.' Josep leaned forward and drained the last of his beer. 'We go?' he said.

'Yes,' Daniel said. 'What about the bill?'

'There is no bill.'

'I can't allow it,' Daniel said. He was drunk.

'Okay,' Josep said. 'You leave the tip. However much you think.' He shrugged his shoulders and gestured to the table in front of them, covered in debris, prawn shells, bits of bread.

Daniel took out his wallet and counted out three ten euro bills and threw them onto the table. Josep gestured with his eyes to one of the passing waiters. 'You are a very generous man,' he said, patting him on the back as they stepped out onto the street. 'Too generous.'

As they sat in the car, waiting for the roof to come down, Daniel said: 'You're all right to drive, aren't you?'

'By the law, no, but by me, yes.' Josep smiled, released the handbrake and sped away from the kerb.

He drove quickly, weaving dextrously in and out of the traffic. On instinct, Daniel put his hand against the doorframe.

'Too fast?' Josep said.

'No, no. It's fine.' Daniel watched the city speed past, people waiting at crossings, hauling luggage down the street in the light of the sun. He looked at his watch.

'It's half past five,' he said, holding it up.

'I know,' Josep said. 'Isla will have had a good rest.'

Daniel thought of Isla, wondering whether he should text her and warn her of his return. He decided not to. They would, he reasoned, be there in no more than ten minutes. It was impossible to think of his life without her in it. This was the lesson of ten years of marriage: to be without her would be unbearable, like falling of a cliff and finding himself at the bottom looking up at an empty space. He would be back soon, would be able to hold her in his arms, for the rest of the day and night if necessary; she wouldn't have to worry about Barcelona, or the things they had planned.

Josep pulled the car up to the kerb. Daniel thanked him and dashed into the apartment building. He couldn't wait for the lift and ran up the stairs, taking them two or three at a time. As he burst through the door, he was panting, hot.

'Darling,' he shouted. 'Isla!' but there was no reply. He passed through the bedroom on his way to the bathroom. The sheets were crumpled, but beyond that there was no sign of Isla. He didn't yet feel a twinge of panic. She would be out the front, perhaps asleep on the balcony, he thought, as he urinated, while at the same time calling out behind him: 'Isla! Darling! I'm back.'

When he finally went through to the front of the apartment, she wasn't there. The doors to both balconies hung open and a faint breeze was coming in. He went out onto the balcony, just to be sure. It was at this point that Daniel began, not to panic exactly, but to feel alert, as if his body or his gut were telling him that he needed to have his wits about him, that something was taking place that needed his attention. He went back through to the bedroom. Nothing. He went through to the second bedroom. Nothing. He went back to the first bedroom. He stood by the bed and called her phone. There was no answer. As it rang, he looked at her bags, which had been neatly placed against the back wall of the room. Alongside them, a small pile of clothes. It was the clothes she had been wearing earlier, neatly folded. It went to voicemail. Daniel dialled the number again; still no answer.

All at once, he felt as if the ground had become unsteady beneath his feet, that it was in fact disappearing, crumbling and falling away and that he was tumbling through the air. But even as he felt that he was tumbling he felt also that he had seen this coming, almost precisely this, that he had, in fact, subconsciously predicted its coming, to himself, as he and Isla had sat at the coffee shop having breakfast that morning, when Isla put the telephone down and told him of Josep's sugges-tion. He had known then – with a cold, iron certainty – that Isla would not be at the apartment when he returned. Despite this sense of having known what was going to happen, he still felt an equal sense of disbelief: this could not be happening; it was impossible.

He went back through to the other room. He called her phone, again, and again it rang through to voicemail. He called the number Josep had left, no answer. Daniel went into a mania, tearing through Isla's belongings, her clothes, her bags, without a thought for what he would say on her return, desperately searching for some evidence of where she might have gone. He went into the bathroom. There was water drip-ping from the shower head, her toothbrush was wet.

Uselessly, he left the apartment and blundered out onto the streets, still trying to maintain an outward veneer of calm, thinking that she would have gone for a walk or a coffee. He went back to the café they had visited that morning, but she wasn't there. He walked on, not really knowing which way to turn, going into every coffee shop he passed, gazing through the windows of pharmacies and grocers. He looked up and down the pavement, wandering into the road between bursts of traffic to get a better perspective. For a moment, he thought he could see her, or her hair, bobbing between the heads of all the other pedestrians, but, in the end, he decided it wasn't her.

The street was busy and hot, the air and movement oppressive. At each junction he seemed to catch the lights at the wrong moment and stood there, almost jogging on the spot, looking this way and that, waiting for them to change. He called her again and again, his thumb hovering over the redial button, but each time it went through to voicemail, and each time the thought that she might be on the phone to someone else receded.

When the street he was on came to a junction with a wide avenue, he sat down on a bench to gather his thoughts. He told himself that everything was fine, that he was overreacting. He phoned Josep, but there was nothing, not even a voicemail. He began to berate himself. He should never have gone for lunch. It was a disgrace to have left her, unforgivable. He would do anything to turn back the clock, to undo what he had done. When he resumed his search, he realised that he didn't know where he was, that he had taken so many turns that now even the direction of the apartment was beyond him. Everything around him seemed both familiar, that he had seen it before, and utterly new, that he had never seen it in his life. His vision started to feel a little strange, as if he were not looking through his eyes alone, but through a telescope turned the wrong way around. The whole thing was futile, a farce.

His phone rang. It was Josep.

'Isla's gone missing,' Daniel said. He could barely breathe.

'What, wait,' Josep said.

'She's not at the apartment. I'm out looking for her.'

'Okay, okay,' he said. 'Calm down. I can explain.'

'What do you mean?'

'I mean I know where she's gone – or where she was planning to go.'

Josep explained: while they were in the restaurant, Isla had telephoned. She felt guilty about not feeling well on the trip and wanted to cook him – Daniel – a meal that evening. She had asked Josep for a good place to buy ingredients and he had suggested La Boqueria at the top of the Ramblas. 'If she walked,' Josep said, 'it will take her a while.'

'Oh Christ,' Daniel said. 'I don't believe it. I was frantic.'

'Relax,' Josep said. 'Go back to the apartment. Have a drink.'

Daniel did go back to the apartment. As soon as he got inside, he felt immense relief, as if the unthinkable had been averted. He went into the bedroom and rearranged Isla's things. His hands were still shaking and he didn't do it right, the piles were uneven, not as Isla had left them, but he would be able to explain.

He went back to the front of the apartment. The air was warm and the evening light came into the room. He stepped out onto the balcony and looked up and down the street. It was a regular Saturday evening in Barcelona. People sat at tables outside cafés. Isla would be back soon. They would cook together, eat, make love.

When he caught sight of her walking along the street, Daniel's heart leapt. He wasn't expecting her to be there at that moment. She was walking up from the cross street, carrying bags from the market. He could see a loaf of bread, a bottle of wine. He looked away and then looked back again, to make sure that his eyes were not deceiving him. It was definitely her. She was wonderful to behold. She moved hurriedly, her hair catching the light, her sunglasses back on her head.

At the pedestrian crossing she stopped and looked up. She saw Daniel and began to wave, a smile breaking across her face. She must have thought that he had not seen her, however, that he was frozen in some reverie, because she began to wave more vigorously, like someone from the deck of a ship. As she did so her arm must have knocked her sunglasses off her head. They fell forward and to the right. Isla's face changed into one of alarm as she stooped to grab them before they fell to the ground. In doing so, like an amateur juggler losing control of her batons, she succeeded only in throwing the sunglasses further forward and up into the air. Instinctively, she made a move to grab them, bringing her foot forward, but it caught against the bag she was carrying. It was going to cause her to stumble right out into the road, Daniel could see.

As Daniel watched all this unfold, the frames began to move more slowly. He had no conscious sense of what to do, but his mind – as if it wanted him neither to witness nor imagine what seemed about to happen – did something that he would not even remember. It went into a sort of delirium, as if spinning rapidly through a range of highly detailed landscapes, so detailed that Daniel could not possibly take them in, the succession of images overwhelming his cognitive processes until everything, including his awareness of where and who he had been, turned completely white.

He was on the patio of a bar, under an awning, having a drink with some friends. Somebody – it was Nando, he thought – was saying something, telling some anecdote. For some reason, Luis could not remember how it started and so he was finding it hard to follow, although everyone else appeared gripped. What was it about, he wondered. As he did so, his telephone rang. He answered it, standing up and turning away from the table. It was Penelope. She was excited, he could tell.

'Things are under way, Luis,' she said. 'My waters have broken.'

'They've broken?' he heard himself say. 'My god, are you all right?'

Of course, she was all right, she said. She was on her way to the hospital, her mother was taking her. Would he please hurry?

'Oh, my darling,' he said. 'I'll hurry all right.'

Luis leaned back into the table. He held up his hand. 'Nando,' he said. 'I'm sorry to interrupt your story, but I have to go.' He paused. He was as calm as he could manage, knowing the importance of the things that were about to transpire.

His friends looked up at him.

'It's happening,' he said, extinguishing his cigarette. 'She's in labour. I've got to go to the hospital.'

'It's happening! Fuck!' Nando said.

They all came forward at once, to touch his arm, to pat him on the back. They all knew that it was possible, but it wasn't expected to happen so soon. This was early, Luis knew.

'Can we help, Luis? Can we do anything?' Christina said.

'No, but I have to leave. This is it.' He could cry, right there, he thought; he wouldn't mind. He knocked back his beer and took his helmet from the table.

'Let me drive you to the hospital,' Roberto said, lighting one of his little cigars. 'My car's around the corner.'

'No it's fine,' he said. 'It will be quicker on the bike.'

'But you shouldn't drive,' Christina said. 'You won't be able to concentrate.'

'I'm fine,' he said. 'I have to go.'

They all stood and cheered him as he left. The bike was parked on the pavement. He straddled the machine and fired it up, testing the engine as he nosed it impatiently across the cobbles, people passing in front of him, unaware of the urgency, until eventually he dropped down onto the road, feeling the give of the shock absorbers.

He was away, out into the packed evening streets of Barcelona, that grand city where his heart had met its match. The sun slanted down through the trees. The machine throbbed beneath him, as if it knew that speed, its speed, was of the essence. He negotiated the cars, packed tight in the narrow side streets, and then turned, with relief, onto Valencia, that wide, beloved avenue, with ample scope to overtake. He wove between the slower-moving cars and buses, slanting his body, releasing the throttle, feeling the machine respond, the buildings flashing past as his speed increased. It wouldn't be long. All he could think of was the hospital and how to get there, what to do when he got there, whether he would have to wear a robe. He could see it all, could imagine it all: Christina lying back on a bed, him by her side, clutching her hand. Fabulous. Fabulous. It would all be fabulous. As he rode through the streets, tears began to rim his eyes. It had been a question of choice, for both him and Penelope, a question of choosing the life that they wanted and leaving behind the ones that they didn't. And now it was happening. At the same time, it was the grandest of sacrifices, giving up one type of life, so that another might be born. He allowed himself to become carried away and let the tears flow freely. At the hospital everything would change.

Up ahead, there were some lights. Out of habit – for all his bravado, he knew that really he was a careful man – Luis glanced at the pavement, to see what was what. To his right, he became aware of a woman walking quickly up one of the cross streets, looking up, not at the road, waving at something above. His fingers twitched against the brake lever. Suddenly, he wasn't sure why, her arms flailed in front of her and she stumbled out into the street, directly into his path. He was travelling fast, too fast. Christina was right. He couldn't believe it. He was going to hit her, this foolish woman, there wasn't time to react. Even as he thought it, however, as if some sixth sense, some instinct, were taking over, he found that he was easing back on the throttle, while putting every sinew into the action of shifting the bike's course. He didn't know how he was doing it, but he was. And then, like that – a flash, literally a flash – he missed her. It was by the narrowest of margins, but he was past her, fishtailing in an s-shape, until he recovered his balance and sped on towards the hospital, towards his wife, towards the woman who had transformed him.

CONTRIBUTORS' BIOGRAPHIES

ELIZABETH BAINES's stories have appeared in numerous magazines and anthologies, and her collection, *Balancing on the Edge of the World*, is published by Salt. Salt have also published her two novels, *Too Many Magpies* and *The Birth Machine*. She is also a prizewinning playwright for radio and stage. She is published online at *The View From Here*.

DAVID CONSTANTINE, born 1944 in Salford, has published several volumes of poetry, a novel and four collections of short stories – *Back at the Spike* (1994), *Under the Dam* (2005), *The Shieling* (2009) and *Tea at the Midland* (2012). He is an editor and translator of Hölderlin, Goethe, Kleist and Brecht. He was the winner of the 2010 BBC National Short Story Award and the 2013 Frank O'Connor Award.

AILSA COX, Reader in creative writing and English at Edge Hill University, is a writer and critic with a special interest in the short story. She is the the author of *Writing Short Stories* (Routledge), *Alice Munro* (Northcote House) and *The Real Louise and Other Stories* (Headland).

SIÂN MELANGELL DAFYDD is the author of *Y Trydydd Peth* (The Third Thing), which won the 2009 National Eisteddfod Literature Medal. She is the co-editor of the literature review

Taliesin and www.yneuadd.com and writes in both Welsh and English.

CLAIRE DEAN's short stories have been published in *The Best British Short Stories 2011*, *Still*, *Shadows & Tall Trees*, *Patricide*, *A cappella Zoo* and as chapbooks by Nightjar Press. Many of these stories, including 'Glass, Bricks, Dust', appeared under the name Claire Massey. An illustrated collection of fairy tales will be published by Unsettling Wonder in 2014. She lives in Lancashire with her two young sons.

STUART EVERS, born in Macclesfield in 1976, is the author of the novel *If This is Home* and the short story collection *Ten Stories About Smoking*, which won the 2011 London Book Award. His fiction has appeared in *The Best British Short Stories 2012*, Granta.com, *Prospect* and SundayTimes.com. This story is taken from his new collection *Your Father Sends His Love* to be published by Picador in 2015.

JONATHAN GIBBS was born in 1972 and lives in London. His debut novel, *Randall*, is published by Galley Beggar Press, and his short fiction has appeared in *Lighthouse*, *The South Circular*, *Allnighter (Pulp Faction)*, and from Shortfire Press. He blogs at tinycamels.wordpress.com.

JAY GRIFFITHS is the author of *A Love Letter From a Stray Moon*, a short novel about Frida Kahlo. Her non-fiction includes *Wild: An Elemental Journey* and *Kith: The Riddle of the Childscape*. She won the Barnes and Noble 'Discover' award for the best first-time author in the USA, and has been shortlisted for the Orwell Prize and a World Book Day award, and is the winner of the inaugural Orion Book Award.

DAVID GRUBB writes novels, short stories and poems. His

most recent poetry collection, *Box*, was published by Like This Press in 2012. Previous poetry collections have been published by Salt, Shearsman, and Stride. He was a winner in the 2012/13 Poetry Business Pamphlet Competition with a sequence, 'Ways of Looking'.

M JOHN HARRISON was born in 1945. His novel *Climbers* won the Boardman Tasker Prize in 1989. His most recent novel is *Empty Space*. He lives in the Midlands.

VICKI JARRETT is a novelist and short story writer from Edinburgh. Her first novel, *Nothing is Heavy*, was published in 2012. Her short fiction has been widely published, broadcast by Radio 4, Radio Scotland and Radio Somerset, and shortlisted for the Manchester Fiction Prize and the Bridport Prize. She is working on a short story collection and a second novel.

RICHARD KNIGHT was born in 1966 and lives in Greenfield near Manchester. His first published work was in *Arc Short Stories* in 1997, followed by stories in *Brace* (Comma Press) and *The Possibility of Bears* (Biscuit). His short story 'Atlantic Flats' was broadcast on Radio 4 in 2009 and he was shortlisted for the Fish Prize in 2010. Richard has also published three children's novels and is currently writing his first novel for adults.

PHILIP LANGESKOV was born in Copenhagen in 1976. In 2008, he received the David Higham Award. He has an MA in Creative Writing and a PhD in Creative and Critical Writing, both from UEA. His stories have appeared in various places, including *Bad Idea Magazine*, *Five Dials*, *Warwick Review* and *The Best British Short Stories 2011*.

ANNA METCALFE was born in Westphalia in 1987. Her work has been published in *Elbow Room*, *Lighthouse* and *Tender*

Journal. She lives in Norwich. 'Number Three' was shortlisted for the *Sunday Times* EFG Short Story Award.

LOUISE PALFREYMAN works as an editor and copywriter in Birmingham. Her short fiction has been published by *The View From Here* and the London School of Liberal Arts. She is part of a thriving community of writers called PowWow. The group meets weekly at a local pub and holds an annual literary festival.

CHRISTOPHER PRIEST is the author of thirteen novels and four short story collections. His 1995 novel *The Prestige* was filmed by Christopher Nolan and his latest novel is *The Adjacent* (2013). He lives on the south coast.

JOANNE RUSH lives in London, where she divides her time between writing and teaching. She holds a PhD from Cambridge University in Renaissance literature and she travels frequently to the Balkans, this year to work with the non-profit theatre company Youth Bridge Global. Her current project is a novel about modern Bosnia. 'Guests' is her first published short story.

MICK SCULLY lives and works in Birmingham. In 2007 Tindal Street Press published his short story collection *Little Moscow*. His first novel, *The Norway Room*, was published in 2014, also by Tindal Street Press.

JOANNA WALSH has been published by Granta, the Tate, the *Guardian*, *London Review of Books* and the *White Review*, among others. Her collection of short stories, *Fractals*, is published by 3:AM Press. She is currently working on a book, *Hotel*, for Bloomsbury's Object Lessons series.

ADAM WILMINGTON is a writer, poet and songwriter born and raised in Wigan. He is currently completing a degree at the University of Nottingham. 'It' was the winning story in the 2013 Manchester Fiction Prize, worth £10,000.

ACKNOWLEDGEMENTS

The editor wishes to thank Gareth Evans, Alison Moore, Gregory Norminton, John Patrick Pazdziora, Katherine Pulman, Rob Redman, Ros Sales, Robert Shearman and Conrad Williams.

'Tides or How Stories Do or Don't Get Told', copyright © Elizabeth Baines 2013, was first published online in *The View From Here* and is reprinted by permission of the author.

'Ashton and Elaine', copyright © David Constantine 2013, was first published in *Red Room: New Short Stories Inspired by the Brontës* (Unthank Books) edited by AJ Ashworth and is reprinted by permission of the author.

'Hope Fades For the Hostages', copyright © Ailsa Cox 2013, was first published in *3AM: Wonder, Paranoia and the Restless Night* (Liverpool University Press/The Bluecoat) edited by Bryan Biggs, which accompanied the exhibition of the same name curated by Angela Kingston and shown at the Bluecoat, Liverpool, and is reprinted by permission of the author.

'Hospital Field', copyright © Siân Melangell Dafydd 2013, was first published in *Beacons: Stories For Our Not So Distant Future* (Oneworld Publications) edited by Gregory Norminton and is reprinted by permission of the author.

'Glass, Bricks, Dust', copyright © Claire Dean 2013, was first published under the name Claire Massey in *New Fairy Tales: Essays & Stories* (Unlocking Press) edited by John Patrick Pazdziora & Defne Çizakça and is reprinted by permission of the author.

'What's Going on Outside', copyright © Stuart Evers 2013, was first published in *The Reader* 51 and is reprinted by permission of the author.

'The Faber Book of Adultery', copyright © Jonathan Gibbs 2013, was first published in *Lighthouse* 1 and is reprinted by permission of the author.

'The Spiral Stairwell', copyright © Jay Griffiths 2013, was first published in *Beacons: Stories For Our Not So Distant Future* (Oneworld Publications) edited by Gregory Norminton and is reprinted by permission of the author.

'Roof Space', copyright © David Grubb 2013, was first published in *Ambit* 212 and is reprinted by permission of the author.

'Getting Out of There', copyright © M John Harrison 2013, was first published by Nightjar Press and is reprinted by permission of the author.

'Ladies' Day', copyright © Vicki Jarrett 2013, was first published in *Gutter* 9 and is reprinted by permission of the author.

'The Incalculable Weight of Water', copyright © Richard Knight 2013, was first published online at manchesterwritingcompetition.co.uk and is reprinted by permission of the author.